Peaches-N-Creamed

by

Karen C. Whalen

The Dinner Club Murder Mysteries, Book 6

Peaches-N-Creamed

Cover Art by *Kim Mendoza*

The Wild Rose Press, Inc.
PO Box 708
Adams Basin, NY 14410-0708
Visit us at www.thewildrosepress.com

Publishing History
First Mainstream Mystery Edition, 2019
Print ISBN 978-1-5092-2599-6
Digital ISBN 978-1-5092-2600-9

The Dinner Club Murder Mysteries, Book 6
Published in the United States of America

Reynard Barre had been alive last night, playing a party game, having a drink with friends, shaking hands goodbye at the door. No matter what he did, if anything, to provoke an attack, he didn't deserve to die. Not that Jane could do much about it now.

He was dead, and her new life was just beginning. She was in love, getting married. She and Dale had finally decided on the date and place for the wedding, and it was time to move forward with their life together.

Staring into the bathroom mirror, she jammed the floss between her front teeth, sawing back and forth. But Olivia was worried about her brother-in-law and the survival of his B&B with a suspicious death on the premises. Olivia knew that Jane would do anything to help her. Olivia knew she was a loyal, true-blue friend who was pretty good at solving murders. Olivia knew Jane wouldn't turn her away.

She unwound the floss and the white tips of her fingers returned to pink. On the plus side, she could save the B&B and wrap up the wedding details. On the down side, Holden's business could go belly up and her romantic wedding could go down the tubes.

She spit into the sink. If she captured the killer, the B&B would receive new bookings and she'd wrap up the wedding plans and finally have the happily-ever-after she needed. She could accomplish one as well as the other. Why not? The two went hand-in-hand, since the widow was both the owner of the winery where the ceremony was to be held and the prime suspect in a murder at the inn where the guests were to stay.

She examined her pearly whites in the mirror. Decision made. Time to sink her teeth into solving the crime.

Dedication

To the Dean and Mary Harris "B&B"
and Betsey, my favorite dog on the Western Slope

Other Dinner Club Murder Mysteries

Chapter 1

Jane Marsh was the murderer.

She was guilty. She'd never get away with killing that lying, cheating, no-account, Mafioso wise-guy.

How long would it take before the others figured it out?

Likely, she was only moments away from being caught.

"Whose turn? Is it yours?" Tommy "Two Guns" waved his machine gun toward the woman assigned the role of Tiaka Powder. None of the suspects looked as villainous as the names of their characters. They appeared to be normal, fun-loving people having a good time in their 1920's costumes.

"No, it's Brynne's turn." Liza N. DeSeat gave Jane an encouraging smile. "That's you."

"Me?" Jane fumbled through her clue book, snapping the pages back and forth. She adjusted her reading glasses, then read in a voice that could be heard by all, "You are the murderer." She sucked in a breath and covered her mouth with her hand, but the words were out before she could take them back.

Olivia swatted Jane's arm. "You were supposed to keep that to yourself. See where it says, 'Do not read out loud.'" She swept the page in Jane's clue book to the correct spot. "And you turned too many pages, too."

Jane squeezed her eyes shut. It was her own fault

she'd given the solution away. She couldn't help kicking herself for living up to her character name, Brynne Less. "Sorry. Pretty stupid of me. Blame it on that second glass of wine, I guess."

A couple of people groaned, and Dane Gerish threw his clue book down. "Time for another drink."

Olivia stabbed her manicured finger close to Jane's chest. "We spent the better part of two hours playing this game, and you blabbed the ending. No one gets to win now." Olivia had rented an expensive-looking, silver beaded dress and a cloche hat. Her straight, jet black hair was cut into a severe, 1920's chin-length bob.

Dale Capricorn sat next to Jane on the long sofa. It seemed silly calling him her fiancé, since both of them were in their early fifties and had been married before—Jane was twice widowed and Dale was once divorced. Calling each other fiancé—or in one month's time, bride and groom—was something the younger set would do.

He choked back a laugh and gave her a squeeze. "Jane, you're a classic!" He didn't usually sport the pencil-thin mustache, but a few days before the party he'd grown the whiskers above his upper lip into a skinny line, gangster-style. She was wearing a black sheaf dress she'd retrieved from the back of her closet and had tied a ribbon around her forehead with a feather stuck into the band. Cheap plastic beads left over from a Mardi Gras party hung around her neck, flapper-style.

She forced a smile. "Classic? Yup, that's me. Heh, heh." She perched on the edge of the sofa as the rest of the scowling guests picked their way past her toward the lounge in the lower level of the bed-and-breakfast where the bar was set up. She stared down at her shoes as one last man scooted around her feet.

She reminded herself the game wasn't her idea.

Olivia and her husband, Doug, were the ones who had arranged for the dinner club to stay at the Ladner B&B during the Peach Festival since Doug's brother, Holden Ladner, owned the inn. The weekend get-away package included the murder game, planned as a dark and mysterious event to coincide with the upcoming solar eclipse. The dinner club was a group of four couples who hosted gourmet dinners in their homes, but only two of the couples were able to make the trip. Jane and Dale, Olivia and Doug.

Jane and Dale also had another agenda. They weren't at the inn in the Grand Valley wine country on the Western Slope of Colorado only for the get-away package. They were there to take a look at the nearby vineyard they'd booked online, sight unseen, for their wedding ceremony. Holden had been thrilled to accommodate the engaged couple for this weekend and again for the small wedding party in September, four short weeks away.

But now, the innkeeper crossed his arms, tapped an angry toe on the floor, and glowered at the ceiling.

Not so thrilled anymore.

Jane's heart sank a little further. Holden was doing her a favor since he was going to give her a discount on the rooms for the wedding. She wanted to be a good guest, especially since he was related to a member of her dinner club. Instead, she'd ruined his mystery game. She ducked her head to avoid looking him in the eye.

Would she manage to mess up her wedding plans as badly as she had the murder party? She had a way of stumbling into *disastrophes*, somewhere between a disaster and a catastrophe on the calamity scale.

The murder game participants who were not staying overnight at the inn gathered at the front door to say their goodbyes, their voices rising as they called out, "so-long" and "adios!" Two of the players, Lisa N. DeSeat and Dane Gerish, shook the departing guests' hands as if they were the hosts instead of Holden. Jane and the other three dinner club members made their way to the second floor. She'd had a long day, between driving over the mountains from Denver that afternoon and driving the murder party to a ruined ending that night.

Thank goodness it was only a game. The guests may have wanted to wring her neck, but Jane was neither a party kill-joy nor a murderer. No one had actually died. At least not yet. Come on, that wasn't such a surprising thought given her track record.

****

The next morning, after reading her devotional and getting ready for the day, Jane descended the steps to the common room. None of the others had shown up this early. She was the first. Even Dale, usually an early bird, hadn't beat her to the coffee. She poured a cup from the urn on the sideboard and stepped out onto the sunny deck where hummingbird feeders cast red prism shadows and aspens fluttered their leaves in the light breeze. The morning air wafted across the patio in small bursts, making it chilly at this early hour. She left her steaming mug on the railing and traipsed up the stairs two at a time for her sweater. But it wasn't in her suitcase. Oh yeah, the sweater was probably in the basement lounge since she'd taken it with her to the

4

party the night before. Bouncing back down the steps, she made the circular route around the landing to the lower level...but stopped on the bottom tread. A man's body lay sprawled in front of the fireplace.

She gave a yelp, fell backwards and sat down hard on the last step, taking deep breaths in and out.

Blood formed a circle on the carpet under his head, and the fireplace hearth was stained with a splash of crimson. The body was clothed in a 1920's costume. One spat-covered shoe hung off a foot, exposing a hole in the heel of the man's sock. Okay, so the guy was lying there like a murder victim, that didn't necessarily mean he was one. This was only someone pulling a prank as a part of last night's mystery game. Right?

"Hey, you can get up. You're not fooling me." She stood and prodded his leg with the toe of her shoe, almost losing her balance, then grasped onto the sofa table and placed her foot back on the floor.

His neck was angled funny, and his arms were thrown out, as if he was trying to catch himself. Something gold was entwined in the outstretched fingers of his right hand. Jane leaned closer and took in the details in a fraction of a second—a gold necklace with a peach-shaped pendant...an orange-tinted glass peach nestled against a translucent, green leaf with tiny vein patterns. Her gaze returned to his face.

She recognized the man, Dane Gerish...he was one of the pair at the front door bidding the departing guests goodbye after the party. This was the man who owned the winery where she was to be married next month.

He was dead.

No joke.

This wasn't a party gag left over from the night

before.

Straightening to a stand, Jane felt her head go dizzy and her vision whirl. Everything appeared as if far away, as if she were looking down on the scene from the top of the stairs instead of the bottom where she stood over the dead man. All the air escaped from her lungs, and her heart pounded out a painful, strong beat.

She turned tail, hastened up the steps, and shouted, "Help! Help!"

Holden materialized from the kitchen with a dishtowel in his hand, and Dale came running down from the second floor at a full gallop almost colliding into her.

Dale asked, alarm in his eyes, "What is it, Jane? Are you hurt?"

Gasping for breath, she held her sides. "No. Not me. It's Dane Gerish."

"Who?" Holden waved the dishtowel like a flag over his head. He pulled her into the kitchen. "Sit down. Sit," he insisted, but she refused to bend and remained standing.

"Dane Gerish. He played the part of the bad guy. At the party." Breathless, she could only recall his character name, not his real name. She patted her chest, calming her heart. "Come on. Follow me."

She twisted back toward the stairs, but Holden stopped her, clutching her arm. "What do you mean? Rey's hurt?"

"Dane Gerish is lying on the floor, not moving. His head's bleeding. We should call an ambulance." Jane shook off his grip and charged toward the lounge with Dale following.

Holden clattered down the steps after them, then

came to an abrupt stop. "Rey! Rey!" His voice came out strangled. All three sets of eyes were glued to the body.

Dale knelt to check the man's pulse, then stood up and slid his cell phone from his pocket. Jane stood by, trying to catch a deep breath. She asked Holden, "What's this guy's real name?"

"Reynard Barre." Holden wiped his forehead with the dishtowel.

Dale repeated the man's name into the phone, along with the bed-and-breakfast's address. After disconnecting, he said, "Do you know him well, Holden?"

"Yes. He not only runs a winery, he's the mayor of Barresville, the next town over from Palisade. A very good friend."

"Do you think he had an accident? Slipped and fell, landed on his head?"

"I don't know." Holden flicked the dishtowel, as if ridding the room of dust motes and bad vibes.

Jane reached out to pat his hands still. "I'm so sorry about this. Are you okay?"

"Yes, I'm fine. I'm fine." He didn't look it, wringing the towel, with beads of sweat popping out on his forehead.

Voices sounded from the floor above, then the other dinner club couple, Doug and Olivia, trooped down the stairs. Olivia's forehead puckered in concern, "What happened?"

"This man is hurt. Dane Gerish from the party. You know, the evil villain," Jane said in a quiet voice, almost a whisper. She didn't want to say outright that he was likely dead. Maybe, since he was still in costume, he had been lying there all night, dead, while they had slept in their beds. A creepy thought.

The couple came closer. Doug fell to his knees next to Dane Gerish, or rather Reynard Barre. As a former police officer, Doug knew what to do. He checked the man's airway, but he did not try to resuscitate him. Olivia's eyes had a wild look as she glanced around the room like she was looking for more dead bodies.

Jane took a closer look herself. The necklace had disappeared…vanished into thin air. Dane Gerish's fingers still curled around an imaginary chain, but the necklace with the pendant was gone. She'd been upstairs less than a minute. Where could it have flown off to?

Dale clasped Jane's hand and gave it a squeeze. He said in an undertone in her ear, "Let's hope this was an accident. How likely is a murder to occur in the same place as a murder party?"

Fear grabbed her stomach into a hard knot. It was altogether too reasonable for their minds to consider homicide because Jane and Dale had encountered murder victims before. She pushed that unwelcome thought aside. "Right. I hope you're right."

A small, choked scream sounded behind them. Liza N. DeSeat, with a pale face and wide eyes, said in a voice wobbly and high, "Reynard! What's the matter?"

"That's his wife," Olivia mouthed to Jane with soundless words.

Liza looked very different from the night before when she was wearing her heavy costume makeup and flapper's dress. This morning her face was scrubbed clean, showing crow's feet at the corners of her eyes, her gray-streaked auburn hair had been pulled into a ponytail, and she sported a long T-shirt with the logo, "Barre Winery," over western style jeans. Her lips trembled as if she were about to cry. "What's wrong with Rey?"

Jane rushed to his wife's side. "Here, sit down. We've called an ambulance."

Shrill sirens blared, coming closer and closer, while they stood listening. Jane recognized the all too familiar *wee-woo-wee* of the ambulance. She'd had more experience with police and paramedics than she wanted to admit. Hard knocks pounded on the door. Holden sprinted up the stairs and returned moments later with several Palisade police officers and an ambulance crew with a gurney.

All but the victim were ushered upstairs. They were able to climb up on their own two feet. He was taken out in a body bag.

*****

Several hours later, the two dinner club couples shared a breakfast table on the outdoor patio. Jane had no appetite, although the food looked and smelled tempting—warm, cheesy quiche; sliced cranberry bread atop a glass pedestal; a fruit mix of bananas, melon wedges, and halved strawberries; fragrant Canadian bacon, crispy at the edges; and glasses filled with four fingers of orange juice. The platters of food scented the air and mingled with the strong aroma of coffee. Holden had kept the breakfast banquet waiting until after the police departed.

The innkeeper held the coffee pot above the table, swishing the dark brown liquid around in the glass globe, the carafe slicing through the air above their noses. He said, "I also have an espresso machine if anyone prefers espresso." He had the same fiery red hair and same height and build as Doug, but the brothers' resemblance ended at the physical plane. Doug's calm demeanor was likely developed during his time spent on the police force. Doug's movements were minimal and low-key, limited to his nervous habit of stroking or chewing on his red mustache. But Holden's gestures were over-the-top, arms waving and legs shifting from foot to foot, quite different from his brother, sitting up straight and tall, still as a pole.

Jane rubbed her forehead, tired and drained from the police interrogation. Coffee was a necessity. She raised a hand for Holden's attention. "Just coffee, please. It's kinda hard to face all this food after what happened."

"Not that we don't appreciate this great breakfast, Holden." Olivia frowned at Jane.

Holden thrust a full steaming cup into Jane's hands. She drank in the heady scent of the brew, craving the energy-giving caffeine. She sipped the hot black liquid while she observed the people around her. Dale had shaved off his pencil-thin party mustache. Olivia and Doug, in spite of Holden's efforts, were just picking at their breakfast. She recognized the three other guests at the next table as Tommy Two Guns, Shamus Onnrue, and Tiaka Powder. She didn't know their real names, but remembered they were the locals who spent the night at the B&B as part of the weekend getaway package. She'd last seen Rey's wife, Liza N. DeSeat, leave with the police, and the wife had either not returned yet or had checked out.

All the guests appeared to have what they needed,

so Holden dragged an extra chair to the dinner club's table and settled himself in the seat. Doug asked him, "Any more news about what happened?"

Holden gave an exaggerated shoulder shrug. "No. I haven't talked to Reynard's wife since the police took her away. I'll call Zeta a little later."

"Is that Liza's name? Zeta? Zeta Barre?" Olivia gave Jane a questioning look, one eyebrow raised, her eyes anxious. "Oh, dear. Isn't that the owner of the vineyard where you're getting married?"

Jane paused with her mug halfway to her lips and lobbed a wide-eyed glance at Dale. She set her cup down with a clunk. "Yes. We were going to meet with her today. Now we won't be able to. Gosh, I was really hoping to finalize the wedding plans this weekend. Do you think I should call her?" Jane cringed. How could she be so self-absorbed? How could she think only of herself at a time like this? But it was pretty hard not to.

Dale said, "Yes. At least leave her a message."

She let out the breath she'd been holding once he'd agreed.

Holden's chin dropped to his chest. "I'm so sorry about everything."

"What happened is not your fault." Olivia gave Holden's left shoulder a pat. Since Olivia was an only child, her brother-in-law was the closest thing she had to a sibling. Doug, who was sitting on Holden's other side, massaged his brother's right shoulder.

"So did the police tell you anything?" Jane tried to speak in a low voice because the local guests were awfully quiet and appeared to be following their conversation.

Holden jabbed an index finger in the air. "Someone

11

pushed Rey and he hit his head. It wasn't an accident. I overheard the police talking. Come with me and I'll show you." He signaled with a jerk of his thumb for the group to follow him.

They threw down their napkins, Doug swallowed one last bite of quiche, and Jane held onto her coffee cup to bring with her. The two dinner club couples, along with the other three guests who must have been just as curious, trailed after the proprietor of the B&B past the common room where the party took place, through the entry hall, windowless and dark, and down the stairs to the scene of the crime.

Chapter 2

Crimson red stained the hearth, and yellow crime scene tape blocked the fireplace. Black fingerprint powder dotted the surface of the wooden sofa table. The room looked every bit like a crime scene out of a *CSI* episode.

"I did think when they were questioning us the police were treating his death as a homicide," Jane said in a *sotto* voice to Dale standing next to her.

He gave her a pained look and whispered, "You were right."

Holden tugged on his brother's sleeve. "I was waiting at this very spot for the police investigator to finish. I heard him talking to the other officers. Look at the sofa table. See how everything is crowded into one corner?" He swept his arm in a wide circle toward the table. An empty bud vase and a silver picture frame were jammed together at the far edge. "The investigator thinks someone pushed everything to the side and Rey hitched his bottom onto the table. From the footprints in the carpet they could tell he propped himself up with one leg on the floor and his other leg dangling." Holden threw out his arms and hopped up on one leg. "Someone shoved Rey hard off the table. It wouldn't have taken much strength, though, since he was unbalanced like that." Holden planted both feet on the floor and pretended to stumble, his arms stretching back, stopping short of the crime scene tape. Then he tugged his cell phone out of his pants pocket. "This is what the table should've looked like. I took some pictures during the party. See?"

Holden jabbed the phone forward. They stared at the image of a vase and a large photo in a silver frame centered on the table, not crammed to the side.

He touched the edge of the wood. "So the investigator found threads from Rey's pants in the crack between the table leg and the table top, here, and footprints in the carpet, there." He directed a finger toward the rug, and Doug bent low to examine the area.

Holden continued, "Rey's head hit the stone hearth in front of the fireplace, catching the sharp corner. And there's something more." He inhaled a quick intake of breath. "There was a peach pit down Rey's throat."

"What?" Doug bolted up from the floor. "I checked his airway." He wore a what-the-heck expression.

"It was there." The accusation came out fierce, but then his brother's shoulders slumped. "But way down."

"Does it matter?" Jane gulped around the muscles constricting in her throat. "He died from the head wound, right?"

The room stopped in that slow way of time stretching. Holden turned toward her. "And how do you know that?"

"We've seen a choking victim before and he didn't look the same." Jane glanced out of the corner of her eyes at her friends. The other three murmured in agreement and they all gave a shudder.

"I don't know what killed him exactly. All I heard the police say was that he bled out and died sometime during the night." Holden tapped the back of his knuckles against his lips and forced a breath out through his nose.

Jane asked, "Why was he even down here? Why didn't he leave after the party when the others left?"

"He and his wife had a room, remember? They were staying the night."

"Oh, I forgot."

Holden bumped his fist on his brother's shoulder. "Doug, I need your help. I've already received cancellations. Rey's death was on the early morning news. They called it, 'murder at the murder party.' I'm worried about the B&B."

Doug nodded, appearing deep in thought, but then Holden focused on Jane. "And it seems you know a lot about this sort of thing. I heard you've solved other murders. You need to help Doug solve this one for me."

Her friends stared at her, as did the three other guests from the party. She'd been unfortunate enough to have come across dead bodies before and had become involved in murder investigations one or two times. Okay, six or seven. Let's just say, more than the average person. Having encountered danger once too often, she'd even signed up for Krav Maga self-defense classes and earned a second level yellow belt. She interlaced her fingers and stretched her arms out, cracking her knuckles. Dale gave her a curious look. Maybe she appeared as if she was proud of her sleuthing skills, so she wiped the smile off her face and dropped her hands into her lap.

She leaned in and lowered her voice. "Who told you that?"

Olivia cast a quick, sheepish look at her husband. "I did."

Because Doug scowled and assumed his cop face, Jane was quick to say, "Doug will help you, Holden." She couldn't help but add, "I'm curious about what else the police had to say, though. Did you overhear anything more?"

Doug took a step closer to his brother. "I'd like to know everything the police told you, too. Did they say why the peach pit was in his throat? Was he eating a peach at the time?"

"No. This is weird, kinky. Are you ready for it?"

Jane swallowed hard. She wasn't sure if she was ready. What could be kinky about a peach?

"Someone crammed the pit down his mouth after he was dead. The police said it was to leave a message. The pit had been cleaned of fruit. It wasn't like he'd just eaten it. He did not choke on it."

Jane sloshed her coffee over the cup's rim and down her fingers. She *was* right. He didn't choke to death. The blow to the head killed him. The group took a collective breath, and Tiaka Powder dabbed a tissue to her eyes. Changing the mug from one hand to the other, Jane swiped her wet fingers against her jeans.

Doug ran his fingertips over his bristling, red mustache. "I'm surprised the police let that information out."

"Well, our police force isn't very big, and we only have one detective. This is such a small town, the police dispatcher is even a neighbor of mine. The detective probably figured I'd find out from her anyway." Holden glanced at the other three townspeople as if seeking confirmation. Tommy Two Guns, Shamus Onnrue, and Tiaka Powder shuffled their feet and nodded. He went on, "But as soon as the state police and the CBI forensic team showed up, I was told to wait upstairs."

Shamus Onnrue rolled his eyes and spoke for the first time. "Of course, the state police would push the locals aside." The two others from the town nodded again. Jane glanced at them with a quick vertical sweep. These three were potential suspects.

Doug explained, "It's common with small departments for the police chief to request help from the county sheriff, especially with the initial homicide investigation, and small agencies need to use the CBI's crime lab. There's a CBI office close by in Grand Junction." Doug would know, being an ex-cop. His eyes roamed the room slowly, taking one last look. "Well, I guess there's nothing more to see here."

After they ascended the stairs to the dining room, the other guests went their separate ways, but Holden stopped the four friends. He lifted his hands in a frantic *help-me, help-me* way. "Doug, you've got to solve this case before I lose any more business."

"I'll find out what I can." Doug clasped his brother's shoulder.

Holden added, "And, Jane, I'd appreciate your help, too."

Doug huffed into his mustache and fired a look that could kill at his wife. Of course, he knew Olivia had suggested Jane's help so she would have an excuse to snoop around, too.

Jane gave Holden a weak smile. "If Doug needs anything, I'll try to be of use, of course, but you're lucky to have a brother who knows what to do."

Olivia jumped in. "We can all lend a hand, right, Douglas?"

"No. You need to stay out of the police

investigation, Olivia. You too, Jane." His jaw was tight and his voice had a hard edge when he said those predictable words.

Keeping both of them happy would be tricky. Olivia wanted to poke her nose in and Doug wanted them to butt out. The last thing Jane needed was to cause family problems.

The weekend was certainly not turning out as she'd planned. She was there to nail down the details for her perfect wedding, not to get caught up in a homicide investigation. But Olivia was giving her that let's-do-this and don't-let-me-down look, as they headed to their rooms to finish getting ready for the day.

*****

"Do you think that man's death had anything to do with the eclipse?" Isobel Ladner was going up the stairs as Jane was coming down.

Isobel, a younger version of her mother, Olivia, had arrived late the night before after the party. She was statuesque, tall, and toothpick thin, with long, shiny black hair and a flawless, rosy complexion, plus red button lips, well-defined cheekbones, and shapely black eyebrows. She'd inherited Olivia's black hair and beauty, together with Doug's vivid blue eyes and pale skin that went along with his fiery red hair. No wonder she was in demand as a fashion model in New York. Always booked for photoshoots, she'd taken the time off from her busy schedule to meet her parents at her uncle's bed-and-breakfast—not to join the dinner club, but as a quick family reunion of sorts.

Isobel touched the inside of her wrist where she had a tattoo of a star, a moon, and the sun with rays flowing out like tendrils of hair. "All kinds of strange things are going to happen during the eclipse, since it's going to be almost total in Colorado, ninety percent, and you know total eclipses are really rare. The last one anywhere near here was thirty years ago. That's before I was born. Even then, I think people had to drive up to North Dakota to see it."

This eclipse-death theory didn't sound as crazy as it would have if Jane hadn't read the sensational articles in the tabloid newspapers...aliens were predicted to arrive on invisible energy beams from outer space and some sort of global psychic power was supposed to be released. She kept herself from rolling her eyes. "I don't think his death had anything to do with the eclipse. You got here after the party ended, didn't you, Isobel?"

Isobel followed Jane back down the stairs. "That's right. Your party was already over."

"But you know about the, umm, the man's death?"

"Yeah, I heard."

One of the townies from the party of the night before, Tiaka Powder, joined the two in the common room. As with many good-looking, well-endowed women, Tiaka wore a deep V-neck T-shirt displaying her generous cleavage. She addressed Isobel with, "Good morning. I don't remember you. You weren't at the party, were you?" Her eyes appeared bloodshot and her eyelids rimmed with red.

Isobel answered, "No, I was just telling Jane that I got here after the game ended. I saw the man, the one who died, though. He was standing at the door when I came in. Holden Ladner's my uncle, and he'd saved a room for me."

Tiaka had on a sad smile. She offered her hand.

"Nice to meet you. My name is Georgiana. What's yours?"

"Isobel Ladner."

Next, Jane clasped Tiaka's hand, or rather, Georgiana's hand, and considered whether this woman could be a cold-blooded killer. Since she was one of the townspeople who was at the party and spent the night at the inn, she had the opportunity. As a local, she probably knew the victim and might've had a motive. She had to be a suspect.

Jane dropped Georgiana's hand. "We met at the party, but you don't know my real name. I'm Jane Marsh." She repeated to herself, *Georgiana, Georgiana, Georgiana*, and tried to erase the woman's character name, Tiaka Powder, from her brain.

The two younger women towered over Jane, who was only five foot two. Georgiana was almost as tall as Isobel, but older, likely in her mid-thirties, Jane guessed, dressed in stylish skinny jeans and kitten heels, along with the low-cut T-shirt. She had long, highlighted blonde hair in layers, and her lips and nails matched the peach color of her shirt. Jane tried not to feel diminished standing between the two attractive younger women.

"Yeah. Mom and Dad told me what happened." Isobel wrapped her arms around her middle as if to shut out all things unpleasant.

Jane asked, "When did they tell you? You weren't at breakfast."

"Uncle Holden brought me coffee while the police were still here. Then my parents showed up in my room just now and told me all about it, too." Isobel yawned and hugged herself tighter. "I'm glad the police didn't ask me any questions. I don't know anything anyway. I was worn out from the flight from New York. I had to change planes in Denver. With all those flights and everything, it was a very long day. So, lucky me, I missed all the excitement."

The police would probably come back at some point and interrogate Isobel, but it was best not to bring that up now. Jane patted the young woman's back. "I'm glad you made it safely."

"Me, too. Just in time for someone to die." Isobel shuddered. "What do you think happened?" Her eyes were wide and fearful, yet curious, reminding Jane all the more of her mother.

Georgiana shrugged, rotating her left shoulder toward them. "Maybe it was some kind of an accident?" Her voice rose at the end in a question.

"And the peach pit was just a weird manifestation of the eclipse." Isobel ended her sentence for her.

"You know about that?" Jane asked.

"Mom mentioned it. That's freaky, huh?"

"The pit's certainly strange, but there has to be an explanation for it." Jane shook her head, then sighed. Even though she did purchase the tabloids to follow her favorite celebrities, there was no way she could believe the incredible alien and paranormal stories. The answer had to be logical. The pit had to have been planted, but what was up with the peach pendant? Was the necklace purposely placed at the scene, too? If so, why was it taken away? And by whom? How did the necklace disappear in the short time it took Jane to run upstairs to the kitchen for help?

"It's so hard to believe that Rey is dead." Georgiana's eyes teared up and she dabbed a tissue to her nose. She took a few steps toward the front door where a compact suitcase on wheels was parked. "Everything about this weekend was a disaster. It was just awful what happened to Rey."

"I heard even the party turned out to be a bust." Isobel chortled and gave Jane a pointed look. Jane drew in a sharp breath. The young woman's laughter seemed a bit insensitive in light of the man's death, but being young and beautiful, Isobel always seemed to be granted a free pass.

"Yes. Someone gave away the murderer…the murderer in the game, I mean." Georgiana's eyes narrowed at Jane. "Oh, that was you, wasn't it?"

"Ur, um." Jane swallowed. She still felt bad about it.

"I'm afraid for what's going to happen next." Georgiana blinked rapidly, then grabbed her suitcase handle and stepped out onto the wide porch.

"Are you going to be all right?" Jane followed her but stopped at the door.

"I guess so." The woman descended the steps with her suitcase bumping behind her. "Well, so long. It was nice meeting you." She rolled her luggage, bouncing and bucking, across the gravel drive to where her car was parked.

Jane and Isobel moved from the door when Shamus Onnrue and Tommy Two Guns approached, one with a leather duffel bag in his hand and the other with a backpack slung over his shoulder.

"Hello again." Jane pasted on a smile.

Their *good mornings* echoed each other and one of the men asked how she was doing.

"As well as can be expected. Before you go, tell

me your real names. I can't keep thinking of you as your party names." She studied the men's faces.

The man whose character was Shamus Onnrue answered first. "Of course. I'm Kirby Potts." He was tall, at least six foot in height, with dark, thick hair, longer on top and shaved shorter on the sides, a modern haircut not noticeable the night before under his vintage fedora. His party costume, a black and white pinstriped suit, black silk shirt, and broad white tie, was almost identical to another character's at the party, Fritz the Snitch, to the extent that it was hard to tell them apart. At breakfast and again now, he was distinctive in a sports coat over fashionable torn jeans and a T-shirt.

The second man spoke. "Skylar Straite, here." Tommy Two Guns' appearance had been a little bit of a surprise. At the party he carried a toy plastic Tommy gun and wore a 1920's zoot suit. This morning he had on well-worn blue jeans and a tie-dyed shirt with, "Think Hippy Thoughts," written across the front. His brown hair, which had also been concealed under a fedora the night before, was uncovered, a shaggy style landing just above his shoulders, giving him a rugged, outdoorsy look. He cast an admiring glance at Isobel.

"I'm Jane Marsh. Nice to meet you." Jane hoped she wasn't blushing at using the trite phrase Georgiana had used. They were meaningless words. What was the appropriate thing to say when you met someone at a murder party where someone was actually murdered? "Hello, how are you? Ever kill anyone?"

"Who's this?" Skylar gave Isobel a warm smile. He seemed to be around her same age, mid to late twenties.

The young woman stuck her hand out. "Isobel Ladner. Holden's niece. Arrived after the party last night."

Skylar shifted his backpack higher on his shoulder and gripped her hand. The two gave each other once-overs that said, *whoa, look at you.*

Kirby headed for the door. "I need to get going." Clutching his leather duffel bag, he bolted down the steps without saying goodbye.

Jane said, "Wow. He was abrupt."

"Nothing personal, Jane. That's his way, and everyone always makes allowances for Kirby." Skylar once more hitched his backpack higher on his shoulder. "He's so important, the famous sculptor, you know." He gave them a peace sign, muttering, "As they say, keep calm and carry on," before sauntering out the door in a laidback, free-spirit kind of way.

Isobel stationed herself at the front window scrutinizing the two departing men. "So tell me about the party guests." Her eyes seemed to follow Skylar.

"You just met three prime murder suspects." Jane guessed that was the case, anyway. They had to be. All the guests at the party were bound to be under suspicion. "They're Grand Valley locals. Your uncle told us he offers discounts to the townies so they can participate in the murder parties and stay one night at the B&B. It's a good promotion because they will spread the word to the tourists."

"Huh." Isobel raised her shoulders and let them fall as if disinterested, yet she watched as Skylar climbed into his VW van parked next to Holden's Subaru Forester beneath the peach trees. When he pulled out of the driveway, she turned toward the kitchen. "I need more coffee. I'll see you later at the Peach Festival. Uncle Holden said I could take one of his bicycles to ride over."

"You aren't going in the truck with us?"

"Nah. I want to get a workout in, and besides, Riverbend Park isn't far. So I'll look for you when I get there." Isobel didn't have an ounce of fat, but that always appeared to be the case—those devoted to exercise didn't seem to be the ones who needed it.

"Okay. Have fun." Jane swung away from the door and scurried up to her room. She unplugged her phone from the charger and glanced around for what else she would need for the day.

A lumpy, flower-patterned down comforter overlaid the four-poster bed, and a bright, cheerful yellow paint covered the walls. A tufted settee was almost hidden under stacks of flowered, mismatched pillows, and an oval rug in a different floral motif protected the hardwood floor. Somehow the dissimilar patterns worked in the shabby-chic style, making her feel warm and embraced in the cuddly, feminine room.

Adding to the comfortable chaos, her suitcase spilled open on the chest at the foot of the bed. The sweater the police let her retrieve from the crime scene was draped over a chair. Two pair of Levi jeans in the boot-cut style were folded on the bed. Should she break down and buy skinny jeans? Did the boot-cut look put her in the old-lady camp? At least she had a fresh haircut and her brown shoulder-length hair was glossy and smooth. Her off-the-shoulder T-shirt gave her confidence that she wasn't too out of fashion.

Dale knocked on her door. "You ready?"

"You betcha. Be right there." She was more than ready to escape the place where she'd found a dead body. But would she be able to avoid the one

responsible for his death in this small town?
Not likely.

Chapter 3

The creep factor was high. Her skin crawled, so she rubbed her hands up and down her arms.

There was a good chance the murder suspects would be at the Annual Peach Festival in Riverbend Park. The whole community attended along with the tourists. The killer could very well walk among them.

Jane assumed her brave face, squared her shoulders, and stepped out of the inn. She inhaled a deep lungful of fresh air that had a tang of something similar to lilac, but not as strong. More like lavender.

The four friends piled into Dale's extended-cab pickup and headed east over the railroad tracks on Glen Oak Drive to Highway 6. They made the short distance into the town of Palisade in a matter of minutes. The hundred-foot high Bookcliffs dominated the skyline from nearly every field of vision—a series of south-facing sandstone buttes resembling the spines of books standing on a shelf, a unique formation, very western, very desert. Jane half expected John Wayne to gallop his horse around the bend in the road and pull up in front of the old buildings with false fronts. Downtown was jam-packed, and Dale's pickup truck took extra space, so they parked several blocks from Riverbend Park and darted across Highway 6 dodging festival traffic.

Isobel had already arrived. She'd locked her bike

and was waiting at the front of the long line, so they jumped the queue and joined her. After paying the fairground fee, the five of them held out their right hands to be banded with wrist passes.

They emerged from the shaded entry tent into the end-of-summer carnival under the bright yellow sun and cloudless blue sky—a setting right out of a Hallmark movie. The scent of wood-smoked barbeque filled Jane's nose, but the fragrance of caramel corn, funnel cake, and farm animals edged their way into the mix. Grass was already trampled underfoot, stomped down to yellow, dead patches by the crowd.

Before being let loose to scout out the rest of the fair, they had to run the gauntlet of the stalls with free giveaways and hard sells. Pitchmen catcalled to attract customers to their booths, and fairgoers' voices shouted with laughter. The men's attention was drawn to a prize wheel and they took turns spinning to win a round of golf. They didn't win the grand prize. Jane continued on while the men collected their prizes of plastic water bottles.

Right in front of her was Zeta Barre, sitting at a table in the shade, wearing a red and white sundress with a blue and white-starred scarf around her neck. Her gray-streaked, auburn hair was swept into a knot at the top of her head. A hefty black, brown, and white longhaired dog lounged at her feet, its tail thumping the dirt. A feather banner that had been poked into the hard ground read, *Barre for Barresville*, and the large, round button pinned to Zeta's dress repeated the message, *Barre for Mayor*.

Jane reared back in surprise.

Zeta rose to her feet and stretched across the table

to shake Jane's hand, looking directly into her eyes. "Hello, Jane. How are you?"

Jane took her hand, which clasped hers back in a strong grip, and found her voice. "Uh, I'm good." She dwelled on Zeta's face for a moment too long, then averted her eyes. "Please know that you and your family are in my thoughts and prayers. I'm really sorry about what happened." She glanced back toward Zeta.

"Thank you. My husband was a wonderful man, loved by many." Her eyes held Jane's, interested and engaged. She had a compelling charm about her. "I got your phone message. I appreciate your willingness to reschedule our appointment today. I can meet you tomorrow."

"Are you sure? You must have a lot of things to attend to." Jane's mind registered that Zeta was sitting in a campaign booth instead of spending time with family or at the funeral parlor taking care of all the necessary arrangements.

"I'll have time after the parade tomorrow." Zeta gave her a solemn nod.

"All right. Thanks." Jane couldn't help but ask the obvious, "So you're running for mayor?"

"I decided to apply to the commissioner to be a substitute candidate. I'm running in my husband's place to honor his memory and as an advocate for his platform." Zeta Barre snatched a brochure off the table and forced it into Jane's hand. "Please read about what Reynard and I stand for."

"I'm not a resident of Barresville. I'm from the Denver area, so I can't vote here."

"I know that, Jane, but you can help get the word out." Zeta's face was hopeful.

"All right. I would like to read your flyer." Jane glanced down at the brochure and back up at the candidate.

"I'm sure you'll find it interesting." Zeta smiled with both her eyes and mouth, raising the corners of her lips and cheeks, causing crow's feet to form around her eyes. She sat tall with her shoulders down and relaxed, not bunched up. She wasn't upset or nervous, what one would expect of a grieving widow, unless her emotions were in check, her feelings in control. No matter what was going on inside of her, she made Jane feel as if she were the most important person at the fair. "So stop by the vineyard after the parade tomorrow and we'll talk about your wedding."

Jane let out a long breath. "Okay. See you then." She knelt down to pat the friendly dog on the head. She was lonesome for her own two dogs at home with the dog sitter.

Dale drifted over from the grass and dirt path clutching his new water bottle. "Hello. What's this?"

But Zeta's attention was now concentrated on another man who'd stepped forward. She was saying, "Good morning, Gregory. I'm contending for mayor in Rey's place. I'm sure I can count on your vote."

Dale and Jane sidestepped away while Zeta talked on. Jane whispered in his ear, "Can you believe she's running for mayor after her husband just died?" Zeta may've been comfortable in her new role, but Jane found it odd.

Dale certainly did, too. He gave her a what's-the-world-coming-to expression and shook his head.

"She said we can meet tomorrow after the parade." Jane threw a glance over her shoulder, but Zeta was in her hand-shaker, office-seeker mode, no longer paying Jane any attention.

"Well, I'm glad for that anyway." Dale wove a path through a cluster of people at a crafts booth, and Jane trailed behind him past another mayoral campaign stand.

A sign rudely demanding, "Keep Barre out of Barresville," swayed in the hot breeze. Several young people manned the booth. Without slowing her pace, Jane snagged one of the campaign brochures for later comparison. Such a bad-mannered campaign slogan bore looking into.

Dale joined Doug at a strongman game, while Jane and Olivia stood back. The barker caterwauled, "Step right up! Test your strength." Doug pounded the mallet with great force onto the rubber mat, but the puck didn't reach the bell. Dale rose to the challenge, too, but was not able to ring the bell, either.

"It's rigged," huffed Dale, and Doug agreed with him. Jane didn't point out that the next player in line, the young man who had taken the mallet from Dale, rang the bell on his first try.

Olivia smirked and wandered to a booth selling jewelry, and the men went inside a cigar stand.

Jane peered down the row of tents displaying peach salsa mixes, peaches in white paper sacks, peach cheesecakes sold in jars, peach relish with peppers, dipping sauces made from peach puree...and a stall advertising, "Stop here for your eclipse glasses."

The cardboard eyeshades were selling fast as customers lined up at the cash register. Jane was glad to note the eyeshades were labeled as compliant with the international safety standard because unscrupulous hustlers were selling unsafe knock-offs on the internet. She entered the deep tent wondering what else was being offered for sale. Chakra jewelry, singing bowls, bells, chimes, and candles. She examined the books on aliens and UFO sightings from around the world.

Isobel appeared at Jane's side. "What are you looking at? Are you going to buy something?"

"I was wondering what 'chakra' means. I see a lot of things having to do with chakras." Jane plucked a candle off a shelf and breathed in the fragrance.

Isobel smoothed a fingertip along her tattoo, tracing the sun rays inked on her skin. "Chakras are like vortexes of energy. If your body's chakras are out of balance you can have health issues. Anxiety or low energy or stomach problems, even."

A stall worker hustled over. "You're absolutely right. People are going to get lightheaded and dizzy when the sun and moon line up, especially here on the Western Slope where the alignment of the land formations are more obvious, you know, between the Colorado National Monument and the Bookcliffs and the Grand Mesa."

"Oh, how interesting." Jane tried to keep her smile from being wooden. "Thank you for the explanation." She already had her eclipse glasses, and her deep-rooted faith gave her all the confidence she needed for so-called alignment, with or without vortexes.

"We're anticipating a lot of cosmic activity. You'll see many surprising events." The clerk was interrupted by another customer and headed back to the cash register.

Jane spotted a pair of eclipse glasses that would be a perfect practical joke, and once Isobel went outside into the bright sunshine, Jane got in line at the cash register to buy them.

After finishing in the booth, Jane caught up with her young friend and asked, "Do you believe in these chakras?"

"I like to keep an open mind." Isobel shielded her eyes from the glaring sun. "Look at that sunny sky. You'd never know the sun is going to be obliterated in two more days."

Jane pointed to the young woman's tattoo. "I love that design, probably because I love sunshine. It gives me a happy feeling."

"Brynne! Brynne Less!" A woman called out her game name. Jane swiveled toward the voice. Georgiana sidled up to them. "I mean, Jane. Are you enjoying the fair?"

"Yes." Jane glanced right and left at the surging crowd. She urged Georgiana and Isobel out of the traffic to the edge of the grass. "I didn't know you'd be here."

Georgiana said, "I can't miss the Peach Festival. I come every year."

"Did you see Zeta Barre's booth? She's running for mayor now." Jane waved a hand in that direction.

"Humpf. I did see that." Georgiana's eyes were covered up by large, dark sunglasses, but her drawn forehead and her deep frown showed contempt. "I can't stand the woman."

"Why?"

"She's not running to honor Rey, you know. She has her own agenda. They didn't have a good marriage, anyone will tell you that."

Jane gave her a startled look but couldn't read the

woman's expression with her eyes behind the dark shades. Georgiana was younger than Zeta by a decade or more. Did they run in the same circle of friends? "So you knew Zeta and Reynard Barre pretty well, then?"

"Of course. Everyone knows them around here. They own a winery and have a big ranch. She cared more about her horses than she did her husband." Georgiana jutted a hip forward and jammed a fist onto her waist.

Jane waited for her to say more, and Isobel stood in silence, too, but Georgiana was staring over Jane's shoulder. Jane turned and followed Georgiana's line of sight toward the "Barre for Mayor" booth where Zeta was shaking the hand of an older gentleman. Jane reverted her attention back to Georgiana.

Sweat trickled down the woman's temple. "Gee, it's a hot one today. I'm going to get out of the sun. See ya' later." She left, zig-zagging between the booths, and disappeared into a fruit stand.

Jane groped her hand up the back of her head to lift her heavy, shoulder-length hair off her neck for some cool air. Perspiration stuck like a melted lollipop in the middle of her back. She had to agree with Georgiana; it was a sweltering day. Was the woman just as spot-on when it came to the Barre marriage? Had Zeta and Rey's marriage been in trouble?

After looking every-which-way and spotting Olivia in a stall hung with western clothes and leather goods, Jane said to Isobel, "There's your mom. Let's join her." She led the way with Isobel following.

"Hey, goils, watcha' doing?" Olivia pronounced "girls" with a silly New York accent as she slid hangers of clothes along a metal rod.

Jane said, "I'd like to get a hat for a little shade, but it's all cowboy hats in here."

"We are on the Western Slope, in wild west country."

Jane glided her fingers across a Stetson made out of stiff raffia straw. She drew it up to her head, John Wayne style, and plopped it on top. "Okay. I'll go with it. Where's a mirror?"

Olivia directed her to a framed mirror hanging on a tent pole. "You look adorable in that hat. It really looks good on you. You should get it." The dimpled crown was not too tall, and the brim curled up on both sides of her head, forcing her hair to curl in under her chin.

A clerk dashed over. "That hat was made for you." She didn't seem to fit the country stereotype with her green-streaked blonde hair pulled back with a green ribbon and dark smudges of green eye shadow across her eyelids. At least she was wearing cowboy boots, but they, too, were green, made of dyed, tooled leather. Jane was surprised her lipstick wasn't green, but it was red.

Jane sneaked in a quick peek at the price tag. "I'll take it."

"Wonderful. Anything else I can help you with?"

"I see you have boots for sale, too." She squinted at Olivia, and her friend gave her a reassuring thumbs up, as if to say, *go for it*. "I'd like to try on a pair. A green pair like yours. They're too cute for words."

It was a good thing she wore her boot-cut jeans, because she purchased the green leather boots along with the straw cowboy hat. Since it was easier to stuff her sandals into her purse rather than carry the new boots around, she kept the boots on her feet. She tucked her hot hair under the cowboy hat and strode behind the two Ladner women down the track between the tents in her fancy boots, her eyes now shielded from the glaring sun under the brim of her cowboy hat.

The sound of music, heavy on the acoustic guitar and violin, drifted over from a bandstand where a country singing trio performed. Dale leaned against a cottonwood tree, watching the musicians.

Jane strutted over to him and showed him her new boots and hat. He gave her an approving smile and held her hand as they meandered across the fairway. He gazed at her with hearts in his eyes, and she ruffled his hair. They were making an end-of-summer memory she could reminisce about during the dead of winter.

They wandered up to a mechanical bull ride surrounded by a crowd of spectators. The bull was centered in the middle of a bouncy mat, and a child around the age of ten was riding it with considerable ease.

"Who wants to ride the bull?" Doug's eyebrows waggled up and down.

"Me, me!" Jane laughed.

"Really? Go for it, Jane." Olivia had on an I-dare-you look. Isobel stood behind her mother with an amused expression on her face.

"You first." Jane stuck out her lower lip like a pouting child.

"Yeah, right. What if I ride the bull, then you chicken out?" Olivia's eyes bulged in an I-double-dare-you look. "Are you a scaredy cat?"

"No. So all right. I'll go first." Jane stepped up to pay the five dollars. Dale's jaw dropped open, and Olivia appeared shamefaced, like someone who wanted to back out. Jane knew that look and that she'd been hoodwinked. She climbed onto the mechanical bull anyway, very much the cowgirl in her blue jeans, cowboy hat, and boots.

Rising to a dare was nothing new. She'd been baited into doing something silly once before…in college…at a time in her life when she was shy and hadn't dated much. The girls in her dorm went on a panty raid outside a boys' dormitory, and she, of all people, caught a pair of boys' briefs thrown from a window. She'd proudly pinned her prize from the panty raid onto the bulletin board over her desk. Later, when using a heating coil to warm water for hot tea, the coil caught the briefs on fire. She'd run down the hall waving the flaming briefs, yelling, "Fire! Fire! Pants on fire!"

"Whoa!" She flew through the air and landed on the bouncy floor, the breath knocked out of her. The mechanical bull wound to a stop with a wheezy noise.

Dale leaned into her vision. "Jane? You all right?"

She stared up, not blinking.

"Why were you screaming 'pants on fire, pants on fire?'"

"Did I say that out loud?"

He nodded and yanked her to a stand, twisting her around. "Are your pants on fire?"

She rubbed her numb posterior to return some feeling to her rear-end along with some dignity to her whole being. "Well, um, no, but the seat felt hot." She didn't want to admit to her embarrassing memory.

"That's not right." Dale made his way to the man at the switch, evidently to complain about the wiring.

An elementary school-aged boy climbed onto the

bull while she joined the Ladners on the sidelines. The boy held on like a child on a mechanical horse at a penny arcade. He stayed on for longer than Jane had the patience to watch.

Doug shoved his cell phone into her line of sight. "I took a video."

Olivia said, "Look at your face. You look like you're riding a real, bucking bull, like a rodeo star. What were you thinking about?"

"Ah, nothing but hanging on, I guess." Her new cowboy hat and boots looked good in the video, at least. The video was titled, "Pants on Fire." There were already a number of "likes," and the number of views had reached forty-nine. "Wait. Where's this posted? Is this on YouTube?"

Doug's hold on the cell phone tightened. "Yes." He refreshed the screen and they watched as the number jumped to ninety.

She slapped his arm. "You take that down right now."

His eyes were glued to the screen. "Too late. The views are over one hundred already." He drew the phone back to his chest and covered his smile with one hand. "No one knows it's you. I didn't tag you, like on Facebook."

Jane glared at him. Olivia and Isobel were biting their lips to keep from laughing.

Dale returned. "The operator said there's nothing wrong with the bull. He doesn't know why you felt it was burning you."

"Thanks, Dale. It doesn't matter. My pants weren't really on fire, but I have an on-fire idea. Follow me."

Chapter 4

"Anything you want. Everything you wish for…whatever your heart's desire…it's all here." Jane pointed to the line of food trucks. "Pizza slices, brats, burgers, barbeque, lemonades…What would you like?"

She wasn't all that hungry herself, so while the others stood in line at the food trucks, she bought a pint-sized bag of peaches from a fruit stand and grabbed a spot large enough for the five of them at an empty picnic table. The men came back with giant turkey legs, Olivia and Isobel carried over Navajo tacos, and they all sank onto the benches to eat. Jane smelled the sweetness of her peach as her teeth sliced through the soft, fuzzy skin and the juice dribbled down her face. After dabbing her chin, she wrapped her napkin around the pit.

"It's kind of creepy that you're eating a peach, you know, since Reynard died with a peach pit in his throat." The edges of Olivia's mouth were pulled down in disgust.

Jane tossed the napkin into the nearby garbage can. "His death isn't going to keep me from eating peaches. We are at the peeeeeach festival." She stretched the word out. "Are you getting bad karma from the peaches, Isobel?"

The young woman crammed a bite of taco into her mouth. She mumbled, "Can't talk with my mouth full."

Doug gnawed on his turkey leg at the same time Dale ripped a chunk of meat off his turkey bone with his teeth. Tearing apart meat like a Neanderthal and nibbling fruit off the pit like a squirrel were disgusting, if one thought about it.

Dale threw down his turkey leg. "If we're done at the festival, let's go check out some of the wineries."

"I'm game." Jane gathered their paper plates and added them to the trash receptacle.

Isobel said, "I'm outta here. See you all later." They gave her a wave as she walked toward the bicycle racks.

The remaining four piled into Dale's company pickup, roomy with the extended cab, and headed out on the Palisade Fruit & Wine Byway, the route locals called the "Fruit Loop." The vertiginous road made ninety-degree turns alongside the irrigation canals connecting the high-altitude vineyards to the Colorado River. Gray netting covered rows of grapevines next to peach orchards, the vines glowing with red grapes, the trees laden with peaches, the variegated colors speckling the green branches, the fruit blooming from yellow to orange to rosy pink.

Jane caught another whiff of the mystery fragrance outside the truck window. "I think I smell lavender."

Olivia prodded the back of Jane's seat. "You do. They grow lavender on the loop, too. We just drove past some. Keep looking. You'll see purple bushes that look sorta like sage." Now that Jane knew what to expect, the narrow stretches of purple tucked among the peach groves were more apparent.

The group clambered out of the truck at the first vineyard. Jane slid her bottom off the seat until her feet touched the ground. While Olivia and Doug went inside to cozy up to the wine tasting bar, Jane and Dale stopped outside to appreciate the view from the terrace. The wind whipped Jane's hair all around. She smoothed it down before taking a few snapshots.

"Don't forget to spit out your wine," Jane reminded her friends once she and Dale joined the Ladners at the bar. Each sample contained about two ounces, not much, but the portions did add up. They introduced themselves to the owner and chatted for a couple of minutes before purchasing a few bottles and moving on to the next winery. By the time they were finished with the Fruit Loop, the back of Dale's pickup held a couple cartons of wine.

"What should we do next?" Dale turned the key to start the engine.

"The Barre Vineyard is just down the road from here. Do you want to drive past and look at it from the outside?" Jane had the GPS app open on her cell phone.

"Sure." Dale swerved onto the road, and Jane pointed the way. He brought the truck to a stop at the Barre Vineyard. A sign was posted on the door, "Closed today due to a death in the family."

They got out to look around. A gravel drive sloped down to a wooden pergola and an outdoor seating area overlooking a panoramic view of the Bookcliffs. Jane and Dale ambled across the lawn to discover yet another breathtaking lookout over the bluff above the winding Colorado River.

"A perfect place to get married." Jane gave her fiancé a broad smile and he clutched her hand. "Of all the vineyards we've seen today, this is my favorite, at least from the outside."

Dale said, "We did a pretty good job finding it on the internet. I'm glad we booked it, in spite of what happened to the owner." He sucked his lips in and scrunched his shoulders up near his ears.

They exchanged nervous glances at the reminder.

When they returned to the gravel parking lot, a long, white passenger van with a satellite dish on the roof drove in and shuddered to a halt. A suited woman and a jean-clad man climbed out. The man braced an enormous, professional-looking video cam on his shoulder. The woman stood with her back to the winery and held a wireless microphone to her lips. "Testing, testing…ready?"

The dinner club members took a few backward steps to shuffle out of view.

The cameraman nodded. "Frame." A red dot blinked on and off, then went to a solid light. He spoke into the sound feed, "Joining us now is special news correspondent, Tracy Weizer of KGND, Grand Junction."

The newscaster went into her report. "We are stunned to learn of the death of Reynard Barre, a respected member of our community and mayor of Barresville. Mayor Barre's great-great-grandfather founded the town which takes its name from the family holdings, Barre Valley Ranch. Several generations of Barres have served on the city council. Many family members have been pillars of the community. Reynard Barre, himself, served for nearly a decade on the Barresville City Council, before taking over from his father as mayor. He was involved in a highly contentious campaign for re-election when he met his untimely death."

Tracy Weizer licked her glossy lips and waved her hand in the direction of the closed sign on the tasting room door. "We are standing in front of the Barre Winery. Reynard Barre's death is still a mystery but appears to be the result of foul play. That he died during a murder mystery game has caused quite a bit of speculation, but the cause of death is not immediately clear, and family members have been unavailable for comment. Law enforcement is looking into possible suspects and motives."

The cameraman clicked off his device and lowered it from his shoulder. "That was good, Tracy. Let's go."

"Hold on one minute." The newscaster gave the club members a speculative look and strode over. "Have you heard about the owner of this vineyard? He was killed last night. What do you think about that?"

Doug spoke up first. "We're not from around here. We're in town for the Peach Festival and we're just visiting wineries this afternoon."

Jane sent him a thankful glance. Tracy caught the look and went for Jane's jugular. "You, the one in the crazy green boots, how do you feel about a person being murdered during your visit to the wine country? Do you feel safe?"

Count on the news to sensationalize his death.

Jane cast a look down at her leather-clad feet and ignored the question but asked one of her own. "You said Mr. Barre was in the middle of a contentious campaign for re-election. What do you mean by 'contentious?' Has the race been particularly nasty?"

"Did you happen to see any of the billboards?" Tracy's eyes lit up, likely hopeful for an interview from an alarmed, out-of-town tourist. "Kirby Potts has been especially negative."

Jane slapped her hands against her cheeks. Kirby Potts? Did she mean the man from the party? The one who was a sculptor? That Kirby Potts? Had to be. His was not a common name. She found her tongue and said, "Kirby was Reynard's opponent?"

Olivia said, "Kirby Potts! Why that was Shamus Onnrue."

"What? What's this? Do you know something shameful about Kirby Potts?" Tracy's voice was giddy with anticipation.

"No, no, that's not what I said. I, I..." Olivia's gaze darted around until her eyes reached Jane. She gave her a *help me!* look. Doug scowled like a husband who was afraid of what his wife was about to say next.

"We met someone with a similar name, that's all," Jane said as she grabbed Olivia's arm.

All four friends turned on their heels to make a run for Dale's pickup truck. They jumped inside, and Dale hit the automatic locks. Tracy stood transfixed with her glossy lips hanging open. Jane barely had enough time to buckle her seatbelt before Dale's truck rocketed out of the parking lot.

"That was close." Dale gripped the wheel and tapped the brakes to slow down at a bend in the road.

Doug rubbed his mustache so hard Jane thought he might tear it off his face. "I certainly didn't want to appear on the evening news."

"Me neither." Jane sliced her hands through the air in a crosswise sign, making an "X" over her chest. "No. Way." Her hands cut an "X" two more times.

"Kirby Potts killed that man, I'll bet." Olivia scooched forward in her seat.

"I'm sure the police will be examining him very carefully." Doug checked his cell phone. Perhaps he was waiting for a call from the homicide investigator. He would be sure to use his police contacts to get information.

"Let's look for the billboards. Everyone keep their eyes out." Jane peered through her window as Dale maneuvered the truck around two bicyclists sharing the road.

Olivia groaned when the truck took a sharp corner. "I need to eat. I admit I didn't always spit."

Jane curled her lip. "What do you mean?"

"The wine. I didn't spit out the wine at the tastings."

"It's a good idea to eat. Head to Barresville, Dale. There's a pizza place you and Jane will really like." Doug eyed his wife and reached past her to crack open her window.

Dale steered the truck north to the expressway. They soon spotted the billboards on the side of Interstate 70 every thousand feet or so.

"Raise the Bar by Defeating Barre."

"Time to take Barre out of Barresville."

"Bar None, Barre Must Go!"

Olivia made tskking sounds. "Wow, that newscaster was right. These billboards are full of negative campaign slogans."

The towering signs blocking the views were disturbing. Jane frowned. "Ugh. I'm already tired of seeing them. Can we get off the highway, Dale? Can't we take a backroad to Barresville?"

He cast worried eyes over his shoulder. "I thought the interstate would be a smoother ride for Olivia."

Olivia took in a bracing breath from the open window. "I'm fine. No problem. Besides, the back way off the highway is shorter."

"Take the next exit and I'll show you how to get there," Doug directed Dale from the backseat.

Dale aimed the truck toward the frontage road to trace the route alongside the Colorado River. The four fell into a silent stupor as the scenery went by. The stunning Bookcliffs on their left towered above the waterway, which wove through the tall grasses and peach orchards on their right. Soon, they descended eastward into a narrow valley, leaving behind the terraced, lush vineyards draped with netting and entering a desolate place with the barren red rock, the dusty brown dirt, and the dry still air of the high desert—the opposite of the green, irrigated, wind-blown vineyards in the wine valley.

After they proceeded down the wide, potholed main street that made up Barresville, Doug said, "Park anywhere. We can walk to the pizza place from here."

Dale pulled in front of an ice cream parlor with windows so dirty it was difficult to see inside. They all climbed out and headed toward the wooden boardwalk. Jane breathed in the smell of rotting wood, like that of a broken-down log cabin or worn-out railroad tracks. The walkway led to the Pizzeria and Brewery where Doug claimed they brewed the best ales around.

"No wine?" Jane teased, but in a half-serious way. She wasn't a beer drinker.

"I'm sure they have a wine list. Barre Valley *is* right next door to Palisade." Olivia shouldered her way through the door. "But I'm having water."

Doug went inside after her. "Let's order, then find

a table outside on the patio. It's too nice to stay indoors." Jane loved to eat outside, so was happy to agree. The place may not have the same views as Palisade, but the high desert had a beauty of its own.

Jane followed Dale into the dark interior where a yeasty smell mingled with the peppery and meaty scent of Italian food. They ordered two pizzas and various ales, and Jane asked for a local white wine.

Once seated outside with their drinks at the cement picnic table against the old brick building, she extracted the campaign brochures out of her purse. "I snagged these flyers at the festival."

Dale said, "Good job, Jane. I'd like to see what the candidates have to say."

"Okay." Jane passed Kirby's over to Dale as she skimmed Zeta's. After only a few moments, she read out loud, " 'Reynard Barre grew up in the valley and saw hardship firsthand. He was named after his daddy and his granddaddy and was the first in the family to get a college education. It's his desire to generate economic wealth in the community by developing Barre Valley and bringing in more jobs.'"

She looked around at the small downtown with several empty buildings across the street, the windows obscured by torn brown paper and "Out of Business" signs. On the far side of the last building, stubbled fields, then arid, parched land stretched toward the distant mesa. The span of hard dirt was formidable. Nothing could grow there.

But nevertheless, the restaurant had plenty of food. Two waiters brought out steaming, fragrant pans of pizza. They each grabbed a slice.

Dale set down his beer and passed Kirby Potts'

flyer to Jane. "Potts doesn't say much about what he's for, but he does say what he's against. He wants to restrict development, whatever that means. It's all pretty vague."

She glanced through the bullet points. "You're right. Potts is against Barre, against development, against, against, against. But there's nothing about what he supports." Jane twisted toward the former policeman sitting kitty-corner to her on the bench. "Doug, is a negative mayoral campaign worth killing someone over?"

"Yes, it is. Definitely a motive."

"Have you heard anything from the Palisade Police?"

"I got a call when we were at one of the vineyards." Doug swilled down a long drink of his cold beer.

"Well...tell us, Douglas." Olivia nudged his elbow.

"All right, already." He wiped the creamy froth from his red mustache with a napkin. "The autopsy was this afternoon. I guess there aren't a lot of deaths in Palisade and they got to it right away. The coroner phoned the investigator with preliminary findings. The cause of death was from a blow to the head as a result of the fall onto the cement hearth. He fell in a freaky way and a blood vessel ruptured in his brain stem. The hemorrhage bled out before he could regain consciousness and he died."

Jane placed her wine glass on the table. "Could he have been saved if someone had called an ambulance?"

Doug drew his lips in. "Probably, yes. This means, at the least, voluntary manslaughter or even murder one."

Dale asked, "What's the difference between voluntary and involuntary manslaughter? I've never understood that."

"Voluntary has to do with the killer's state of mind, like killing someone in the heat of passion. Involuntary is when it was an accident, not intended. This smacks of intent, though, and if the killer intentionally left Rey to die, the charge could be first-degree."

"What about the peach pit?" Olivia tapped her husband's arm.

"The pit was forced down his throat after he was dead. That means the killer stayed to make sure he died or came back afterwards. That action alone could be evidence of intent."

Each one set their slices of pizza on their plates, and Dale swirled a finger around the neck of his shirt.

Olivia said with a sniff, "Oh, dear. I've lost my appetite. And, now we have peach pit paranoia."

"No, just a problem with peach pit placement." Jane made a pppppppt sound, like a jalopy trying to start. "Too many 'Ps.' That's hard to say." No one laughed. Even Olivia didn't snicker. Jane stared out at the desert vista. "Why is Grand Valley so green and fruitful, and this valley so dry and barren? They're close to each other, just separated by the mesa."

Doug knew the answer. "Grand Valley has a unique climate. Warm winds blow in from De Beque Canyon. The chinooks keep the grapes from freezing in the spring, even when there is still frost over here in Barre Valley. Then, during the summer, heat radiates off the Bookcliffs. There's nothing over here to give Barre Valley that same warming effect. The cliffs don't stretch this far east."

"The pizzas and the brews are good here in Barrestown, anyway." Dale slid another gooey slice from the pizza dish onto his plate, his hunger obviously returning.

"It's Barresville, Dale." Jane suppressed a smile, then asked Doug, "What do the people over here do for a living?"

"There are a few ranches, including Barre Valley Ranch. But the ranches are struggling, it's so dry, the land can't support large herds. The Barre Winery in Palisade is where Reynard and Zeta make their living." Doug must know all of this from his brother who had lived in Palisade for many years now.

Dale raised his eyebrows. "Life has to be tough over here, a stark contrast to the lucrative life in the Palisades."

Jane slapped his arm. "The town is called 'Palisade,' not 'the Palisades.' It's like saying 'the Denvers.' Doesn't that sound wrong?"

"Oh, yeah. Sorry." Dale laughed. "Olivia keeps making fun of me for calling the Bookcliffs the 'Bookends.'"

Olivia snorted. "Yes, Dale. You're an easy target."

Jane took a sip of her wine. "What's Isobel doing tonight, by the way?"

Doug shrugged and washed down his pizza with another mouthful of beer.

Olivia answered the question. "You know how kids are, they only hang out with you for so long, then they want to be on their own." Disappointment threaded through her words.

"She's not a kid, she's an adult." Jane flicked a palm skyward. "Besides, she showed up at the Peach

Festival and spent all morning with us. And she came all the way here from New York, don't forget that."

"I know, you're right." Olivia gave out a deep sigh. "I'll be ready to head back to the B&B when we're done here. Maybe Holden knows more about this raging war between Barre and Potts."

"Good idea," Doug said, grabbing one more slice. "I'll bet he does."

"And he'll know about the other townies, too." Jane had had her fill, so she threw her napkin onto her plate and stretched her arms over her head.

Dale said, "We should get a to-go box for the rest of the pizza. There will be a couple of pieces left." Once he finished, he went inside the pizzeria for a box.

Soon they were back on the road to the Ladner Bed-and-Breakfast for the lowdown on the local scene.

Jane may not have the small-town scoop, but she was darned sure going to find out. Likely soap opera secrets waited to be revealed. Time to rip the covers back and expose the naked truth.

Chapter 5

"Look! There!" Olivia's voice came out high and loud, causing Jane to yell, "What? Where?"

"Dale, pull into this peach stand!" Olivia rapped a knuckle on her window.

He yanked the wheel and skidded to a halt in front of a ramshackle adobe hut with "Peaches and Pie" hand lettered on the side facing the road.

"Ouch!" Jane's shoulder bounced against the passenger door. She let out a long breath and let go of the death grip she had on the door handle.

Doug rocked back in his seat. "Didn't we just eat?"

"And?" Olivia's hand made a spiral, urging him to get to the point.

Jane added, "How can you be hungry after that pizza?"

"Pie, Jane. Peach pie. Can't turn that down. Remember, you were the one who said we're here for the festival. Come on, let's go." Without waiting for the others, Olivia sprang her door open and hopped out, then jogged toward the building that had peeling stucco, a roof that dipped, and a cracked and broken window.

"It looks like a dump," Jane said under her breath. "A shack." But the air, wafting through the truck door Olivia had left yawning open, was perfumed with the scent of baking fruit and cinnamon.

Dale sang the lyrics to "Love Shack." He gave his

head a quick jerk toward the pie hut, as if mirroring Olivia's *come on, let's do it!* and said, "We might as well go inside."

Jane dutifully shut the truck's doors and followed the two men in. The smell of fresh baking—cherries and cinnamon and nutmeg and brown sugar and…peaches—made her mouth water. A hunger pang shot through her stomach, so she must've saved room for dessert after all.

An industrial-sized cooler buzzed against one wall, looking like it was salvaged from a 1950's grocer. Rips in the dirty and worn-out linoleum exposed the subfloor below, and scuff marks had eroded the pattern and color. Even Jane's housecleaner couldn't dig out the grime embedded in the corners, not even with Mr. Clean and a mega power spray.

But the heavenly, mouth-watering scent of baking pie overruled her hesitation.

A woman with a weathered face, wearing a large bibbed apron over a flowered cotton dress, like Andy Griffith's Aunt Bee, appeared from a back room. "Good evening. I just took a peach pie out." Her voice was melodic, as homey and pleasant as the smell of the baking pies.

Another group of tourists burst through the door with, "Mmmmm. What smells so good?"

Before the new arrivals could cut in, Olivia hollered out, "We'll take the peach pie."

The Aunt Bee lookalike smiled, giving away an imperfect set of teeth with several missing. "I'll be right back." She disappeared from sight through an ill-fitting door to another room.

Jane examined a crowded wall with wooden

shelves holding dusty potted plants. Under the shelves, photographs hung haphazardly. The plants were flourishing, but the lopsided picture frames looked like they could fall off the wall at any moment. Jane stepped closer to straighten a photograph of a horse, perhaps one from the wild horse refuge. Another photo portrayed the pie shack at the foot of the soaring Bookcliffs, a charming, lazy setting belying the obvious hard work of baking that went on inside. Both photographs shared a particular sun-lit glow, shafts of light extending golden from the ball of flame in the sky, the oblique, long, sloping beams of light bathing the desert, the slanting rays intensifying the sunset. The pictures must've been taken by the same photographer, one who had a particular, distinctive eye for the light. In both pictures, a woman gazed at the horses, but only the side of her face was caught on camera. Her blonde hair and jawline looked familiar.

Aunt Bee returned with an oversized, high-crowned pie. Doug tugged a wallet out of his back pocket and asked in his polite way, "Do you have plates and silverware?"

Aunt Bee gave them a puzzled look. "You're going to eat it here?"

"Yes, the pie's hot now." Olivia's voice was sing-song, as if the answer was obvious.

"Well, let me look around." Aunt Bee found four paper plates of the flimsy, thin variety, the kind that could disintegrate upon impact with food, and four plastic forks sealed in cellophane, looking like they were left over from someone's take-out bag.

Olivia carried the heavy pie outside to a picnic table under an old cottonwood tree. The table was splintered and bleached gray by the sun, but after dusting broken bits of branches and debris off the wood, they all took seats. Using a plastic knife, Olivia cut the pie into six generous sections and lifted the pieces with her bare hands. Jane didn't mind, since Olivia constantly scrubbed her hands with a miniature bottle of sanitizer from her purse, and her fingers were more disinfected than a serving piece straight from the dishwasher.

Once her flimsy plate was in front of her, and in spite of being stuffed to overflowing already, Jane dug in along with the others. No one said a word as they gobbled up the yummy pie, tasting sweet in a sugary, flaky crust, enhanced by warmth and freshness, just out-of-the-oven goodness. The guys ate the two extra pieces and the pie was gone.

"We creamed that peach pie." Olivia passed around her pocket-sized bottle of hand cleanser and they all squirted a dollop onto their sticky palms. Jane's fingers tingled as the alcohol-based gel evaporated.

"Peach has to be my favorite pie." Jane couldn't seem to get enough of the peaches.

Dale wiped his hands on a tissue. "Apple for me."

"This peach was sooo good, oh yeah, but my fav' is pumpkin." Olivia smacked her lips.

Doug had on a dreamy look. "My mom made a wonderful banana cream pie. I'd have to say that's my favorite."

"I thought I was stuffed after the pizza, but now I can hardly move." Jane patted her full belly. "Should we head back to the B&B?"

"Yes," they all said at once. At least everyone agreed on that.

The return trip took only fifteen minutes since Dale remembered the back country short cut. Once in the door, Doug stowed the to-go box of pizza in the refrigerator, and they all waddled outside to where Holden was enjoying a cigar on the L-shaped, wraparound patio overlooking the Bookcliffs at the long end and the front parking lot on the short end.

"Mind if I have a smoke, too?" Doug asked his brother.

"Not at all. Do you need a stick?" Holden blew a smoke ring. "I've got plenty."

"No, I brought some." Doug hurried to his room and returned moments later. The group settled into the row of comfortable patio chairs with their feet propped on the railing facing the cliffs.

Honeybees made their droning sound among the peaches that had fallen and split open on the ground. A sprinkler from an irrigation system rent the air with a sh-sh-sh-tik-tik-tik, then repeated, sh-sh-tik-tik. A dog barked and a plane rumbled overhead. All comforting sounds of late summer. One of those crisp Colorado evenings that made you love the west.

Jane brought up what the others were probably wondering. "Holden, we found out today that Kirby was running for mayor against Reynard. Isn't that odd? He's an artist, not a politician."

He nodded. "That's right. He's running for mayor."

"And Zeta is running in her husband's place now." Jane toed off her cowboy boots and they clattered to the wood deck. She slid farther down into her seat cushion and planted her petite bare feet with her pretty pink toenails up on the rail.

"I did hear that." Holden placed his cigar in the

ashtray.

Jane shook her head. "I'm surprised you invited both candidates to your party."

Holden inhaled a deep lungful of air. "I know, I know. But look. One will win. One will lose, and no matter what, we all still have to live in this small valley. We all have to get along."

"Are you sure they got along?" Olivia leaned forward, her eyes bright. "Maybe it was Kirby who killed Rey?"

Holden waved his index finger back and forth in a broad gesture. "That seems like a drastic measure."

Jane added, "Still, we need to consider it."

Doug gave both women a look that could silence the drone of the bees. Everything did seem to go quiet. The sprinkler shut off with a sputter and a ratchety sound. The dog stopped barking. Doug laced his fingers behind his head and crossed one foot over his knee. His cigar hung from a corner of his mouth and bobbed when he spoke. "Tell us about the people at the party. Especially the folks from town, the ones who didn't have rooms who were only here for the mystery game. Did any of them have a reason to kill Reynard?"

It was all right with Jane if Doug asked the questions. Just as long as he didn't cut her out of the investigation.

"I don't have a clue about that, Doug, but even if they did have something against him, they had no opportunity because Rey saw them all out the door. Everybody else left before he died, except those staying the night. Kirby, Georgiana, Skylar, and Zeta." Holden jabbed a finger in the air four times, once for each name.

"What about Dee Lish? I thought she was obnoxious." Olivia screwed her face into a scowl.

"Who was she?" Jane shifted in her seat to look at Olivia.

"The one who kept laughing really loud."

"Oh, yeah."

Dale added, "Or how about 'Ratatatat' Touille, the guy who brought a Nerf machine gun? Or 'Fritz the Snitch?' I thought he was a little weird. He was dressed in the same costume as Kirby."

Holden said, "The guy who played the Snitch character is a professional photographer. He's a bit of a nerd with all his camera equipment, but he's very talented. You'll see his photographs for sale everywhere. But remember, those guests had all left, they were long gone." Holden stared at his hands, which were unmoving in his lap for once.

Olivia knifed Jane with a sharp elbow. "I'll bet that Snitch took pictures of the party if he's a photographer."

Jane rubbed her arm. "Good thinking, Liv. I'll bet he did, too. I wonder how we can find out and get a look at them." She rested her head on the back of her chair, sleepy-full from pizza and peach pie. The buzz of yet another bee whizzed past her ear, cutting across the deck in line for the orchard. The breeze played in the trees, and the branches shook as birds took off in flight. The sweet, ripe peaches scented the wind, and the descending sun lit up the cliff face with a radiant yellow glow. "Could Liza, I mean Zeta...jeez, it's hard to remember their real names...have killed her husband? The murderer is often the spouse."

Holden dropped his feet from the railing and sat

forward, elbows on knees. "No way. Zeta is incapable of killing anyone. She's the most amazing person in the world." His voice was heavy as he added, almost as an afterthought, "She loved her husband."

Whew. Holden seemed to be her number one fan. Jane closed her eyes, the better to concentrate, blocking out the distracting beauty of the cliffs soaring to the sky, the grandeur of the steep rocks looking so different in the evening light. "Why didn't Zeta notice when her husband didn't come to bed last night? I mean, it didn't look as if he made it upstairs. He was still wearing his party costume."

Holden said, "I don't know. I'm sure the police asked her that question."

Olivia raised an eyebrow. "Well, I think that's very suspicious."

Doug said, "There could be an explanation. Some people are sound sleepers. Zeta could be one of those."

Jane asked Holden, "Apart from the wife, what do you think about Skylar as the killer? Or Georgiana since both of them were here all night?"

"I can't imagine either one of them hurting Rey." Holden threw his arms up in the air. "But I don't know. What are your thoughts, Doug? You're the expert."

"We need to make sure someone else couldn't have sneaked inside." Doug stood and set his cigar on the edge of the patio table, the burning end directed outward. "I'm going to check all the windows in that room where Reynard was killed. I'll be right back."

Jane jerked upright. "I'm coming." She bounded out of her chair. The rest of them had on a resigned look and stretched up to follow Jane and Doug to the lounge.

The police tape was down, and the fingerprint powder wiped clean, but a faint rusty brown stain was evident in the carpet. The hearth had been scratched where someone, perhaps Holden, had scrubbed it hard to return the surface from blood-red back to stone-cold white.

Doug tugged the latch on the only window in the room. "This window is locked up tight now, but was it last night?"

Jane lifted up on her tippy-toes to peer outside through the ground-level window. Bicycles leaning together were stacked against the glass outside. The undersurface of the deck obscured the evening sky. A curled garden hose, gardening gloves, and a couple pair of rain boots were scattered in the dirt, and beyond that a lawn stretched over to the peach orchard. Holden's Subaru was parked under one of the fruit trees.

"I watched the police check this window myself." Holden crossed one arm over the other. "I don't think a person could get in or out, at least not very easily, not with all the bikes in the way."

Olivia yanked a thumb behind them at the stairwell. "Could someone have gotten in through an open window upstairs? Then come down here and kill Reynard? Then go back upstairs and escape the same way." She popped her eyes open wide, in a dare-to-contradict-me expression.

Holden stood a little taller. "The rooms were all occupied. Someone would've heard or seen something."

"What about the front door?" Jane piped up. "Isobel was able to walk right in the front door after everyone else left."

Holden flapped his hands. "I saw Isobel come in and I gave her the key to her room. Then I locked the doors and went to bed myself. There was no sign of forced entry. I'm sure the police suspect one of the guests, not an intruder."

Jane agreed with him, but there were more than guests at the inn. She studied the B&B owner. He may look a lot like his brother and Jane's good friend, Doug, but she didn't know him at all. He had the most knowledge of the layout of the inn, he was acquainted with all of the guests, being the one who invited each of them, and he had the most opportunity to run into Rey in the lounge...perhaps he had a reason to kill the man and took advantage of the moment to do it. She swallowed hard. Did she really suspect Doug's brother?

She paced in a circle, preferring to concentrate on the guests. "So the suspect list is Zeta, Kirby, Georgiana, and Skylar."

Realistically, Jane had to include herself and her friends, even though they were innocent, of course. There was no way around it. They were all suspects. She might as well get the uncomfortable truth out in the open. Jane said, "Add to the list the four of us, and Holden and Isobel, since we were all at the inn during the time Reynard died."

Olivia extended her arm to stop Jane in her tracks. "What do you mean?"

"We might need alibis, that's all." Jane shrugged out of her friend's grasp and wouldn't meet her eyes.

"Let's check out the upstairs windows in the bedrooms just to make sure no one broke in." Doug made it to the steps in three quick strides and said over his shoulder, "Holden, can you let me inside the vacant rooms?"

"Wait, before we go, can we look around for the missing necklace?" Jane's words made the others stare her way. "Maybe whoever killed Reynard realized he, or maybe it was a she, dropped the necklace, went back for it, and then hid it in here somewhere." She gazed around the room taking everything in.

The corners of Doug's mouth turned down. "What's this about a necklace?"

Oh, right. No one else had seen the pendant. "Reynard had a necklace in his hand when I found him. And after I ran upstairs to get help, by the time we got back down here the necklace was gone. I told the police about it. The chain was gold and there was a glass peach dangling from it."

"Why didn't you mention it to me before now?" Doug rubbed his mustache hard, flattening it against his upper lip. His police contact must not have shared this clue with him.

"Sorry. I just thought of it." Jane lifted one of the cushions off the couch and rammed her fingers between the sections.

Dale had on a puzzled expression. "She didn't say anything to me about the necklace, either, Doug."

Doug seemed resigned. "All right, then. The investigator probably looked for the necklace already, but let's search anyway. This room first, then after that we can split up and go over the whole B&B. Describe the necklace again."

"It's gold with a peach-shaped pendant. The peach looked like it was made out of orange glass with a tiny green leaf." She straightened up and headed for one of the club chairs.

The rest of them joined in, looking under furniture, in table drawers, even in the dirt in the potted plants. They separated to search the guest rooms and the rest of the B&B for the necklace, or for any other way in or out, even testing the locks on the small bathroom windows. One by one they returned to the lounge area and sat down in the same seats where they'd sat during the murder party. No one had found the necklace. No signs of forced entry, like Holden had said. No smoking gun clue.

"I told you the police already looked over the whole place." There was a note of frustration in Holden's voice, and Jane could understand that.

Doug nodded. "There was a small chance we'd find anything. The windows could've been opened, shut, and locked many times since last night, but it was worth double checking."

Olivia said, "Nancy Drew always found a torn scrap of someone's clothing stuck in the window. Darn it, why couldn't we?"

Jane put on her thinking face and nibbled her lower lip. "Holden, you said you took pictures during the party, remember?"

"Yes." He tapped his chest. "I did."

Jane swiped her cell screen. "I took some photos, too." She scrolled through dozens of shots. "How about we all share our party pictures so we can look through them for clues?" Her fingers stopped flicking at the bottom of the camera roll. There she was, pictured in her costume standing next to Olivia, who was a good five inches taller. Yes, she was short, but she was always amazed at how much shorter she was than everyone else. In her mind she always looked other people directly in the eyes.

"What do you mean by sharing photos? How do we do that?" Olivia patted her pocket, as if trying to locate her phone. "Pass our phones around?"

"No." Jane didn't look up. "I'll upload mine to a photo sharing site and send you the link. Each of you can load yours."

Dale scratched his head. "That sounds like a lot of work."

"I'll do mine tonight and all of you can do yours tomorrow. It's easy." Pictures from that photographer would be nice to have, too, but at least they had their own photos to look at. "I wish I could get ahold of pictures taken by the other guests. There's bound to be some clues."

Doug frowned at her. He probably didn't like her inserting herself into the investigation.

"Great. Now we'll get somewhere." Holden's face crinkled into a smile. "How about we head back to the patio and I'll open a bottle of wine?" His smile slipped a bit. "Except, our cigars have probably gone out by now."

Doug puffed out his cheeks. "They're not as good when you relight them."

Olivia didn't hesitate. "I could use a glass of wine." Her husband gave her a silent are-you-sure look, and she shrugged her shoulders. "I didn't have any at dinner and the wine tasting this afternoon was a long time ago."

Jane excused herself to run to the bathroom. Then she stopped in the kitchen for a glass of water for hydration to drink along with the glass of wine. When she approached the door leading to the patio, she overheard Dale saying, "I wish we were married already so the two of us could share a room. I'm ready to have this wedding over with."

"Wow, Jane is really old-fashioned." Holden made a duck face, flattening his lips together in a you've-got-to-be-kidding kind of expression.

"She's a churchgoer."

Jane took a deep breath and stepped outside. She gave her chin a determined upward thrust. "It's nice to hear my love life is the topic of your discussion."

They became so quiet the grandfather clock could be heard ticking inside from the common room.

"What took you so long, Jane?" Olivia's voice boomed out in an attempt to recover from the awkward conversation stopper.

"I went upstairs to the bathroom and I wasn't gone that long."

Olivia sputtered, "It seemed like a long time. Or, no, I mean, it's good to take your time. Or, everyone should take that long in the bathroom…umm, whatever you did, you look really nice, good job, Jane!"

She bristled. "I'm sure there's an attempt at a compliment buried in there somewhere."

Dale patted the chair next to him. "Come here and sit down." She lowered herself onto the chair, and he handed her a glass of wine. "I was just asking Holden if he had any more cancellations. He's had a few. The weekend of our wedding next month is the only one where he's full up." He slung his arm over the back of her chair in his protective way. A warmth seeped into her stomach. His comments were actually flattering, not insulting, and she had a happy feeling of belonging, of being half of a pair, of oneness with this handsome man.

Holden rubbed his chin. "My B&B, along with every hotel in this town, was booked all the way through the third weekend in September. That's the weekend of the Colorado Mountain Winefest." He frowned with a grave face. "Except, after Rey's death made the news on television, I've been getting cancellations, a lot of cancellations."

Olivia flicked a bleak look toward Jane.

She forced herself to put on an encouraging smile. "Maybe those cancellations aren't even related to Rey's death. Sometimes people have to switch their plans."

"That's a lot of people changing their minds." But Holden looked a little more hopeful.

"We've booked the entire inn for the wedding and we aren't cancelling." She gave him a wide smile full of teeth. They had invited eight couples, and their reservations filled the place. The B&B was a perfect location and so was the winery. But...what if Zeta Barre was the killer? Zeta might have the compelling charisma of a politician, but she was still a prime suspect, a possible spouse-killer. If she was a murderer, would they need to cancel the wedding ceremony at the Barre Winery? Would they need to cancel their reservations at the inn, too?

Jane couldn't hold her wedding at a vineyard that was owned by a killer. That wouldn't work at all.

Chapter 6

"Jane, can you come into my room for a minute?" Dale had on a sly grin as he held the door open.

"Yes, but remember I'm a churchgoer." Jane made a screwball face when she slid past him.

"I'm sorry I talked about what should have remained between just the two of us." He shut the door with a click. His room was a mess, with clothes piled on the bedspread and shoes scattered over the floor, but she found a place to sit on the end of the bed. He sank down next to her, the edge of the mattress dipping under his weight.

"I did walk in on you at the wrong moment."

"You sure did." He laughed. "I hate waiting, but if waiting means being with you, then I'll wait as long as it takes." He stroked her back up and down. "No pressure."

Yeah, right. "We haven't had a chance to talk about the Barre Winery. You liked it when we saw it from the outside, didn't you?"

"I did."

"It sure looks perfect. There's a big problem, though." Jane chewed a fingernail. "It's important to solve the homicide first, don't you think?"

"No, no, it is not. We didn't know the victim. His death has nothing to do with us. His wife seems to want our business." He wrapped his arms around her

67

shoulders and drew her in tighter. "We booked the place a month ago. It's a little late to change it now."

"What if Zeta's the killer? What if Zeta's arrested?"

"Holden doesn't seem to think it's her. You don't think it's her, do you?" Dale's chin rested against the top of her head as her arm snaked around his waist.

She snuggled deeper into his embrace. "I don't know. This is affecting our plans whether we want to admit it or not." Her breath swelled against her ribs and she forced a big breath out. "If Zeta's arrested, will the winery close? And even if it didn't close, I sure wouldn't want to get married at a place owned by a murderer." She drew her head back and looked her fiancé straight in the eyes. "And I know you wouldn't either."

Dale deflated.

Jane said, "Say Zeta is arrested and the winery is shut down…if that happens, we should have another place in mind as a backup. We need a contingency plan just in case."

Dale sat up straighter. "That's not a bad idea. What about right here at the B&B? We already have the rooms reserved. We could get married on the deck and arrange for a caterer. Heck, Holden might even want to supply the food."

"Don't forget Holden is a suspect, too, same as Zeta. Would it help any to move from one suspect's place to another?"

"You're right. We should probably find a backup place that is not connected in any way to Rey's death."

Jane rubbed the back of his neck. "I agree. But even if Zeta isn't the killer, we still need to solve the murder because we"—she waggled a finger between the two of them—"could be suspects along with everyone else."

He stared deep into her eyes without blinking and gave her a light kiss on the lips. He murmured into her ear. "That's true enough. But the police have left us alone. We haven't been questioned any further."

"It's only been one day. Mark my words, they'll be back to see us."

"Let the police and Doug handle this investigation. Don't forget about you and me, the two of us and our future together." Dale pulled her into a long, passionate kiss. When he released her, she almost slid off the bed onto the floor.

"Um, what were you saying?" Her voice came out hoarse as she elbowed herself upright. "Oh, yeah. We need to concentrate on the wedding."

"Let's not borrow trouble. The police might have someone in custody right now. There's no reason to panic and change our plans. But if we do need to cancel the winery, we should have a backup."

Jane agreed, "It's a go, then. I'll forget the investigation and focus on the wedding, Plan A being the winery and Plan B a contingency." She'd be married in a month come hell or high water. A thrill went up the back of her spine and down her chest—making her heart thump faster—and the zing went into her stomach landing with a wallop of fireworks.

After several more steamy kisses, Jane emerged from his room and plowed right into Olivia in the hall.

"What have you two been up to? Your hair is all messed up, your lipstick smeared, and you have a silly smile on your face."

Jane felt her cheeks burn. She'd likely blushed red, adding to her mussed look.

Olivia nailed her with a scowl. "Jane, you can't be distracted from this homicide investigation. You heard what Holden said, he's getting cancellations. After you and Dale left, he told Doug that the bed-and-breakfast might be empty on the biggest weekend of the year, during the Winefest. I'm afraid of what might happen if his business continues to take these kinds of hits. You really need to solve this murder and fast."

Jane touched her fingers to her temples. "I hear what you're saying, Olivia, but people will start booking rooms again soon, you'll see."

"What if that doesn't happen? Barre is pretty well known around here, and the story made national news. A video of the outside of the B&B was on television. I'm sure it's on the internet, too. Murder at a murder party. You know how that sounds."

"Oh, dear. I'll look over my photos tonight and upload them to a shared site. You upload yours tomorrow and tell Doug to do his, too, and we'll all go through the photos. Maybe there's a clue there."

"Okay, then what next?"

Jane's gaze darted up and down the hall as she searched her mind for other ideas. "Can you ask Holden to talk to his neighbor on the police force, the dispatcher? Ask her who the police have been talking to, if she knows. That way we can get a feeling about the suspects. I mean, it's not like you and I know the people in town, the ones who might have a motive. And the police could be focusing on someone already. It'd be a relief to know."

"Yes, I'll ask." Olivia pushed out her lower lip and

blew out a breath of air, blasting her bangs off her forehead. "Thanks, Jane." Her friend's face softened.

"We'll need to keep it on the down low. Don't say a word to Doug. Or Dale."

"I agree. It's a plan." Olivia squeezed Jane's arm. "See you in the morning." She continued down the hall as Jane went into her own room. So, yet another plan…

Dale wanted Jane to concentrate on the wedding, but Olivia asked her to solve the man's murder. How could she please both of them?

Toothbrush in one hand and toothpaste in the other, Jane stood at the bathroom sink. Time to brush and floss. This was what she did every night, but her hand hesitated. She could bail out of both the investigation and the winery if she wanted to. She had no real reason to nose around, and she and Dale could simply cancel the winery and get married somewhere else, even by a justice of the peace. For Heaven's sake, this wasn't the first wedding for either of them.

She squeezed the tube until it looked like a flat tire, then brushed, up and down, up and down. Setting the wet toothbrush next to the sink, she strung out a long piece of floss and wound it around her fingers, cutting off the circulation.

But what about Reynard? Reynard Barre had been alive last night, playing a party game, having a drink with friends, shaking hands goodbye at the door. No matter what he did, if anything, to provoke an attack, he didn't deserve to die. Not that Jane could do much about it now.

He was dead, and her new life was just beginning. She was in love, getting married. She and Dale had finally decided on the date and place for the wedding, and it was time to move forward with their life together.

She jammed the floss between her front teeth, sawing back and forth. But Olivia was worried about her brother-in-law and the survival of his B&B with a suspicious death on the premises. Olivia knew that Jane would do anything to help her. Olivia knew she was a loyal, true-blue friend who was actually good at solving murders. Olivia knew Jane wouldn't turn her away.

She unwound the floss and the white tips of her fingers returned to pink. On the plus side, she could save the B&B and wrap up the wedding details. On the down side, Holden's business could go belly up and her romantic wedding could go down the tubes.

She spit into the sink. If she captured the killer, the B&B would receive new bookings, and she'd wrap up the wedding plans and finally have the happily-ever-after she needed. She could accomplish one as well as the other. Why not? The two went hand-in-hand, since the widow was both the owner of the winery where the ceremony was to be held and the prime suspect in a murder at the inn where the guests were to stay.

She examined her pearly whites in the mirror. Decision made. Time to sink her teeth into solving the crime.

Doug, as an ex-cop, who now worked in corporate security, had contacts with the Palisade Police, but he was not likely to share everything he learned. No. Jane needed to do some research on her own. In her job as a paralegal, she knew how to investigate. Doug wasn't the only one with resources. In fact, she'd helped solved murders before with her paralegal know-how. The first place to look was in public records. In Colorado, most criminal court records were public. And bankruptcy records, civil lawsuits, property liens, domestic violence, divorce decrees, all were at her fingertips.

Sitting in the window seat in her pajamas, she opened her tablet computer and got busy. To start with, she searched the criminal court dockets, then the news sites. She quickly discovered this group of suspects didn't have any criminal records, darn it, but luckily they were well-known locals who were often in the press.

Photographs of Kirby Potts and both of the Barres graced the social pages in the *Daily Sentinel*. The Barres attended many social functions since the winery had won a few awards, including the "East Meets West Wine Challenge." Georgiana's photograph was posted on the Peach Festival's sitelink because she'd been the Peach Festival Queen many years ago. Of course, the bitter mayoral battle was mentioned several times, and in particular, commentary on the rude billboards. It was amazing the two opponents had gotten along at the mystery party at all. That is, they'd seemed to get along as far as Jane could tell. Maybe they really hadn't...

The social scene and the political campaigns weren't the only things newsworthy. Skylar's name came up in half a dozen search results due to his attendance at rallies and forums at the college on environmental issues.

A search for Kirby Potts yielded a business webpage for his art studio. Jane scrolled through all the images on the site. She recognized the headshot of mystery game player "Fritz the Snitch" included with the studio's affiliated artists. His real name was Adam Aemes. He'd been dressed at the party in a costume similar to Kirby's, but they looked nothing alike, otherwise. Adam's nose was wider, his eyes closer together, the shape of his face narrower. His hair had a similar cut as Kirby's, though. It was as if he was trying to look like the sculptor, like an adoring fan trying to emulate a movie star.

Jane next searched Facebook and sent "friend" requests to all of the names on her list. Friends, indeed. Murder suspects, more likely. What she really needed to do was interrogate a few of these people—Kirby, Skylar, Georgiana, Zeta, and Adam—she'd decided to include Adam Aemes.

She pulled her eyes away from the computer screen and picked up her phone. She created a photo album on a cloud site and scrolled through her pictures, tagging them for upload. Then, she set her computer and phone aside, screen time over. She logged out for the night— done with the internet, the portal for all the data on the earth—and crawled between the sheets, closing herself off from all the concerns of the world.

She fell asleep into a dream about a killer hiding in the peach trees, peach pits falling from the sky, and a peach colored moon covering the sun, casting the planet into total darkness.

*****

After completing her devotional time the next morning, Jane checked Facebook. Her friend requests had been accepted. She examined the party pictures the other guests had posted on their Facebook pages, copied them to a folder on her tablet computer, and then uploaded them to the shared site. One particular photo was very interesting. Very.

She tripped down the steps two at a time and made

rapid strides to the patio. "Good morning, one and all!"

Doug had a newspaper propped open on the table in front of him, but he raised one finger in acknowledgement. Olivia and Dale both had coffee cups to their lips and put them down to return her greeting, "'Morning."

"What do we have to eat?" Jane slid into a chair at the table. Unlike the day before, she had an appetite for breakfast this morning.

Olivia answered, "Since we're the only ones left staying, Holden made 'fruit soup' and instead of using berries, he sliced fresh peaches for the topping."

"I can't wait to try it." Jane filled a bowl with the breakfast soup. She tasted orange juice, yogurt, honey, and, of course, the peaches.

Delicious!

Each one made yummy sounds as they slurped down the mouthwatering creation.

After they clanked their spoons against their bowls for the last drop, Jane said, "I need you all to upload your party pictures, don't forget."

"I did this morning, hon." Dale gave her a warm smile.

She returned his grin with one of her own. "I didn't see them yet. You must've done that after I loaded the ones from Kirby and Skylar."

Doug paused over his bowl. "Where'd you get their pictures?"

"From their Facebook pages. Georgiana had a few, too, so hers are on the site as well." Jane gave him an excited look that said, aren't I clever! "You've got to see the profile picture I found on Georgiana's page...you just won't believe it..." she trailed off…building the suspense.

The other three pulled out their cell phones to check out the photo site.

"Georgiana is wearing a peach pendant necklace!" Olivia's voice was fired up.

"That's right. It's the same necklace I saw in Rey's hand." Jane beamed at them. "At least it looks the same to me. So Georgiana has to be connected to the murder. Is she the killer? Did she go back to the scene to remove the evidence that proved she was there? But what is her motive?" She rubbed her hands together.

"Hold on, Jane." Doug chewed on one corner of his mustache. "We don't know if Georgiana lost the necklace, or if it was stolen, or if she gave it to someone else before the crime was committed. Or there might even be two of those necklaces. There could be an explanation that doesn't place Georgiana at the crime scene." He dashed her certainty with his police logic.

Holden stepped out onto the patio carrying a fresh pot of coffee, which he set on the table with a heavy thump. "Who wants more? This coffee has a cinnamon flavor." He gave an air kiss to the tips of his fingers.

"Me, me." Jane emptied her mug down to the dregs and raised her now bone-dry cup in the air.

"You've had two cups already. You want another?" Olivia's voice had a slight note of reproach.

"Don't be silly. Of course, I do." Jane made a *gimme-gimme* sign with her free hand. "I'm having more caffeine because smoking crack is bad for you."

"Ha. Ha. I've heard that joke before." Olivia had a smirk on her lips.

Jane didn't have another comeback, so she just shrugged.

Holden peered over his brother's shoulder at the profile picture of Georgiana. His eyes appeared tired and drawn. "Are you going to talk to the police investigator about that necklace, Doug?"

Doug said, "I'm sure they've already seen the photo, but yes, I will. When I get a chance to talk to them again, I'll mention it."

Dale swiveled his phone screen around for all of them to see. "Look at this. Jane uploaded pictures of the vineyards from yesterday, too."

"I must have tagged my winery photos to upload without realizing it." Jane took a sip of her fresh coffee.

Isobel sauntered out from the kitchen onto the patio. Wearing sweatpants and a tank top and devoid of makeup, she looked twelve instead of twenty-something. The back of her shoulder was exposed, showing a tattoo of a lotus flower. The sun, moon, and star design winked a happy greeting from her wrist. She gave up a big yawn. "Good Morning."

"Morning, sweetheart." Doug's whole face lit up.

Isobel gave her dad a smile. "I need some of that coffee."

Her mother indicated the seat next to her. "Sit down. Don't just have coffee. Eat some of this fruit soup, too. It's mostly yogurt, and it's good for you."

"Maybe later." Isobel took the seat. "Hey, Jane, I looked through your pictures on your photo site. You have some fantastic shots, but I have a question for you." She thumbed her cell phone, then handed it to Jane. "What's in this one?" The selfie picture was taken off the corner of the B&B's patio, capturing the rows of peach trees, the branches bending under the heavy fruit. "Look at the tree behind your head. There's a ghost child right there."

Jane lowered her face to the screen and pinched the photo to enlarge it. She had to admit what looked like a child's face appeared in the tree. The photo gave her the willies. "That's really strange." She passed the phone around so the others could see the ghost, too.

Olivia shook her head at her daughter. "That's just a peach."

"Nuh-uh." Isobel's stubborn look mirrored her mother's.

Jane found the original image in her camera app, then slid a finger across the screen to the preceding images. "It has to be a peach, but that photo was taken with the quick action function. Four or five pictures were snapped all at once, nanoseconds apart, and look, the face is not in the photos before or after." She shivered, and not from the cool morning breeze.

"The eclipse manifestations are starting. It's in two days." Isobel thumped the table. "This is bad juju."

For once the young woman's words described exactly how Jane felt. Wigged out. The world was going to be cast into semi-darkness for a minute or two as the moon blocked the sun on its journey across the sky. Would the animals forget it was daytime and behave as if it was night? Would the morning glories close their flower petals? The hummingbirds go into torpor? The bats and owls appear in the eclipse-induced night? What other strange phenomenon would occur?

Holden waved his hands over the dishes of food, tugging Jane away from her speculations. "You all finished here?" He plucked up an empty plate. "The Peach Festival Parade starts at nine. If you don't want to miss it, you need to head over to Third and Main.

Parking won't be easy since the entire town will show up, plus a whole lot of tourists."

"I'm not going to the parade. See you all later." Isobel headed back inside.

The adults screeched their chairs away from the table.

"Meet at my truck out front in five minutes." Dale put his hand on Jane's back. They were the first through the patio door.

*****

"Hurry up and wait. Isn't that the way it is?" Olivia blew out an exasperated breath. "We're early by half an hour. What should we do now?"

"Let's walk around." Jane was ready to stretch her legs.

The group meandered down Kluge Avenue to Palisade Memorial Park where the Lions Club was holding a pancake breakfast. A man wearing a "Barre for Mayor" button on his golden Lion's Club vest caused Jane to stop and stare, then she saw Zeta roaming through the crowd, her distinctive gray-streaked, auburn hair coiled at the top of her head, a broad-backed, longhaired dog at her side. She was shaking hands, focusing intently on each individual, and sporting her Duchenne smile—the one that raised the corners of her mouth and cheeks and formed crow's feet around her eyes. She appeared to be working the gathering, like the politician she was.

Dale and Doug stepped into the line for pancakes. Dale gave the excuse, "Might as well sample the breakfast. There's warm peaches for the topping. It's only six bucks a person, and you get sausages and eggs, too."

"You can't afford not to." Jane laughed. "Spoon on extra and I'll have a taste of your peach topping."

Four or five immense metal drums occupied a corner of the lawn, each spinning on its axis in a slow orbit, each manned by several cooks. Steam rose off the flat, circular tops of the drums, and bubbling pancakes sizzled on the surfaces, going for a ride as the drums rotated like merry-go-rounds. The cooks, in ball caps, purple shirts, and yellow aprons, and armed with metal spatulas, flipped the pancakes as they circled in front of them.

A tap on her shoulder got Jane's attention.

"Good morning, Jane. Would you sign my petition?" Skylar wore a shirt sporting the slogan, "Bring Life into Balance," and a campaign button, "Kirby Potts for Mayor." He gripped a clipboard in his hands, and several more stuck out from under one arm clutched to his side.

"What's it for?" Jane hitched her purse strap higher on her shoulder. She wondered why Skylar supported Kirby for mayor.

"This one is to enact legislation to ban the use of bee-killing pesticides. If we lose the honeybee, our whole food chain could collapse."

"Oh dear, that would be a disaster. I'll sign it." She took hold of his pen and scribbled her name on the form.

"I've got some more here. This one is to preserve a valley in California from corporate development and"—he juggled his clipboards around to bring new ones forward—"This one is sponsored by Greenpeace to promote sustainable energy solutions."

Jane scratched her head. "Gee, Skylar, that all

sounds super, but I don't know enough about these causes, and I really should read up on it before I sign anything else. Now is not the time. Maybe you can point me to some websites or something." She found her business card in her purse with her email address and pressed it into his hand.

He looked like he was about to open his mouth to argue, but Olivia seized Jane's arm in a tight grip. "What's Isobel doing here? I thought she wasn't coming to the parade."

"Oh, she's helping me out. Bell! Bell! Over here," Skylar hollered and gave the young woman a wave. Olivia appeared to be sucking wind. The man was calling her daughter by the nickname only Isobel's closest friends used.

"Oh, hi, Mom, Jane." Isobel walked up and handed a clipboard to Skylar. "Look at how many signatures I got." Her smile lit up her beautiful face. She curled her fingers to beckon him to follow her. "There's some people over there who've got questions. Can you come with me?"

Olivia gave Skylar a long, appraising look, then stood in silence as the two young people made their way past the cooking drums, crossed the green, and darted out of sight between families with strollers and dogs on leashes.

"Well, Isobel does love a good cause." Jane tried to be upbeat. "You know our kids don't even buy a bottle of water unless a portion of the money goes to dig a well somewhere. That's how they are. And that's a positive thing, right?"

Her friend's eyebrows drew together. "I guess so." Then she shook her head. "She could have anyone she wants, and she picks this hippy dude. I think she just likes to yank my chain."

The men walked up to stand next to them, and Dale handed Jane a small paper cup of the peach topping, then he slung an arm over her shoulder. "Time to find a place to watch the parade."

They pushed through the crowd to head toward downtown. Jane slurped up a taste of the peaches, then tossed the cup into a garbage bin. At the edge of the park, they passed Kirby Potts surrounded by a coterie of young people handing out flyers.

He was saying, "You don't want to elect Zeta. She'd be nothing but the same as Rey, and maybe worse. She can't be trusted, I tell you…" but the rest of his speech was drowned out by the traffic noise on Main Street.

They made their way several more blocks, other parade-goers in front and behind, a line of people proceeding all the way to Third. The four of them separated from the pack and turned west to stop with their toes on the curb at Third and Peach Avenue, as good a corner as any to watch a Peach Parade.

They arrived in time to catch the first float rounding the corner.

The home-grown pageant looked and sounded like a scene in a movie set in a small town with an all-American, apple pie kind of feeling, except the pie would have to be peach instead of apple. Floats displaying brown corrugated boxes of peaches, crates of peaches, and jars of peach preserves reminded them all that they were celebrating the peach harvest. But rather than peaches, the scent of popcorn mingled with sweet cotton candy creating a carnival smell. The maroon clad

Palisade High School Marching Band high-stepped down the street with their toes up and instruments angled skyward. John Philip Sousa types of songs filled the air. Next came proud owners with their antique cars, business proprietors in decorated floats, and hilarious clowns on goofy bicycles. A man in an Uncle Sam's costume carrying an oversized American flag followed in line. Jane joined the onlookers in clapping and cheering as the floats rolled by.

A Volkswagen van with a banner across its bumper and a megaphone on its roof was near the end of the procession. A recorded voice, "Potts for Mayor of Barresville. Keep the Barres out of Barresville," sounded over the din made by the large assembly watching from the sidelines. The very next vehicle, blasting patriotic music, sported a different banner, "A vote for Barre means a vote for Barresville."

After the campaign vehicles inched past, this year's Peach Festival Queen rode by on a firetruck, waving a gloved hand in queenly style. Bringing up the rear was Georgiana on horseback. Pink ribbons fluttered from the horse's mane, tackle, and tail. A man standing next to Jane shouted out, "Hey there, Peaches!"

Jane caught his eye. "Why did you call that woman on the horse, 'Peaches?'"

"That's her nickname. She was the queen of the festival years ago. Ever since then, she's been known as Peaches."

Jane blinked at him for a moment. "Are all the former queens called that?"

He gave her a puzzled look. "No, just her."

Maybe she should find the former Peach Queen at the end of the parade to ask her about her nickname.

Georgiana's title could be one explanation for the peach pendant. Jane needed to know more about this woman. How well did Georgiana know Rey? Just what did she do for a living? Was she married? Did she have a family? She appeared to be single, the same as Kirby and Skylar. Jane was itching to get her fingers on a pen and write down the questions, but there was no time at the moment.

Dale grasped her hand and tugged her along after the retreating parade. "I guess there's going to be a marching band competition at the end of the street. Let's follow them and watch."

"There's a coffee shop on the way if you want a latte, Jane." Olivia knew her so well, and of course that's where they all headed.

Soon Jane had a mocha latte, two-pump, non-fat, no whip in her hands. When they stepped out of the crowded coffee shop, the drummers were performing cadences together in the street, and it looked as if the whole town surrounded them to watch. The brrrummm brrrummm brrrummm sound of the drums resonated off the old buildings.

The last note played.

The drums stilled.

The crowd lifted their hands to clap.

But before their palms could meet, Kirby Potts' voice exploded out of the sudden quiet. "You purposely positioned your pickup truck to follow my van so you would drown me out. I should've known you'd resort to those underhanded tactics. What did you do, bribe the parade organizers?"

"Kirby, settle down." Zeta placed a light hand on his arm. "The parade spots were decided months ago.

Don't you remember that we rolled the dice and you won? You got to go first and I came after you." Zeta's calm manner could soothe the most outraged malcontent, but her protector, the immense black, brown, and white mountain dog, lifted a lip in warning and gave out a low growl.

A man Jane recognized, Adam Aemes, stepped from the line of onlookers and snapped a picture. Zeta gave him a sharp glance.

Adam displayed the image for Kirby to view. "Look at your expression, Kirby. This will make a great picture for one of your flyers." Jane peered around his arm to catch a glimpse of the photo of Kirby's serious face looking intense and a rare moment when Zeta looked wishy-washy and weak.

Kirby said in an undertone, "I'll beat you in this race, Zeta. I'll get rid of the Barres once and for all."

Zeta turned away to squeeze her shoulders through the crowd. A moment later she'd disappeared. Georgiana was nowhere to be seen, either.

That left one option.

Chapter 7

Off they went to the Barre Winery. At least one of the suspects would be easy to find, since they'd already made plans to get together with Zeta.

The Bernese mountain dog greeted the two couples in the parking lot alongside rows of grapevines. This time the dog's tongue hung out of the side of its smiling mouth, looking eager to please. You'd never know the happy tail-wagger was the same growling beast as the one at the parade. As if the dog wasn't friendly enough, Zeta herself gave Jane a warm welcome, wrapping her in a half hug, a quick one arm squeeze-and-let-go, before she opened the enormous barn door into the showroom.

"What's your dog's name?" Dale bent down to pat the animal on the top of its furry black head.

"Betsey." Zeta ushered them past crates of wine-themed merchandise—corkscrews, wine charms, decanters, and wine glasses with the Barre Winery logo. Photographs of the Bookcliffs, the Grand Mesa, and the Colorado National Monument were displayed under a sign stating the pictures were taken by a local photographer and were for sale. A walk-up bar was anchored against the far wall with four or five barstools tucked under the counter.

Skylar was pouring samples, and Isobel occupied one of the stools in front of him.

"So now we know where you've been hanging out." Jane had to say something, since Olivia seemed to be speechless. Jane was a bit surprised herself, because Skylar had on a "Kirby Potts for Mayor" button at the pancake breakfast, yet he appeared to work for Zeta Barre. He didn't have a campaign button on now.

Isobel just raised her eyes to the ceiling and twiddled the stem of her wineglass. Her parents slid onto the stools on either side of her, and Skylar set them up with pours.

"So let's talk about your wedding plans." Zeta gave Jane and Dale another of her Duchenne smiles. "Usually couples have the ceremony on the patio outside. The wine tasting room in here will be open afterwards for you and your guests. I offer an all-inclusive, which means I hire the caterer." She flapped a hand toward three high top tables in the corner. "Samples of the finger foods are over there for you to taste, and that's where the food will be served, too."

The three of them strolled over to the tables and gathered bite-sized portions on appetizer plates. Jane munched on the baked brie with figs and walnuts and nibbled on the morsels of cheese and fruit that included roasted peaches. They'd already decided not to have a wedding cake. At her age, Jane wasn't wearing a traditional gown either. She'd purchased a simple, sleeveless, biscuit-colored, tea-length dress that was feminine, flowing, and flattering. It was hanging in her closet at home ready for the big day. The plans were coming together at last.

Zeta asked, "Have you hired a photographer?"

"Oh, I'll ask my son. He'll take the pictures on his cell. He's quite talented." Jane's older son, Luke, had a good eye for the camera.

"I'm sure he is, but you should hire a professional. Having a family member take the pictures on their phone is like drinking a one-dollar jug of wine. You need a pro. I'll call one I know and see if he's available, an excellent photographer. Besides, your son won't want to be tasked with a job to do. He should enjoy himself."

Jane chewed thoughtfully, then swallowed. "I see what you mean. Thank you for taking care of that."

"What are the total charges?" Dale's eyes were eager and wide, as was his smile.

"The photographer will send you a separate bill, depending on how many pictures you order. I only charge for the caterer and the bottles of wine." A smile formed on Zeta's lips in a way that invited everyone to smile with her. "I find these events pay for themselves, since the guests will want to buy a bottle, or two or three, to take home as a souvenir."

Dale chuckled. "What do you think, Jane?" His voice was animated and his eyes were shining.

Jane entwined her fingers through his. "Yes. Where do we sign?"

Zeta handed them a couple of pages of paperwork. Dale read through the fine print, wrote his signature with a flourish, and handed her a check for the balance. He said, "Time for a celebratory glass. But let's take it outside." It was another one of those days, too nice to be indoors.

Skylar poured them generous measures and carried their wine flights through the raised overhead door. The Ladners, *sans* Isobel, followed them outside, along with Betsey, who slumped down in the shade of the pergola woven with grapevines next to a cat stretched thin and long on the cool paving stones. A calming sound filled the space—trickling water from a fountain with Zen-like stacked rocks.

When Skylar returned indoors and the four friends were seated around the table overlooking the Bookcliffs, Doug made a ting-ting noise with his fork against his glass. "Here's to Dale and Jane. To wedded bliss." They all raised their wine glasses in the air.

"You're still wearing your wrist pass from the festival yesterday, Doug." Olivia tugged the orange band around her husband's wrist.

"Oh, yeah. I forgot to take it off." He pinched the band between two fingers and yanked hard. The plastic stretched tight against his skin but refused to break. He jerked the band with more force, and the plastic burst apart with a loud snap. His wrist flew down to smack the table and his other hand flew up to punch himself in the face. "Ow! What the…" Bright red blood poured out of his nose.

Olivia rummaged through her oversized handbag for a tissue, and Jane jumped up and hastened inside for a cold towel. Once Doug had tissues stuffed inside each nostril and a cold towel on his swelling wrist, he glanced around as if in a daze. "That was the weirdest thing. Those bands are really, really strong."

"You should've cut the plastic with scissors. That's what I did." Olivia spoke in her bossy voice.

"Here, have more wine. It will help with the pain." Dale glided Doug's wineglass closer to his elbow.

"But don't spill it." Olivia was going a bit too far now.

"When I asked for the towel I had to explain what

happened. Isobel said the wrist pass attack was another manifestation of the upcoming eclipse." Jane snickered, trying to lighten the mood.

"Isobel! Don't get me started." Olivia looked as if she could spit the wine's bitter tannins right out of her mouth.

"Relax. Isobel's just having fun." Jane smelled the bouquet, sliding the rim of her glass under her nose. The varietal had a dry, bold aroma. This could be her favorite wine of all time. She'd be sure to ask Zeta to serve this one. Wait. Were she and Dale getting carried away? How could she forget that she still had a homicide to solve? And Zeta could be the killer. She swallowed a lump back in her throat.

"What's the matter, Jane?" Olivia must have caught the look on her face.

"I seem to have forgotten all about the murder of that poor man." Jane gave Dale a sideways look. Her gaze followed his as he took in the pergola, the dog and cat, the view, the table with their scattered wine glasses. A sad look crossed his face. Jane knew that look. Dale would be disappointed if they couldn't get married at the Barre Winery, but she reminded herself they were going to have a backup plan. Being married was more important than getting married. No matter what happened, they would be together. All the same, she said, "I hope whoever killed Rey is caught soon."

Olivia jumped on that. "Now that your wedding plans are finalized, we can concentrate on solving the murder." The wedding plans did seem to be coming together, except for the back-up plan, the what-if contingency, the alternative if the bottom dropped out—always a possibility when Jane was in charge.

Doug went into full-on cop mode. "No detecting. No playing Bond. Let the police do their job."

His wife's face took on a stormy look. Before her friend could start an argument with her husband, Jane said, "I really like these wine samples. How about you guys?"

Olivia sneaked a look at Jane and mouthed, "We'll talk more later." Her friend's near-silent communication told the story. Olivia was ready to snoop. Bond was about to meet his match.

Doug kneaded his sore wrist. "The second red wine in the flight is foxy."

"This white at the end of the row is silky, not chewy." Olivia set one of the sample glasses on her flight board and picked up another.

"Silky? Foxy?" Jane furrowed her brows. She thought she'd heard all the ways wine could be described, but these were new to her.

Dale slid his arm over the back of her chair. "Foxy means the wine smells wild and musky."

"Chewy is when the tannins are not overwhelming. You really need to read up on wines, Jane." Olivia tskked.

"Ooooh-kay. You guys are such cork dorks." She tried to shrug off her ignorance. She barely knew what tannins were and never cared to study the guidebooks. And here she was, planning a wedding at a winery. A winery which might be owned by a murderer.

Doug swirled his glass under his nose. Could he smell the wine with tissues still stuffed in each nostril? "I'm going to buy a couple of bottles of this first red."

"That's the Pinot Noir. I want at least one of this Chardonnay." Olivia fumbled in her purse for her wallet. "Let's go inside."

Dale squeezed Jane's shoulder. "Do you want any?"

"Sure. We should buy some bottles after these generous pours. I have to admit the grapes are good." She finally felt like a wine aficionado, saying it that way.

They stood and followed the Ladners inside. Isobel left Skylar and joined Dale and her parents on the other side of the room to ask Zeta for her recommendations.

Jane sat on the stool across from Skylar. "Should I go back outside for our glasses and bring them in?"

"No, no. I'll get them."

"Thanks." She shifted in her seat and cleared her throat. She cast a look over her shoulder, but the others appeared busy. Now was her chance to sneak in a few questions. She'd wanted to interrogate Zeta, but this young man would do. "Skylar, what do you think of the way Rey died? Who do you think put that peach pit in his mouth? Why would anyone do that?"

He shook his head solemnly. "It's a message, but what?"

"What significance is there in a peach?"

"The only thing I can think of, it points to the festival."

"But what, specifically, about the festival?"

His eyes narrowed and he pursed his lips. They both fell silent for a couple of moments, thinking.

Jane asked, "Maybe it's not the peach, maybe it's the pendant that's important. Maybe the killer put the peach in Rey's throat and the necklace in his hand, both. Maybe the message is the pit and the pendant, together. But what does it mean?"

"That sounds like, 'The Pit and the Pendulum.'" He let out a half-hearted laugh.

She gave him a weak smile in return. "And just as scary. Gee, do you think there's a clue there? I haven't read that story since I was in junior high." When he didn't answer, she went on, "More likely the clue points to Georgiana. I just found out her nickname is Peaches."

"Right. That's what people call her. But what did you say about a pendant?" Skylar quirked an eyebrow in a question.

"You don't know?"

"No. What about it?"

"When I found Rey, he had a necklace in his hand, a necklace with a glass peach pendant. It disappeared when I went upstairs to get Holden. And this is significant, Skylar. The necklace was Georgiana's." Jane studied his reaction.

His eyebrows went up and his lips turned down. "Wow. I hadn't heard anything about that."

"The police investigator didn't tell me to keep it a secret. I'm surprised you weren't questioned about it." Jane chewed on a thumbnail. What were the police doing? She knew what they weren't doing. They were not asking the right questions. "Skylar, did you hear anything during the night?"

"No, I'm sorry, I didn't." The young man gave her an elaborate shrug, rolling his shoulders forward.

"Who do you think killed Rey?" Jane heard the pleading in her own voice.

"I don't know. But the clue is the peach pit. And the necklace, too. It has to be." His eyes widened and his face lit up. "I know. We came out with a new peach wine this year. Maybe the killer was trying to leave a clue about the Barre Winery."

"Peaches are everywhere you look, though. Why would anyone think of the Barre peach wine?" Jane really wanted to know. Maybe there was something to this theory. But Skylar just wiped the counter with a rag and shook his head. She urged, "What about Georgiana? Could she have killed Rey? It was her necklace, you know."

"Gee, Jane. I don't think so. And I don't remember seeing her wear it." The young man looked as perplexed as Jane felt.

The others trotted over carrying full tote bags with "Barre Winery" stamped on the sides. Skylar rang up their purchases on a tablet computer using a credit card reader. He thanked them and told them to have a good day. They waved goodbye, and Doug insisted on carrying his wife's heavy tote to the truck. Olivia gladly handed it over to him.

As Olivia crunched up the gravel incline to the parking lot, rocks slithered out from under her feet. Jane said, "Be careful," at the same time Olivia fell forward, landing on her knees and the palms of her hands. "Liv! Are you okay?"

"Yes. I'm fine." She rocked back on her heels to examine her palms then checked her nails.

"It's a good thing I'm carrying the bottles of wine." Doug held out his free hand to help his wife to a stand.

She dusted her fingers together, then swept off her pant legs. "I think my right knee has a strawberry." A drop of red blood bloomed on the knee of her slacks.

Doug's nostrils still sprouted white tissues and now Olivia's knee required a Band-Aid.

"Isobel will say I fell because of the spooky, woo-woo eclipse." She laughed it off. Betsey had trailed after them and was now nosing her way next to Olivia, as if offering sympathy.

"First Doug gets a bloody schnozzle, now you get a bruised kneecap. Maybe there's something to the eclipse effect, like Isobel said." Jane snorted a laugh as she gave Betsey one last rub. "Well, little Ms. B, you need to go home now." Betsey appeared to understand, since she hightailed it back down the gravel path heading toward the cool interior of the showroom.

After they clambered into Dale's pickup, Jane felt unsettled for some reason. Who would get hurt next? Were the vortexes between the cliffs and the mesa exerting energy and throwing people off balance? She shook off the wonky feeling and fastened her seatbelt.

Dale performed a three-point turn around. He hit the gas and sped onto the Fruit Loop. His grin made his dimples deepen and his fingers danced across the steering wheel. "Problem solved. We've finalized the place to get married."

Olivia locked eyes with Jane. She knew her friend wanted her to solve the murder, too. And hadn't she better? Otherwise Plan A could fall through and there was no Plan B in place yet.

*****

The four of them spent the afternoon walking the length of the quaint downtown in nearby Grand Junction, from the bicycle store to the bagel shop, past the bank with the silver buffalo sculpture called, "Chrome on the Range," past the corner of Fourth and Main with the metalwork, "Girl on a Bike," past other unique pieces, some granite, some bronze, some whimsical, some modern. Jane stopped to take a picture of a metal sculpture of a cowboy perched on a black horse, the wizened man looking out from under his broad hat. The sculpture was for sale by Kirby Potts, and the plaque indicated a steep price. She was surprised there wasn't a campaign sign with an ugly slogan hanging from the horse's mane.

Jane and Olivia entered an antique shop while the men went into a sporting goods store. As Jane placed bunches of dried lavender sprigs and a bottle of lavender hand lotion at the cash register, Adam Aemes hustled through the front door pushing a large, flat crate on a dolly.

"Good afternoon, Adam." The clerk gave him a wide smile. "Do you have more photos to sell? We're down to about half a dozen."

"Got some more right here. Thanks, Mavis." Adam gave her a wink. He smacked the front wheels of the dolly onto the hardwood floor, exposing a "Keep Barre out of Barresville" button pinned to his shirt. "Do you want me to hang them up?"

"No, we can do that. Just take the box through to the stockroom."

Adam angled the hand cart back onto its wheels and propelled the dolly across the hardwood with a rumbling sound, crossing paths with Olivia as she made her way to the front.

"Who was that? He looks familiar." Olivia also had a sprig of dried lavender in her hands.

"Fritz the Snitch. You recognize him from the party. His real name is Adam Aemes."

Olivia's eyes lit with recognition. "Yeah, yeah. I remember him now."

Jane clutched her friend's arm. "Can we hang around and wait for him to come back? We can ask him some questions."

"Good idea."

The two examined all the impulse purchase items at the cash register—refrigerator magnets, lavender sachets, candles, potpourri, incense, notecards, and earrings made of gold flaked aspen leaves. Jane had to add to her purchases a refrigerator magnet that read, "Yay Sunshine," and Olivia added some notecards with pictures of the Bookcliffs. Finally, the man came strolling back through the store with his empty cart.

"Adam, you may not remember us, but we met at Holden's party. I played the part of Brynne Less"—she put on her brightest smile—"and my friend, here, was Marybelle Moneymaker." She touched Olivia's arm.

Adam's gaze darted between the two women, then he settled his eyes on Jane. "Are you Jane Marsh?"

"Yes. You remembered my real name."

"Not really, but Zeta called me. She said you played the part of the brainless character who gave away the solution to the game. I'm your wedding photographer."

Chapter 8

"You? You're the wedding photographer?" Jane looked at him with interest. "Zeta gave me your card, but it didn't have your name on it. It said something like, 'AA Photography.'" Jane slid her fingers into her purse. Was the card handy?

"That's me. Adam Aemes. Should we talk about what kind of shots you want?"

"There's no need for much of a discussion. We want to keep it simple. We've both been married before. This isn't our first wedding. I only want a few pictures of Dale and me with that fantastic view from the winery, and then some candid shots of the guests, that's all. I'm afraid it won't be a big job."

"I won't plan to be there more than an hour, then."

"That'll work. Do you do a lot of weddings for Zeta?"

"Yes. There's a whole crew of locals she keeps busy. The caterer was at Holden's party, too. Skylar Straite."

Jane's eyebrows rose up. "Skylar's the caterer? My, oh my. I didn't know." She gave Olivia a wide-eyed look, as if to ask *what-next*? One of Olivia's eyebrows went up, too, in silent understanding. Jane tried to relax her face so they both weren't standing there with shocked looks. But it was incredible that everyone involved in the wedding was connected to

Rey Barre's death.

Jane stared at her feet. This wedding was probably not going to happen. How could it? Her wedding vendors were the most obvious suspects. She needed to solve this murder more than ever, not only to help Holden get his customers back, but to make sure the wedding was on track. Plan B was looking more and more likely. She'd better get to work on it.

Adam broke into her thoughts, "If you hadn't given away the identity of the murderer at the party, I was going to guess you were the killer. I would've won the game."

Olivia, not to be topped, said, "I figured out the murderer was Jane, too. We would've tied."

Jane stepped a few inches closer to Adam and said in a low voice, "Wasn't that awful what happened to Reynard Barre?"

His face took on a sad countenance, but he stared over Jane's shoulder and tilted his dolly onto its wheels as if to steer for the door. "That was a shock."

"Did you take pictures at the party?" Jane crossed her fingers behind her back and hoped he had. Maybe his pictures would have the smoking gun clue.

"No. Taking photographs is what I do for a living, such as it is." He laughed, short and sudden. "I was out to have a good time, not to work, and I left my camera at home." He rapped his knuckles on the counter and said, "Bye, Mavis. Talk at you later," then to Jane, "See you at the wedding," before rolling his cart out the door.

Doggonit. That was a dead end. Jane and Olivia's eyes met and their shoulders both slumped. Olivia stepped up to the counter. "I'm ready to check out."

While the clerk rang up her friend's purchases, Jane prowled the length of the store past the antique furniture until she came to the wall of framed photographs. Most of the images were the same with slight variations—photographs of the wild horses and the Bookcliffs she'd seen on display at several different places now. One was a duplicate of the fruit stand, not more than a shack, where they'd bought the pie the day before. All the pictures had a similar style, the same gilded sun with slanting rays. The wild horses playing among the light beams; the beacons of light illuminating the rocky red clay and stubborn green tuffs of grass. The photographs were for sale nearly everywhere, from upscale wineries to ramshackle fruit stands to antique shops, all taken by the same photographer, Adam Aemes.

One photograph caught her attention. Turning toward the camera was a woman with light-colored hair, her hand shielding her familiar-looking face as she gazed at the wild horses. The rays of the fading sun bent toward the horizon and cast her features into shadow. Was the woman Georgiana? Jane scanned the other pictures again and found several more with the same woman. One photo showed Georgiana full in the face. It was her. Definitely.

Jane returned to the front and asked the clerk, "Adam sells his photographs at several places around town, doesn't he?"

"Yes. I think he's trying to generate a following. The photos are quite good, but people take their own pictures on their cell phones now to post on Instagram."

Jane said, "You probably sell a lot of them anyway since the prices are reasonably low."

"That's true. I'm not sure how he can make a living at it."

"Perhaps that's why he does weddings." Olivia stuffed her credit card back into her wallet and took hold of her bag.

The clerk went on, "I'm sure you're right. But weddings are not what he wants to do the rest of his life. He'd like to become as well-known an artist as Kirby Potts. He rents a little space from Kirby for his photo studio hoping to sell at the art gallery."

"You know Kirby and Adam well?" Jane gave the clerk a long hard look.

"This is a small town. Most of the business owners know each other." The clerk tallied Jane's purchases. She waited for the woman to say more, but all she said was, "Have a nice afternoon," when she handed Jane her sack.

Jane decided to be on the lookout for more Adam Aemes photographs.

After they left the antique shop, Olivia stopped in front of a jewelry store with a door framed between two bay windows. The old building might have once housed a movie theater. "Let's go in and ask about Georgiana's necklace. Maybe she got it here. Or better yet, maybe someone bought it for her as a gift. That might be a clue."

That would be quite a stroke of luck. Jane followed her inside. The store was depressingly empty of customers, no photographs graced the walls, but two young, pretty blonde teenage girls were working the counter. "May I help you?" they echoed each other's words.

Olivia elbowed Jane. "Show them the picture of the

necklace."

Jane fumbled around on her phone until she found the icon for the photo app. Locating Georgiana's photo, she enlarged the image so only the necklace could be seen. She held the phone out to show the two clerks. "Do either of you recognize this necklace?"

The first clerk said, "Sure. We sell that here. It's a popular seller during the Peach Festival."

The second clerk took a closer look. "But wait. That style is old. The one we sell now is a bit different." She reached under the glass counter and brought out a similar necklace. "See here, the green in the leaves is a different shade and the peach is quite a bit larger."

"Are the necklaces made by a local artist?" Jane asked, since the Grand Valley was home to an entire community of artists and craftsmen.

The clerks looked at each other. The first clerk shook her head. "No, these came in with a shipment from a manufacturer in New York," and the second one added, "There's probably a lot of stores that sell it."

"Shoot." Jane closed her lips in a tight line.

"Would you like to try this one on?" Clerk number two held out her palm, the chain dangling from her dainty fingers.

"I would." Olivia lifted her hair while the clerk wrapped the chain around her neck and snapped the clasp shut. Olivia fingered the glass peach as she stared into an oval mirror sitting on the counter. "Can you tell us who bought the necklace in the picture? I don't want the same necklace as someone I know, even if the style has changed."

Clerk number one laughed. "I've only been working here a few months, and the store doesn't keep records of who buys what."

"I haven't worked here very long either." Clerk number two unhooked the necklace and slid the chain off Olivia's neck quick as a flash.

Jane tapped on her phone and reduced the photo to normal size to reveal Georgiana's face. She gave both young girls an entreating look. "How about this woman? Do you recognize her? Do you remember if she came into the store?"

"No." Both clerks moved their heads from side-to-side.

"Do you know when you received the shipment with this new style?"

"We just got it in right before the Peach Festival." Clerk number two returned the necklace to the display case.

"Thanks, girls." Olivia gave them a curt nod and followed Jane out the door. "That didn't help us any," she said after they moved down the sidewalk.

"Yes, it did. We know whoever bought the necklace probably got it in town, I mean, why not? And it was purchased before this year's style came out."

"That could've been a year ago during the last festival."

"You might be right." Jane gave her friend a conspiratorial look. Were they on to something? Or was she grasping at straws?

Olivia said, "I did catch a glimpse of the price, it's a lot, fifteen hundred dollars. Write that down with your other clues when we get back."

"I will." Jane stopped in her tracks. A street lamp held notices for various musicians playing at clubs, and under an appalling poster of a zombie playing a guitar, a tattered sign read, "Stay away from the Ladner Bed and Deadfast."

"Oh, my God!" Olivia practically screamed in Jane's ear, her voice charged with fury. She ripped the paper off the post. "Very funny. Deadfast. Ha. Ha. Who did this?" Her eyes blazed at Jane, as if expecting her to know.

Trying to give off calm vibes, Jane said, "Take a deep breath, and let's walk up and down Main and see if there are any more flyers." Olivia immediately stormed off and Jane hurried to catch up with her. They found two more on other lamp posts. Olivia tore them to pieces. No doubt, if Olivia found the culprit she'd cut him to shreds as well.

Once they completed their circuit, they met up with the guys at the coffee shop, Main Street Bagels. Entering the fragrant café was like coming home. She headed to the barista for an espresso even though it was late afternoon. She couldn't resist the smell of coffee beans mixed with the garlic and onion scent of the "everything" bagel.

They wasted no time explaining to their men about the flyers they'd found. The men were outraged, too, but Jane couldn't help relaxing—the aroma therapy of the coffee and Dale massaging the back of her shoulders were stress busters.

"Don't eat too much," Olivia warned her husband when he ordered a pastry with his coffee. "It's almost time for dinner."

"Oh, I'll be hungry then, too."

"We're going to the Bookcliffs Cowboy Steakhouse." She shook her head at him.

"Oh, yeah." Doug changed his order to just coffee.

"I'm looking forward to a ribeye."

Steaming mugs in hand, they found seats at a large, round table in the front window. Jane sent text messages to her sons to let them know the wedding at the winery was a go. Holy Cow! She was going to be a married woman in just a short month—that is, if the vintner, the caterer, or the photographer, any one of them, wasn't the murderer. She better get to work on a Plan B.

Her younger son replied that he checked on her dogs and they were doing fine with the dog sitter. Just thinking about her pups warmed her heart. The dogs had no idea they were about to welcome a new member into the family—Dale. And her sons and their wives didn't have a clue Jane was involved in another investigation of a murder victim—Rey. Outside of this town and apart from this short weekend trip, life would go on. No difficulties. No drama. No death.

Until the next misadventure, anyway. Every journey had its share of setbacks. Happiness came when one accepted the struggles along with the good times. The hurdles were part of the story, overcoming them often the most memorable part.

She beat Doug to the toast. "To this wacky, adventure-filled weekend. Hear. Hear." They clicked coffee cups and Dale gave her a radiant smile. The men showed them the fishing flies they'd purchased at the sporting goods store, then Jane leaned her head back in her chair and closed her eyes while the guys went on to discuss secret places to fish and Olivia took a phone call from her daughter. After that tranquil break in their busy day, it was time for dinner.

Jane and Olivia stopped in the restroom before

heading out. In the hallway were framed photographs for sale, more of the same by Adam Aemes, catching the yellow beams of the slanting sun across the red desert floor. Jane pointed them out to Olivia. "These photos are everywhere."

Olivia skimmed a finger along the wall as they strolled past. "We're going to see the wild mustangs tomorrow ourselves."

"I can't wait." Jane had never been to the wild horse refuge before.

After leaving the coffee shop, they stopped at the bed-and-breakfast to change for dinner. Jane got into character by wearing her cowboy hat and boots. Isobel was lounging on the patio, bored and hungry, so she decided to grace them with her company. The five adults were able to squeeze inside Dale's pickup with the extended cab, and they hit the road.

Passing through the Redlands, then the national conservation area with staggering views of the surrounding mountains—all nooks and crannies chiseled by the powerful wind—they made the drive north on Hampshire Road, past the trailhead to the North Fruita Desert. The Bookcliffs Cowboy Steakhouse seemed to be in the middle of nowhere, but pickups bearing Colorado and Wyoming license plates filled almost every spot in the parking lot. Dale had to troll back and forth searching for an empty space.

The interior was roomy, so the wait was short. Outside, Dale's dusty pickup truck and inside, Jane's cowboy hat and boots fit right in with the western ambiance. Booths lined the four walls, and square tables with red-checkered tablecloths took up the rest of the room. A buzz of conversation hummed in her ears, and the scent of fried onions hammered her nose.

A middle-aged, bird-like, high-energy type of woman, in tight jeans and a low-riding apron, said in a cigarette smoker's low voice, "Follow me this way to your table."

They wound through the restaurant to a booth. While the others scooted their bottoms across the bench, Jane hung her hat on a nearby hook like all the other cowboys.

The waitress described the special for the evening, tender buffalo steak with sautéed mushrooms. Jane paused when she learned that the beef was locally raised and the cattle auction house was nearby. The waitress said it was within "chucking distance." Farm to table was a popular trend, but she preferred not to think about how beef got from the cow to her plate. She almost ordered a salad but changed her mind and requested a small filet. Even Isobel asked for the steak. Each of them ordered a Coors except for Jane who wanted lemonade.

After the waitress gathered the menus and left, Doug twisted the ends of his mustache and asked, "Is chucking distance the same as, 'yonder over that 'a way?'"

Jane smiled. "For criminy sakes."

"Don't get all-fired up." This was Dale.

"Go to blazes." Olivia covered her hand over her mouth. "Whoops. Did I just tell someone to go where I think I did?"

"Yes, you did, Gol-darn-it." Jane laughed out loud this time.

Isobel gritted her teeth as she stared at the plaque above their booth that read, "Always drink upstream from the herd." Jane examined the other walls for the familiar photographs, but the local photographer didn't have his pictures for sale at the steakhouse. She only saw photos of John Wayne scattered on the walls here and there.

"I need to tell you something, Dale. And Isobel, you'll be interested to hear this, too." Jane tapped the young woman's arm. "Skylar's the caterer for our wedding."

Dale's mouth dropped open, but Isobel did not appear surprised. She said, "You'll love him, Jane. Everything he prepares is from locally grown, organic ingredients."

"Is catering what Skylar does for a living?" Doug asked.

"Yes. Plus, he sells produce from his organic garden. And as you already know, he works in the tasting room at the Barre Winery." Isobel seemed to be well-informed about him.

"So Skylar's the caterer and Adam Aemes the photographer. He was at the party, too, in the role of Fritz the Snitch," Jane pointed out.

"In a small town everyone's lives, or livelihoods, are intertwined." Doug didn't seem to notice his wife's look of disgust. Skylar was certainly not Olivia's top pick.

A couple of moments passed before Jane realized the diners at the other tables had fallen silent. The only sounds were the chinks of silverware and dishes from the kitchen and the words of a song over the sound system, the singer wailing on about a loaded shotgun.

Jane understood the sudden quiet when a waiter led Kirby Potts, Skylar Straite—speak of the devil—and

Adam Aemes past a table where Zeta Barre was seated with another woman. Zeta and her dinner companion sported "Barre for Barresville" campaign buttons. Kirby had on a "Kick Barre out of Barresville" badge, as did Adam. Kirby gave Zeta a deathly glare, but she inclined her head and gave him one of her soothing smiles, while tucking a strand of her graying auburn hair up under her bobby pinned French knot.

"Talk about small town, look who walked in. And I didn't see Zeta sitting over there before." Olivia spoke with stiff lips and gave her head tiny, quick jerks toward Zeta as if she was afraid the woman would hear her name and know they were talking about her.

"I didn't either. Holden did tell us this is where the locals ate. It certainly looks like they all showed up tonight." Jane took a sip of her lemonade. Were the two opponents packing heat? Would they have a shootout with those guns the country western singer was crooning about? An old-fashioned cowboy face-off?

Isobel rose from her seat at the end of the booth. "I'll be right back." She stopped for a few words with Skylar before snaking through the tables toward the restrooms.

Kirby's gaze wandered over the dining room. Zeta was busy in conversation with her table companion, yet appeared to be canvassing the room with her eyes, too. Kirby left his chair to chat up diners at a booth across the aisle, and Jane continued to scan the room herself. Her attention was drawn to the waiters who appeared from the door to the kitchen, carrying dinner plates, hot and steaming with steak and potatoes. The waiters halted at the dinner club's booth, and they all made room in front of them for their plates. Five or ten minutes later, Isobel returned to her seat.

"Your steak is getting cold," Doug said around a full mouth.

Isobel appeared not to care as she made slow work of her meal while the rest of them attacked theirs like scavengers on carrion. Conversation centered on the tender, juicy, and flavorful steaks in the out-of-the-way place at the end of the road. A well-kept local secret.

Dale whispered to Jane, "Should we consider this steakhouse for Plan B? What do you think?"

She made a so-so gesture. "Meh." Of course a man would think a steak and a brewski appropriate wedding fare.

Before long they were patting their mouths and throwing down their red-checkered napkins. Isobel claimed to be full after eating only half of her steak and picking at the rest.

"Should we head 'em up and move 'em out?" Jane joked.

"Yup. Let's skedaddle and mosey on outta here." Dale helped her out of the booth.

"I'd like to check out the auction barn." Olivia drained her glass before standing. "I've never seen one before."

"I did hear it's a landmark." Doug slid across the bench seat. "Might be worth seeing. Since it's Saturday night, there's probably nothing going on right now."

The evening was young, only seven, and they were on a western adventure, so Jane said, "Game on. It's early yet. Let's go."

Dale said in Jane's ear, "How about checking out the barn for Plan B?" He gave her a wink.

"Very funny." Jane gave him a gruff laugh.

Olivia's eyes sparkled. "Time to part-tay."

"Let's take the bull by the horns, saddle up, and rodeo on," Jane teased, stuffing her cowboy hat on her head.

The group proceeded to the checkout by the front door. Kirby was still giving Zeta the evil eye while he forked a piece of meat into his mouth. Zeta appeared to be ignoring him by giving her dinner companion her complete attention. Jane thought she heard someone say, "Check out those boots. Green. Did you see that?" and she whipped her head around but couldn't tell who spoke those words. After the guys paid the bill, they all went outside, and Jane was glad to leave the formidable mayoral contenders and the traditional brown-booted cowboys behind.

After Dale steered the truck down a few wrong turns over rutted, dirt lanes with cattle guards, they found the auction house—a long, rectangular building with an empty stock yard in back. Jane shivered, buttoning her jacket against the cool air from an early evening wind blowing across the desert. Tumbleweeds and a torn plastic grocery sack were caught on the barbed wire between the wooden fence posts. Jane's boots made clouds of dust in the gravel as she walked toward the entryway. The outdoors smelled a little like manure mixed with alfalfa, dusty and baked, even though the heat of the day had fizzled out hours ago. The air tasted gritty, full of dirt the wind stirred up from the dry prairie.

The building was not locked, so they entered into a cool, quiet space. The barn had stadium-like seating around a straw covered arena. A metal railing embedded in a cement floor enclosed the animal pen.

The concrete made the indoors smell like an unfinished basement, but with a touch of antiseptic and barnyard animals overpowering the aroma, as if they'd passed a strong-smelling cattle truck on the highway. Light was dim, like a windowless crypt.

Jane's spine tingled as if someone had walked over her grave, and the hair on her arms stood at attention.

Was the impending eclipse causing this creepy feeling?

Isobel let out a scream, an almost inhuman sound. Olivia dropped her purse, and it hit the floor with a bang that echoed in the empty building. Both mother and daughter stared into the pen, their faces a picture of shock.

Dale gripped her arm to hold her back, but Jane took a few steps closer to the railing for a better look. "What? What is it?"

Georgiana lay crumpled in the bits of straw. Unmoving. Lifeless. In a dead-eyed stare.

Doug said in his cop-voice, "Everybody, stay where you are." He catapulted over the metal railing, like a bronco rider being chased by a Brahman bull. He fell to his knees but darted a sideways look at the group while sliding his fingers across his throat, the universal sign for *croaked*.

Chapter 9

Georgiana may have departed for that last roundup in the sky, but her body was taken away by an ambulance service out of Grand Junction.

The police requested their written statements. The officers were particularly interested in their movements over the last hour and quickly confirmed their alibis with the staff at the steakhouse. Jane told them, other than when Isobel left the table, they were in each other's company the whole time in full view of the wait staff and the other diners. Several hours passed before the police finished, and they were finally allowed to leave.

The late-night drive back to the inn was quiet and subdued. Jane felt cold and her teeth chattered, so as soon as she got to her room she climbed into her pajamas. It was only ten, but she was no longer in the mood for a rodeo.

Dale knocked on her door. "Jane, Holden's opening a couple of bottles of wine. Don't you want to join us?"

She gave the bed with the blankets turned down a longing look. She didn't want to leave the down comforter, the fluffy pillow, the new cozy mystery open on the table, but she said, "Coming." After all, wine would help her sleep better. She drew a baggy sweatshirt over her head and tugged it down past her hips. A glance at her pajama bottoms assured her they looked like pink leggings with a little lace trim around the ankles. She sprang open the door and descended the stairs after Dale.

He held her hand as he led the way. He said with an apologetic tone in his voice, as if making an excuse, "We didn't drink that much wine at Barre Winery and none of us had more than one beer at dinner."

"Actually, I had a lemonade, but a tall Merlot sounds good to me right about now." She squeezed his fingers.

Holden was in the kitchen standing at the counter with a bunch of cherry tomatoes on the vine laid out on a cutting board. His jaw was grinding, his temples moving under his skin. The other Ladners leaned against the wall, all three with their arms crossed, as if unsure where to put their hands and uncertain what to say. Holden extracted a knife from the block. "We'll feel better with a snack. Does someone want to cut up these tomatoes while I make the hummus?"

"I'll cut the tomatoes." Jane's energy was returning. Dinner was hours ago and the police interrogation stressful and long, but food preparation was pleasant busywork that brought comfort with its familiarity. "So how do you make hummus, anyway?"

"With canned chickpeas, a couple of tablespoons of olive oil, some nut butter, lemon juice, garlic, salt, and pepper. Dump it all in the blender, and that's all there is to it." The muscles of Holden's face eased as he explained the process.

Olivia nudged away from the wall. "I'll help with the hummus." The strain at the corner of her eyes diminished, too, as she plugged in the blender.

114

The guys took stools at the kitchen island. Dale rested his elbows on the granite. "I'll just stay out of the way."

"Is that your excuse for not helping?" Olivia chuckled and a couple of the others gave a relieved laugh.

In short order, the counter became crowded with hummus, quartered pita bread, sliced tomatoes sprinkled with oregano, fresh avocado spread on rice cakes—Isobel assembled those—and the inevitable slices of ripe peaches.

Holden elbowed the patio door open, a bottle of wine in each hand. The rest of them followed him out carrying the trays of snacks. A blustery wind had kicked up with the setting sun, and Jane was glad for her thick sweatshirt.

"Fill a plate and nosh away." Olivia set a platter on the patio table.

"So, tell me. What happened to Georgiana? The details, please." Holden's voice was back to low and strained.

Doug extracted the bottles out of his brother's grasp and set them on the table. Clamping one hand on his shoulder, he directed Holden to a chair and lowered him down. "I'm sorry to bring you this news. She was murdered, Holden."

"At least this time the death doesn't involve the B&B." Olivia patted his arm.

"But it does." Doug's eyebrows were drawn in and he chewed on the ends of his mustache.

Olivia gulped in a sharp breath. "How can it? Georgiana wasn't killed here."

Doug pinched the bridge of his nose. "There was a

peach pit shoved down her throat."

Jane's blood ran as cold as the evening breeze, and she folded her arms across her chest. Of course the murders were related. Two people killed. How many more would die before the police found the killer? Or would Jane have to find him first?

Dale reached for the wine and muscled the cork out of the first bottle. He poured glasses and handed them around.

Holden shook his head in a helpless way. "Another peach pit?"

"Another blow to the head, another peach pit in the throat." Doug looked into his wine glass as if searching for the answers to another senseless death.

"I thought one of the bulls had trampled her." Isobel covered her face with her hands. Her sleeves fell away, exposing her tattoo with sunrays stretching out in waves. Olivia put an arm around her daughter's shoulder. The horror of finding Georgiana with her skull crushed was all too much to take in.

Doug added, "Her body was still warm and limber when we found her, as if she'd only been dead a short time."

"You know, the same person who killed Rey had to have killed Georgiana." Jane hugged herself tighter, and Dale rubbed a circle on her back in his comforting way. "We need to get serious about the suspects. We should make a list."

"I'll get a pen and paper." Isobel jumped up and dodged inside. She returned moments later and forced a pad of paper into Jane's hands. "You do it."

Jane stared at Doug. "You go ahead, Doug. Tell us what you're thinking and I'll make a list."

Doug swirled his wine around and legs formed on the sides of his glass, then he set it down in one smooth motion. He mimed *after-you-my-dear*. Maybe the second death had rattled his sangfroid because he didn't appear to care if she asked the questions.

"Okay," Jane said. "We need to know more about Georgiana, like what she did for a living."

Holden answered, "She worked at the stable at the Barre Valley Ranch. With the horses."

"Really?" Olivia's face showed the same astonishment Jane felt.

"Another connection." Doug laced his fingers in his lap.

"So that was why Georgiana was at the auction barn." Jane drubbed the pen on her tablet. This was an interesting piece of the puzzle, but where did it lead?

Dale pointed out, "The auction barn was for cattle, not horses."

"Oh, right. I heard the word, 'barn,' and thought horses." Jane was showing her ignorance.

Doug said, "The question begs to be asked, was Georgiana the intended victim all along?"

Dale said, "That's an idea, but that doesn't bring us any closer to the killer, does it?"

No one had an answer for that.

Jane tapped her pen against her chin. "What if Georgiana witnessed something? Maybe she was there. Maybe Rey was protecting Georgiana from the killer. He grabbed her necklace as she escaped, leaving him behind to face his own death. But why wouldn't Georgiana come forward and tell the police?"

Doug brought his tented fingers up in front of his mouth. "Right. That makes no sense. And way too melodramatic."

Jane tried a new theory. "How about this? Georgiana didn't actually see the killer push Rey to his death, but she saw something suspicious. She confronts the killer at the barn, and he or she murders her." She sat forward, her voice coming out fast and high. "Georgiana knew who was down in the basement with Rey."

But Doug wasn't buying into it. "If the woman had seen something, she would've told the police, Jane. No one would keep dangerous information like that to themselves." The others nodded in agreement, and Jane slumped back in her chair. Doug said to his brother, "We need to know more about the victims, Holden. Tell us everything you know about both Reynard and Georgiana. Now is not the time to keep anything back."

Holden's face was pale and his lips worked as if he was having difficulty finding the words. His chest shuddered with uneven breaths. "All right, but what I'm going to say doesn't leave this room. Certain people could get hurt. So nothing is to be repeated."

Their heads all bobbed up and down at the same time in pack mentality.

"Reynard and Georgiana were lovers." His eyes were aimed at the ground.

They seemed to gasp all at once, except for Isobel, who took a bite of rice cake and chewed with crackling sounds.

Jane poised her pen over the page. "Why keep this a secret? Why would you protect a married man who was having an affair?"

"He was a good friend, and so is Zeta. I don't want news of the relationship to get out." He lifted his shoulders in his dramatic way, then let them fall. Sadness flitted across his face. "I wouldn't want Zeta to be hurt."

Dale tapped Jane's pad of paper. "That is a pretty strong motive for Zeta to kill both of them."

"No, no, no, no. It can't be Zeta. She would never do such a thing. She's not capable." Holden's hands flew around, cutting through the air in great big arcs.

Olivia stopped him with a hand on his wrist. "Listen, we're just brainstorming here. She has an alibi for Georgiana's murder like we do. She was at the restaurant, same as us."

Holden shut his eyes and gave his head a quick jerk, signaling yes.

Jane hated to upset him, but said in a soft voice, "I saw her leave her table. She disappeared from sight."

"That's true. Zeta was gone for a good fifteen minutes or so, right about the time Isobel went to the restroom." Doug traced a finger across the face of his watch. As a trained officer of the law, he probably noticed more than most people.

So Zeta didn't have an airtight alibi, and Holden didn't look happy about it. Jane didn't want Zeta to be the killer, either—what would happen to the wedding?—but the owner of the winery was a top suspect, no denying it. "Zeta has another motive, too, besides jealousy over the affair. Political ambition. She wants to be the mayor of Barresville." Jane got busy jotting down her theories.

"Zeta would never kill her husband." Holden's face was stricken and his head fell to his chest. Why was he so adamant, so concerned for this woman? Just how well did they know each other? Was there more to their relationship? Friendships between men and women were complex things.

Jane studied his expression for a clue and made a guess. "You have feelings for her, don't you?"

"No, of course not." His voice came out strangled and he looked at her with haunted eyes. "We're just friends, that's all." His words did not ring true.

Jane pressed, "Holden, is there any reason for you to be a suspect?"

"Whaaaat?" Olivia acted like she wasn't sure she'd heard that right.

Holden lifted both hands up, as if in surrender. "Maybe."

Doug fixed his gaze on his brother. "What do you mean?"

"Remember, no word to anyone. Swear it." Holden crossed his own heart. The group stared at him.

"Right, right." Doug sucked his lips in until they disappeared.

"I was engaged to Zeta before Rey came along and stole her away. That was years and years ago. Over time the hard feelings were forgotten, and Rey and I became friends. But in the past we were enemies because of Zeta." His voice came out shaky and grew even more so the longer he talked.

Olivia's jaw dropped. "You never told us you were engaged." She huffed out a breath, her irritation clear.

Jane interrupted with, "If it was so long ago, why would it matter now? Why would you make us swear not to say anything?"

"I don't want Zeta to be reminded of the past. She's got enough to deal with at the moment. She's been running the vineyard singlehandedly, just about, while Rey worked on his campaign. And now that he's dead, her plate is especially full."

"Okay, but Holden, you had no reason to kill Georgiana. Granted, the police may consider you a suspect in Rey's death." Jane caught the glare from Olivia. "But what reason would you have to kill Georgiana? None."

"To protect Zeta from finding out about the affair?" His voice went down an octave, as if reaching to the bottom of the barrel for an excuse no matter how farfetched. Jane made another note because she found it to be believable. Perhaps his feelings for Zeta had kept him from getting married to someone else all these years.

Olivia tried to peer around the hand Jane was using to shield her notes from view before she cast a worried glance at her brother-in-law. "There are other suspects, right? Jane? Doug?"

They all looked from Doug to Jane, then Doug asked, "Are we done with the snacks?" They all nodded. He brought out three cigars from the inside pocket of his pullover and passed two to the other men. "Ladies, do you want a cigar? I have some of the girlie ones you like, Jane." He patted his pocket.

"None for me." Olivia didn't usually smoke. She grabbed the food trays to run them into the kitchen.

"I don't want a cigar, either. Thanks, anyway." Jane turned the page in her notepad. "Back to Olivia's question. I made a list of suspects. Do you want to go over them?"

"Yes." Olivia was quick to answer as she resumed her seat.

"Okay. First up, Kirby Potts. He had a motive…to

kill his rival for the mayor's office. Maybe he didn't know Zeta would step into the race. Then, after he killed Rey, he had to kill Georgiana because she knew something or saw something." Jane glanced at the others with a defiant look. "Well, she could have. So anyway, Kirby had the opportunity, he was in the vicinity of both murders. He could have sneaked out of the restaurant just as easily as Zeta. Motive. Means. And opportunity, as they say."

"Skylar had opportunity, too." Dale puffed on his cigar at the same time he lit the end.

"No! He doesn't have a motive." Isobel spoke for the first time. "Now you're getting way off base."

"Skylar has to be included on the list since he stayed the night at the inn." Jane shied away from looking at the youngest Ladner. "Don't get mad, but let me just put this out there. I saw Skylar with a campaign button supporting Kirby Potts. Yet he works at the Barre Winery. That's odd. Here's a theory. Skylar cares about all kinds of environmental issues. So maybe Kirby's agenda is more in line with Skylar's, more concerned with conservation, than the Barres'."

"Right. Blame the environmentalist! Someone has to look out for the Earth, you know." Righteous anger lit Isobel's eyes. They were all probably thinking the same thing...that Isobel was crushing on Skylar. "Who else is on your list?" Isobel's voice was thick and tight.

"Zeta, as you know. Remember, a woman could've pushed Rey. He was off balance when he fell and hit his head in that freakish way. The police told you, Holden, didn't they, that a woman could've done it? And a woman could've sneaked up on Georgiana and bashed her on the head, too." Holden gave her a dark look. Jane added, "So to continue, Adam Aemes is the next suspect on my list." She didn't mention Holden's name was the very last, and under motive she'd scratched down, "jealousy."

Dale interrupted her thoughts with, "Adam who?"

"The photographer, Fritz the Snitch. Now, I know we think he left before Rey was killed, but he could've hidden himself in the basement, pushed Rey and left him for dead, and then escaped out the door. He was dressed so similarly to Kirby that no one would've noticed." She flashed a triumphant look.

"Good thought." Olivia gave her a fist bump.

Doug held his cigar between two fingers and stabbed the air. "The photographer needs a motive."

"True." She put her chin in her palm, then sat up straight, letting her hand fall to the table. "Could there have been two killers, Doug? The first one and then a copycat?" Jane's mind was spinning with theories. "Maybe Georgiana is the first killer. She killed Rey, say out of jealousy, or better yet, he was going to dump her. You know, a lover's quarrel. Then someone kills Georgiana and leaves the pit as a copycat clue."

She could picture the whole thing. The lovers planned a rendezvous in the basement after the party. Georgiana confronted Rey. Told him he needed to leave his wife. But Rey was in the middle of a political campaign, not the best time for a separation and divorce that could distract voters from the important issues. He refused to end his marriage, or maybe he just put Georgiana off, and she got angry and shoved him. He grabbed her necklace as he fell and hit his head. Maybe she didn't even mean to kill him. She left him, thinking he'd recover. But he died. Then, Zeta figured it out. She confronted Georgiana. She had a vendetta against her husband's lover, her pride was injured…but…why put the peach pit in their throats? Did the pit have anything to do with the pendant necklace and Georgiana's nickname, Peaches?

Jane still liked her other theory better. Georgiana witnessed something, she had secret knowledge, a clue, and one killer silenced both Rey and his lover.

Doug broke into her reverie. "That's actually a plausible theory."

"Which one?"

"Two killers. It could've happened that way. And if so, it will be harder to solve." Doug tapped a knuckle to his mustache.

Cigar smoke hovered under the patio roof, smelling like an old man on a park bench, like Jane's grandpa. On her plate were leftover tomatoes with oregano, an old-fashioned dish, smelling like her grandma's pasta sauce. The scents together evoked a memory of childhood, although as far as Jane knew, her grandparents never ate hummus or rice cakes. What was the appeal of rice cakes? Eating a rice cake was like eating air. The younger generation didn't care for comfort smells or comfort foods. No, the more unfamiliar, and sometimes even the more unappetizing, the better.

Isobel spoke up. "Did you look at the party pictures Jane posted? I did, but I couldn't come up with anything new."

They sat with their eyes glued to their cell phones, like a bunch of middle-schoolers checking their messages for a text, something more important to them than a real conversation.

Isobel said, "Adam Aemes does look just like Kirby Potts in their matching striped suits, black shirts, and white ties."

"The costume stores are probably limited in Palisade. We rented ours in Denver." Olivia shook her head as if she couldn't imagine living in a city without a fully stocked costume shop.

Dale stubbed out his cigar, drained one last swallow of his wine, and set his glass on the table. "I'm beat."

Isobel had been busy on her cell phone, but said out of the corner of her mouth, "It's only eleven."

Jane nodded. "Right. Time for bed."

The party broke up. Dale made sure Jane wasn't too upset to sleep—she assured him she was fine—then he left her for his own room.

She slid out of the warm, smoky-smelling sweatshirt she'd put on over her pajamas and climbed under the blankets. But her thoughts wouldn't settle. Holden was a serious suspect. She couldn't discuss him with the others, but she couldn't rule him out, either. There was something in the back of her mind nagging just below the surface. Something about the party pictures? Something in the lounge.

She tossed off the blankets and tiptoed out her door and all the way back down to the basement.

The faint blood stain on the carpet was still visible in the circle of light from the lamp. The candle and the silver-framed picture were once again arranged in the center of the table. The photograph showed the untamed mustangs in the Little Book Cliffs Wild Horse Area, the sun slanting across the horizon, a wild, very western scene, with the tawny copper colors of the

125

desert and the golden yellow glow of the setting sun. One of Adam Aemes' photographs. His signature style. Nothing new about that. She shook her head, muttering to herself.

She went on bare feet to the kitchen to make a cup of Sleepytime tea. The deep voices of men came through the kitchen window. Holden and Doug were still seated on the patio deck. The brothers were close together, facing each other. Doug's expression was flat, but Holden's showed deep concern, like he was listening with all his attention.

She sidled up next to the door and squished her back against the wall, holding herself still, closing her eyes and concentrating.

Doug said, "The police told me that Zeta inherits everything, and Reynard had quite extensive holdings in Barre Valley in addition to the winery in Palisade. She has more motive than anyone else."

"I suppose so."

"Holden, did you see Zeta go down to the basement with Rey? I know you don't want to say anything, but you can tell me."

"No way. She didn't go down there. Why would she choose my place to kill her husband? She would've had plenty of opportunities at home, don't you think? But she didn't do it, of course."

The sound of a chair scraping back caused Jane to jump, so she plastered herself tighter to the wall. She took another peek, then jumped again when Doug flicked some ashes off the end of his cigar causing it to glow red in the dark. Was Holden lying to his brother? Did he see Zeta with Rey that night? Or worse, did either of the Ladner brothers spot Jane snooping on them? Not a very nice thing to do to friends, but she couldn't help herself.

"Did you talk to Zeta about her marriage?"

"No."

"Did you talk to her about finances, the winery, the ranch?"

"No. But I heard through the grapevine they had no life insurance. See, she didn't have a motive to kill her husband."

Nothing more was said while Jane listened a few extra moments to the beats of her own heart. She chanced another quick glance out the patio door. Doug had his arm around his brother's shoulder, a hand on the back of his neck, and their red heads were together. A private, personal moment between siblings.

Then, strange flashing lights lit up the inky black sky outside the patio door and a shiver went up her spine. Rain began to hit the side of the building with soft splatters.

She slid along the wall until she was sure to be out of their line of vision and tiptoed to the stairs. Racing back up to her bedroom, she locked her door and jumped under the flowery down comforter, pulling it up to her chin. She tried to turn her thoughts away from the unsolved murders. To think about something else. To sleep...

The lights flashed again.

The eclipse was going to happen in two days, close to noon on Monday. Would the day really go as dark as the night? Would crickets come out and chirp, thinking it was time to begin their mating call? Would birds head toward their nests and animals to their burrows, tricked into believing it was time to go to sleep? Jane worried about her dogs. Without her there to comfort them would they be as confused and upset as she was right now?

Maybe tomorrow would turn out to be a calm, relaxing Sunday, the day of rest it was meant to be.

But Jane was to have no such luck.

Chapter 10

Jane was caught up in the crazy street scene at the Farmers Market in downtown Palisade Sunday morning after church, the frenzied crowd a far cry from calm.

Third Street was jammed with townies and tourists alike, buying fruit and vegetables offered by natural produce growers. Booth after booth displayed the typical white paper sacks of peaches. She might have caught a glimpse of Ratatatat Touille and Dee Lish from the party, but couldn't be sure. She expected to run into Skylar. Didn't he sell local, organic produce? But she didn't see him among the vendors.

"I've got to pick up a few things for Holden. Follow me." Olivia plowed through the other shoppers, carrying a straw tote bag over her arm in search of the best fruit and vegie stand.

But Jane had another mission.

She was certain the local politicians would make the most of every opportunity to campaign, so she scanned the tents for Kirby or Zeta, but didn't spot them before trailing after Olivia into a stall holding bins of vegetables. While her friend picked through the purple varietal tomatoes labeled, Black Krim, Jane lifted a white paper bag by its flimsy handles from one of the crates. She couldn't resist buying a bag of the delicious peaches.

Olivia was going to be some time yet, so after

paying for her peaches, Jane proceeded down the length of the street. Sure enough, Kirby had erected a tent with a banner, "Keep Barre out of Barresville." Jane made her way over.

"Hello, I'm Kirby Potts. I'm running for mayor." Unlike Zeta, he didn't seem to recognize her.

"Remember me? I was the one at the party who gave away the solution to the game. Heh, heh." She chuckled, like it was a small thing, even a kinda cute thing, charming even. She carefully omitted the word "murder" from the name of the game.

"Oh, yes, of course. Brynne Less. Why are you still in town? I thought you were only here for the party. Aren't you from Denver?" He probably wanted her to move along since she was not a member of his constituency and could not vote for him in the election.

"My group is staying for the whole weekend, through the eclipse tomorrow."

He nodded and gazed past her, but the stream of people continued to march on by, no one else was stopping at his booth. His eyes flicked back to her. "Can I help you with something? Answer a question?"

"Yes, as a matter of fact. I'm curious why you're running for mayor."

"Someone has to do it. It's time for a change."

"You have an art gallery to take care of, a business to manage."

"Local businessmen and women often serve as mayors of small towns. Giving back to the community, you know. I'm only running to get the people around here to move on from the Barres. The Barres have always controlled the town like a bunch of money-grubbing old ranchers." His words sounded battle-ready and condescending.

"What do you mean, money-grubbing?"

"The Barres are only interested in lining their own pockets. They aren't looking out for what's best for their neighbors. It's time to kick the Barres out of Barresville." That same old slogan.

Jane could sense his impatience, almost hear his silent message telling her to move along. But no one else was paying them any attention and now was her chance. "About the night Reynard was killed, after the party did you see anyone come in the front door or go down to the lounge?"

"No. I did not. I already told the police all of this."

She leaned in, her words low. "I'm sure you're aware of the latest homicide, and I'd like to ask you about that, too."

"Georgiana." The name came out as a whisper. A deep frown cut across his face, real emotion this time that didn't seem to come from Barre-hate.

"That's right. Horrible, just horrible, isn't it?" She quailed at the thought herself, the memory of finding Georgiana at the auction barn.

His eyes were no longer roaming the crowd. He was staring down, silent, at the table piled with brochures, bumper stickers, and pens bearing the slogan, *Keep Barre out of Barresville.*

"I saw you at the steakhouse last night. You and Skylar and another man, that photographer, Adam Aemes. I was wondering"—she took a breath and held it before letting it out in a big puff—"if any of you left your table during the meal?"

His shoulders stiffened and he went rigid. "You're checking my alibi."

She didn't deny it.

"I didn't leave the restaurant. A lot of people stopped to talk to me, and the staff out there know me well. People will remember me." He gave her a scornful glance.

"You never got up to go to the restroom?" Eek. Was that question too personal?

"No." He shook his head.

"Did anyone else from your table?"

"Well, Skylar did. He was gone a while, and I just assumed he was talking to Isobel."

Jane's throat constricted. "You know Isobel?"

"Just through Sky. Small world, you know." His gaze returned to the crowd as if desperate for someone else to stop at his booth.

"I suppose you knew Georgiana, too, because, like they say, everyone around here knows everyone else."

"I met her through Adam. They grew up together, went to the same school."

"Yes?" Jane gave him an encouraging smile, but he didn't say more. She tried another tactic. "I just found out Georgiana worked for Zeta." Best not to mention the affair in deference to Holden.

"Zeta! I can't believe she's taking up the race against me. Who knew she'd do that? You just can't trust those Barres." Kirby's eyes flamed with anger, and he spoke through clenched teeth. He looked as if he wanted to beat his opponent, not only at the polls, but with a bludgeon. He appeared capable of killing someone. All of a sudden, his stormy expression changed to a bright smile, and he half stood to shake the hand of a woman behind Jane. "Hello. My name's Kirby Potts."

Jane backed away from the table and made strides in the direction of the fruit and vegetable stand where she'd left Olivia.

Her ears were sharper than normal, listening to the voices in the crowd. Kirby would be disappointed no one was talking politics. Shoppers converging in the street were discussing the eclipse and preparing for the eclipse and buying extra supplies because of the eclipse…just in case…because you never knew what could happen. A couple of bystanders were planning to attend a gathering on top of the Grand Mesa to view the celestial event.

She drifted past a tent with eclipse products—sun protection glasses, pinhole projector kits, and books on the history of cosmic occurrences and flying saucers landing in Roswell, New Mexico. Next door, the vegetable stand had a long line and Olivia was at the end of it, so Jane turned around and went into the eclipse booth.

She picked up a book entitled, *Little Known Facts About the Total Eclipse*. The introduction provided some teasers. You could experience bad health if a solar eclipse happened on your birthday. Pregnant women should refrain from watching the eclipse because radiation exposure could impact a fetus inside the womb. Contrary to the doomsday warnings, another so-called expert claimed the eclipse could have favorable effects on plants…flowers planted during the eclipse would be more vibrant and colorful. These predictions sounded like silly superstitions.

Nothing was mentioned about falling down and getting hurt, accidently punching yourself in the face, or seeing manifestations of ghosts in the backgrounds of pictures. Or finding dead bodies. She strode out of the booth to go look for Olivia.

She glanced back at Kirby Potts and happened to catch him glaring at her.

Surely politics were more dangerous than the eclipse.

*****

Back at the inn, Olivia set the bags of organic peaches and tomatoes on the kitchen counter. "Here you go, Holden. I got these for you at the market."

"...and then Kirby said he never left the table at the restaurant last night." Jane hiked herself onto a kitchen stool. She'd just finished recounting her conversation with Kirby Potts.

"Thanks for picking these up." Holden stowed both bags in the refrigerator. "So we should check out Kirby's alibi. Dale and Doug will be busy fishing for another hour or two." The men had taken off early that morning for a fly-fishing lesson on the Colorado River. "Do you want to go? The steakhouse is open for lunch." Holden waved his hand toward the door.

Olivia's eyes lit up and she gave Jane an excited grin. They made quick work of gathering their things and climbing into Holden's Subaru. The three arrived on the dot when the restaurant opened at eleven.

Jane, with the pair of Ladners hovering at her elbow, asked if she could talk to the waitresses who worked the shift the night before. They were directed to a work station with menus, coffee pots, and silverware in tubs.

The same bird-like waitress, once again dressed in tight jeans and a low-riding apron, said in her gravelly voice, "Yes, I remember. Both Kirby and Skylar left their table for a time. Skylar seemed to be gone longer. Kirby worked the room, you know, talking up the other diners about running for mayor."

"What about Zeta?" Jane felt Holden's eyes boring into the back of her head.

Another waitress, wrapping silverware in paper napkins, didn't miss a beat, plucking down the silverware, rolling up the napkin, tucking in the ends. "Zeta, she disappeared for about, let's see, fifteen minutes, maybe. I remember 'cause I took two orders and delivered food to the table next to hers, and that's about how long that takes me."

Holden gave the waitress a hopeful smile. "Do you know where Zeta went?"

"Nope." Both waitresses shook their heads. Neither one knew where she'd gone.

Jane poked her head in the kitchen to ask the cook who was busy with prep work, but he had nothing to add.

"Let's check out the restrooms." Jane jerked a thumb over her shoulder to the signs for the little cowgirls' and little cowboys' rooms. She led the way down a narrow, dark hall past a dirty mop in a wash bucket.

"You look in the girls' and I'll look in the boys'." Holden flattened his palm against the men's room door.

"Brilliant idea, Holden. I'm glad you didn't ask the women to search the men's room," Olivia deadpanned, crossing her eyes and twirling her index finger near her temple. Jane chuckled. She could afford to laugh, since she wasn't the recipient of Olivia's sarcasm this time.

"I've been in a little boys' room before." Olivia entered into the windowless restroom with worn

135

wooden stalls, broken and chipped ceramic tiles covering the floor, and a rust-stained basin hanging off the wall. "Usually the women's rooms are so much nicer than the men's, but this one is pretty nasty."

"I wonder if Isobel talked to anyone when she was in here. Maybe she ran into Zeta." Jane peered into the mirror. Why did the mirror make her appear about ten years older and as if she had deep bags under her eyes?

"I'll ask her." Olivia recoiled from the mirror, too, so it wasn't just Jane. They glanced over the space but there wasn't much to see. After only a minute or two they met Holden back in the hall outside the restrooms.

He aimed a finger down the length of the dingy corridor. "That door at the end opens to the outside."

"It does?" Jane's voice reached a high note. Would they find a clue? "Let's look."

They hustled out the door. The bright sunshine hit Jane's eyes with a blinding glare. A tin bucket held cigarette butts, but the gravel underneath was a magnet for most of the crinkled stubs. A rickety metal folding chair leaned against the weatherworn back of the building. Dumpsters, enclosed by a high chain link, locked fence, were also encircled by foraging birds and the odor of rotting lettuce. The gravel turned into clay, and the clay transitioned into a desolate field of red dirt, patches of yucca plants, and tumbleweed rolling before the breeze. On the other side of the barren tract dotted with craters of prairie dog burrows was a long, rectangular cement building and next to that, a holding pen filled with cattle.

Jane hazarded a guess. "That can't be the auction barn, can it?"

Holden said, "Yes. That's the barn."

Olivia shielded her eyes from the sun with one hand across her forehead. "Well, the barn's in chucking distance after all. Jeez. And Dale drove all around trying to find it. It seemed a lot farther going by road."

Holden dug his hands through his red hair, rifling it. "Let's time how long it takes to walk across the field. I'll bet fifteen minutes wasn't enough for anyone to meet someone and get back." He was undoubtedly thinking of Zeta.

Jane set the timer on her cell phone, then jogged the distance with Olivia close behind. Wind was in her ears and dust in her nose. She needed to watch her feet to avoid the prairie dog holes and the washboard of ruts. She tripped a little in an attempt to maintain her footing. Holden seemed to saunter as he covered the same ground.

Jane timed both herself and Holden. A minute and three seconds to run and a minute and a half to walk. "So let's say two minutes to walk over, maybe five minutes to speak with Georgiana and bash her on the head with something, then five seconds to take a peach pit from a pocket and shove it down her throat." Jane winced as that image came to mind. She blinked away the vision. "And another two minutes to get back to the restaurant." Her mouth formed the words, "Two, five, two," as she counted off on her fingers. "That's only nine or ten minutes. Skylar or Kirby could've done it." She lowered her voice and covered the side of her mouth to add, "Or Zeta. None of them has an airtight alibi for the entire time they were at the steakhouse. Not like us. We never left our table."

Olivia raised her palms up. "What was Georgiana hit on the head with? Do you know?"

"I didn't see a weapon that night, but none of us other than Doug went into the pen to get a good look. Holden, can you ask your brother? Will you do that when you get a chance?" Doug didn't need to know Jane and his wife were the ones behind the question.

"I will." Holden stood at the door but didn't make a move to go inside. A dozen or so pickup trucks were scattered over the parking lot. The fast, up and down voice of the auctioneer's song escaped through the wooden door. Holden cocked an ear. "Sounds like an auction is going on."

The heat of the sun blasted Jane's face. She squinted her eyes and scanned the horizon. "The police must've released the scene already. We won't find any clues inside the building if animals are in the pen where we found Georgiana."

Holden agreed with a nod. "But we might find clues outside. What if the killer made arrangements to meet Georgiana? She was waiting for him in the barn. He scooped up a rock from the ground on the way in. Then afterward, he threw the rock across the pasture so no one would find it."

"He chucked the rock." Olivia made a joke, but neither of the other two laughed.

Jane said, "If the killer used a rock, he had to've hit Georgiana a couple of times, I would think. Just knocking someone on the head once wouldn't necessarily kill a person. Her skull had a lot more damage than that."

Olivia shivered. "Right. It looked like there was a lot of anger. Be glad you didn't see it, Holden."

His eyes were to the ground. "Let's spread out, walk about ten feet apart, and scan the field for anything that could've been used as a weapon."

"What are we looking for?" Olivia's brows were knit in suspicion.

Jane stared at the dirt. "Blood. Hair. The usual."

"Eugh!" Olivia stretched her lips down in disgust. "Bleeck. This is too much."

"You always wanted to investigate, my dear, and now's your chance." Jane bumped shoulders with her friend.

Holden grabbed Olivia by the arms and directed her to a spot, then he did the same to Jane so they ended up standing in a line about ten feet apart. He took his own position. They crept along with small steps, their gazes glued to the ground.

About halfway across the terrain, Jane almost tripped on a heavy gray rock, not round, more in the shape of a disc, easy to grip in a strong hand. The rock was covered at the sharper end with a brown stain that almost matched the red clay in the pasture. She let out a hair-raising shriek. "Here! I found something!"

"Don't touch it." Olivia's voice boomed equally loud. She careened over, practically pushing Jane out of the way, then Jane did the same to Olivia, taking a deep knee bend to get a closer look. Holden yanked her back, and she rolled over onto her backside. Olivia helped steady her to a stand, while Holden drew his cell phone out of his pocket.

"I'm calling the police investigator. Can one of you go back to the restaurant? When the police show up, direct them to this field. I'll stay right here until they arrive."

"I will." Olivia tucked a strand of her windblown hair behind her ear. "Come with me, Jane." She tugged her arm. Jane nodded and stumbled after her friend, who practically trotted back inside the restaurant. Olivia nabbed a table and ordered two coffees. "We can stay inside right here. Why do we need to go out front?"

"Fine by me." Jane's nerves were jangling. She didn't really need the caffeine, but somehow hot coffee was comforting anyway.

They hadn't long to wait. Before they finished their coffees, a team of officers entered the restaurant. Jane and Olivia both rose from the table and walked them to the back door where they could see Holden standing sentinel in the pasture. He spotted them and waved his arms wildly as if they couldn't see him there.

One of the officers said, "You two, stay inside."

After about twenty minutes the officers returned with Holden in their wake.

Jane asked, when they climbed into Holden's Subaru, "Do you think they can get fingerprints off that rock? Did you find out if the police asked Georgiana about her necklace? Did they ever find it?" Jane propped one knee over the other and picked at the clay stuck to the soles of her cowboy boots. "Did you tell the police to check the suspects' shoes for that red clay from the field?"

"Wait up, Jane. I didn't think to ask them any of those questions. Sorry." Holden gripped the steering wheel. "I can ask Doug, though, because he has an 'in' with the homicide investigator. We need to tell Doug about the bloody rock we found anyway. The officers did seem excited when I showed it to them, saying something about how they were short-staffed or they would've found it themselves, although one of them mentioned that the blood could belong to an animal or be quite old. It was dried."

Jane's eyes turned to Olivia sitting in the back seat. "How are we going to tell Doug what we did...questioning the wait staff?"

"He'll get over it. Don't worry." Olivia examined a fingernail, not looking as confident as she sounded. "Let me handle Doug."

"I'll let you." Jane snorted. "I'll give that little meeting a sideslip."

Olivia snickered along with Jane, but hers was more of a nervous twitter. "We found an important clue. Ha! That'll show him." They laughed together like they were sharing a joke, like before everything turned so serious, like before the murders happened. Olivia's laughter wound down, but when Jane gave her a slanted look, she started back up.

"Girls, girls, this isn't funny." Holden frowned.

"Sorry, bro." Olivia patted his shoulder from the back seat, then started chuckling again. "Jane's looking at me. Make her stop."

Jane gave her a goofy grin. Laughter relieved stress and was good for the soul.

"The police told me I have to go to the station tomorrow morning and give them a formal statement. I'm sure they'll talk to the waitresses and the cook and find out we asked them questions. They'll probably want to talk to you, too, Jane, and you, Olivia." His voice had a somber tone, and the tension in the group returned.

"You can ask the police what they found out about the necklace while you're there." Jane stationed both boots on the floorboard and grasped her knees. "Maybe you can even find out who the police questioned, and if they don't tell you, can you ask your friend, the dispatcher?"

"I asked her that already, I meant to let you know, Olivia. The police questioned all the guests at the party, including those who left before Rey was killed." His glance darted over to Jane and up to the rear-view mirror to catch Olivia's eye. "They questioned Georgiana three times and Zeta twice."

"They probably know about the affair. They might ask you about it tomorrow, Holden." Olivia's voice had turned serious. She took several deep breaths, then said in a lower tone, "Are you still having the eclipse party tomorrow?"

"Of course. First the police, then the party." Holden pulled into the bed-and-breakfast alongside Dale's pickup. "The fishermen are back."

Jane sucked in a breath. Time to 'fess up.

What would the two men think of the three of them laying hold of the murder weapon? What was the worst thing that could happen?

That Doug would be so frustrated he'd chew off his mustache completely?

Chapter 11

Doug didn't rip the hair off his upper lip, but he did roll his eyes back so far that Jane thought his eyeballs would pop out the top of his head.

She left Doug in his wife's capable hands and knocked on the door to Dale's room. "It's me."

"Come in." He opened the door. "You have to see the pictures of the fish I caught." His eyes shown and his voice held a happy note.

They sat together on the loveseat under the window overlooking the peach orchard. She scanned his pictures of staring fish laid out on the ground. He explained it was catch and release.

"I have some news for you, too." Jane cleared her throat, took a deep breath, and told him about the rock they'd found in the field.

"I'm glad you took Holden with you and I'm glad you called the police." His voice was tender.

His concern was a load off her mind. "We didn't expect to find the murder weapon. That was providential."

"More like divine intervention. Do you really think you happened to stumble across the actual weapon?"

The scenario played over in her imagination once again. The killer picked up the rock, strode inside the barn, struck Georgiana before she had a chance to defend herself, and fled back to the restaurant, dropping the rock on the way. "Yes. I think they'll find it's her blood." She gave a shudder.

He rubbed his forehead before glancing at his watch. "It's time to meet the others. Grab your jacket."

Back in her room, she stuffed sunscreen and lip balm into her pocket, slung her binoculars around her neck, and changed into hiking shoes. She had to go back for her cowboy hat and windbreaker and was the last to arrive at the truck. Doug explained which way to go, and they were soon headed to the rugged canyons and plateaus that made up the wild horse country.

While on the road, Doug started in with his warnings about letting the police do their job, blah, blah, blah. While Olivia stared out the window, Jane exchanged some texts with her dog sitter.

She gnawed on one of the peaches she'd bought at the farmers market. They were soooo good, sweet and juicy, just the right texture, not too soft or too hard, the furry skin breaking easily under her teeth, the cool body of the fruit tasting tangy closer to the pit. Jane moaned at the utter yumminess.

"What is it, Jane?" Olivia strained forward from the backseat. "Did you think of another clue?" She cast a glance at her husband. "I mean, uh, did you remember something?"

"No, not a thing. It's just that the peaches are so delicious. You want one?" She suppressed another *yummy* sound as she chewed and swallowed, then grabbed a second furry peach from the bag to hand to her friend.

"No, none for me. But be careful. You've been eating a lot of those. You'll make yourself sick." Olivia sat back once more. Jane sneaked one more peach out of her bag and stowed the rest under the seat. The peaches were on the small side, not softball sized, closer to racquetball sized. So she didn't feel guilty for eating so many. Two were more like one big peach. Or so she told herself.

She enjoyed the scenery on the long ride over the dirt road into the North Soda past High Lonesome Ranch on the Roan Plateau. She loved the views of the high desert, such a contrast from the Front Range, which was all green and lush and cedar smelling with tall lodge pole pines and spruce trees. The desert canyons were mostly brown, but if one took a deeper, longer look, the color variants in the strata were evident...tan, russet, carmine rose, smoky topaz, burnt umber. Even black from ribbons of coal and white from threads of marble. Add the big blue sky to the palate of hues. So big, the breadth of the sky made her heart swell, as they cut across the high plateau among the hoodoos or fairy chimneys, columns left behind when smaller rocks eroded away from the harder cap rock, and deep cliffs, so deep she couldn't see all the way to the bottom.

Once they reached an old cabin, she unfolded herself out of the truck. Dale opened the tailgate and handed around cold bottles of water out of a Yeti cooler. Doug marked the time—just after one in the afternoon, then led the way on a dirt and gravel track that turned into a trail behind the cabin.

Jane watched her feet for snakes. She didn't spot one, but was glad she'd kept a look out anyway, since tall stacks of horse manure dotted the sides of the trail. She asked anyone within hearing distance, "Why would someone rake the manure into piles? I thought this was a wild area."

Doug said, "No one raked the manure. That's how the stallions mark their territory."

"It is?" She stepped around another mound that was about a foot high.

They made their way down to the valley floor. White blooming bushes called Service Berry scented the air. Long grasses covered the lowland, and towering mountains provided a magnificent backdrop.

Four or five groups of wild mustangs were spread out over the wide valley.

Olivia held her binoculars to her eyes. "See how the stallions and their mares form different bands?"

"I do. And look, there are some colts, too."

"The babies are about three months old." Olivia had the *Little Book Cliffs Wild Horse Range* website open on her cell phone. "It says here some of their names are Bolt, Rascal, and Jetta. They're so cute."

Jane tore herself away from the vista in front of her to take hold of Olivia's phone screen. "Is 'bookcliffs' one word or two? This website shows it as two words and I've seen other places where it's one."

Olivia answered, "I know. It's not consistent. You'll see it spelled both ways."

Jane returned her attention back to the valley. The horses had mostly brown with white faces, but many were red-brown, brown-black, gray, roan, chestnut, and all-white, too. She shot a couple dozen photos on her cell phone.

She said to Dale, "Too bad we can't get married here. That would be some Plan B, wouldn't it?" Jane was half serious.

"No can do. No restrooms around here, so it

wouldn't work." He gave her a smile, then touched her face and caressed her cheek. Jane knew that look in his eye. He was having fun. They were getting married in a month! And on the beautiful Western Slope of Colorado.

Once they'd arrived back at the truck, Dale said, "I'm not ready to call it a day. There are some four-wheel drive trails outside the wilderness area. Anyone up for a ride?"

"I'd love, love, love that!" Excitement churned in the pit of Jane's stomach. Could the day get any better? She'd almost forgotten about the double homicide. It was too peaceful in the wild horse refuge to think about. But she frowned anyway, since it had crossed her mind.

"What's the matter? You're scowling." Dale brushed a strand of her hair behind her ear.

"I'm not scowling." Jane gave him a broad smile. "Doug, would you like a turn at shotgun? I'll sit in the back with Olivia." She was feeling magnanimous, so they changed places.

The backseat turned out to be a poor choice when the truck bumped over pot holes in the washed out, cratered four-wheel-drive road, practically rattling her teeth.

Primitive hardly described the rocky track. The truck's wheels ascended up the flat limestone slate and crawled over boulders that appeared too steep to scale, sometimes forcing the vehicle into what seemed like forty-five degree angles. Jane hung onto the grab handle above the window like it was the only thing keeping her from falling off the edge of the plateau and bit her tongue so she wouldn't scream, "Holy Frijoles!"

or a few stronger choice words.

She did have to holler, "Dale, stop the truck," after he reached the top of another ridge. "I need to find a bush."

They all stared around at the rubble that was bare of trees or shrubs. Dale was right, there were no restrooms on the plateau.

Olivia came to her rescue. "Come with me. There's a boulder over there." She pointed toward a tall outcropping that might offer some privacy. She handed Jane some tissues from her oversized handbag before Jane skirted the megalith and entered a carved-out, grotto-like area.

Her friend stood lookout, but on Jane's side of the slab she caught a glimpse of the head and shoulders of a man approaching on foot from behind a stunted piñon pine. He was encumbered with a large backpack, his face aimed her way. Jane only had time to stumble back before he appeared on the near side of the rock, and a second later a small boy came into view clambering over the boulders.

Jane waved her arms in a cross motion, then crossed her index fingers in an "X" warning. The man's eyes widened as he took in Jane's position with sudden understanding. He held out his arms to shield the boy's view and the two did a one-eighty to dodge back through the groove in the rocks that Jane now recognized as a trail. A rock cairn even marked the beaten path. Olivia had picked out a well-used hiking destination for Jane's privy, and her friend was standing guard at the wrong end.

Heat flushing her face, Jane scrubbed her hands with the wet towelette, also courtesy of Olivia, and decided not to mention her near total exposure to anyone.

"I appreciate your keeping look out, Olivia. You're the top bud, sista'." She was really thankful to have a friend watching her back, even if facing the wrong way. Jane crossed over to the truck with Olivia at her side. "Thanks for stopping, Dale. Too much coffee, I guess. Heh, heh." She chuckled, as if her most embarrassing moment *ever* had not just occurred.

A know-it-all grin broke out on Olivia's face and she presented Jane with a *you-re-not-fooling-anyone* kind of look. But Jane wanted to move on to her other news. "I think I saw weird crop circles over that-a-way." She waved her hand out the window toward the ridge overlooking a shallow canyon.

"There aren't any crops in that valley." Doug's eyebrows huddled together and his lips flattened in disbelief.

"Let's find out." Dale turned the steering wheel. "See those tire tracks? Other trucks have gone this way before. Let's take the trail over." They topped yet another moraine, one Jane didn't think was possible to scale, and Dale came to a stop. Far below them were circles in the dirt and full-sized pickups looking like toy trucks. "Give me your binoculars, Jane." She handed them over and Dale peered at the sight. "Those trucks have logos belonging to an oil exploration company."

"That's Barre Valley Ranch land." Doug rubbed his mustache as if in deep thought. "What are they doing down there?"

None of them had an answer. Dale tossed the binoculars into the console.

Grinding gears sounded in the distance, but soon

grew louder and louder. They sat still, listening, as if wondering in one accord if that was the sound of an oil rig. But an ancient VW van, covered in dusty red dirt, burst over the top of a long, flat rock, bumped heavily across the splayed formation, scrabbling the loose, unstable shale, jouncing over indents and ruts and broken bits, then roared out of sight around a bend, before anyone could ask, "what the heck was that?"

Jane dropped open her mouth, then snapped it shut. She rubbed her eyes. "Whoa. Was I the only one who saw that Volkswagen van? Tell me someone else saw it, too."

"Your eyes aren't deceiving you. I saw that van." Dale scratched his head. "How in the world did an old minibus get up here on the plateau? This four-wheel truck barely made it. Truth really is stranger than fiction."

"A ghost van. A phantom VW…" Olivia's eyes were wide.

"Isobel would say it's a manifestation of the eclipse." Jane laughed. "It was a funny sight. Did anyone catch a glimpse of the driver?"

"No, it was such a shock seeing the old junker speed by, I didn't even look to see who was driving it." And this was Doug, trained to be observant from his law enforcement days.

"The van's windshield was really dirty, almost impossible to see through." Olivia sucked water from her water bottle. "And we didn't see the driver because we were too busy smoking out the oil company."

"Yeah, what's up with that?" Jane's gaze went from one to the other of them, as Dale turned the truck in a circle to head back down to the Little Book Cliffs

Wild Horse Area, and from there to return to Palisade.

*****

Sunday night had arrived along with another wine event—the Sommelier's Dinner—a special affair held at a local restaurant prior to the Winefest Weekend. Several winemakers were going to describe the wine chosen by the head chef to pair with each course of the meal.

At least the dinner club hadn't attended any wine tastings that day, so Jane could allow herself a little fruit of the vine with her meal that night. She'd consumed more this weekend than in the previous six months. But since they could walk to the Sommelier's Dinner from the B&B, there would be no worries about drinking and driving.

She studied the outfits she'd thrown across her bed. Now that they'd been at the B&B for four days and she'd only brought a small suitcase, her choice in clothing was starting to become limited, but the burgundy skirt with navy tights underneath would match well with the navy shell. She wiggled into her outfit and slid her feet into a pair of navy ballet flats.

The four met in the common room, ready with jackets and purses. Holden waved them on their way, telling them to enjoy themselves. When the dinner club members filed inside the restaurant, they were instructed to take a seat at a long table in the center of the room. The place was closed to the public for the occasion, and all the participants were told to sit together at one table.

Zeta's winery was not represented, but in this small town and for this big of an affair, it was no surprise when the photographer, Adam Aemes, walked in the door. He lowered himself into the seat next to Jane and they exchanged hellos. On her other side sat Dale, then Doug, and then Olivia.

The first sommelier talked about the appetizers. Riesling paired well with grilled vegetables and fruits, Pinot Grigio with antipasto, and Sauvignon Blanc with the stronger tastes of the chicken, shrimp, and cheese appetizers. She should be taking notes. By the time Jane had a swallow of each pairing with the corresponding appetizer, she was ready for coffee, but there were still several courses to go.

A break was given between the winemakers' presentations, so the men chatted about their fly-fishing lesson that morning and Olivia began a conversation with the woman next to her. Jane turned to Adam, who seemed to be on his own, since the woman on his other side was busy talking with the man across the table from her.

"So, Adam, we meet again." Jane smiled.

"Hi, Jane. Is that your fiancé next to you?"

"Yes." Jane pressed deeper into her chair and they both stared at the back of Dale's head, but he was busy with a fishing story. "Tell me about yourself, Adam. How did you get started in photography?"

"When I was a kid I loved to take pictures with old cameras I found at garage sales. Joined the AV club in high school. I was a bit of a nerd. Took pictures for the school newspaper. Then, I decided to make a career of it." He laughed, but there was no mirth in it.

"Are you from around here?"

"Yes. Grew up in Clifton."

"You share a studio with Kirby Potts, right?"

Squirming to sit up straighter, he seemed to come

alive and his face crinkled into a smile. "Kirby rents space to me. I'm really lucky to get a spot in his studio. He's so talented. I'm hoping some of his talent and success rubs off on me, I guess."

"So Kirby's successful?"

He set down his wineglass and turned to gaze at her fully. He said with a slight note of reproach and a cold look, "Of course. He's a famous artist. We're lucky to have him here on the Western Slope. I only wish I could be half as good of a photographer."

"You are! Your photographs are amazing." She gave him a big grin. He rocked back in his chair, appeased. Encouraged, she continued, "Kirby told me you introduced him to Georgiana. That you went to the same school."

He took a big swallow of wine, downing the glass then lowering it to the table. He touched a finger to the corner of his eye. Was that a tear there? "We graduated from high school together, knew each other all these years. It's hard to believe she's dead."

Jane dipped her head, deliberating how to ask another question. The next sommelier began to speak, right when Jane said, "I'm so sorry." Olivia made a shushing sound, so Jane and Adam turned their attention to the program.

The winemaker spoke with enthusiasm. Bold tasting wines should be paired with bold tasting entrées. Wines higher in tannins matched well with fattier meats, and wines high in acid shouldn't be served with certain sauces. Tannins? Acid? This was getting into unfamiliar territory.

Jane didn't want to taste yet another wine when she had two samples still in front of her. "Dale?" She

153

nudged his elbow. "Do you want my wine? I'm not going to be able to keep up."

"No. I can barely drink my own. Just leave them." Dale jerked his face back to the speaker who was demonstrating how to aerate red wine. The winemaker swirled a glass in the air while explaining why wine needed to aerate. Jane couldn't remember why reds required aeration and not whites.

At last the main course was served. She unfolded her napkin in her lap while the waiter placed a plate of pork tenderloin in front of her and poured her a glass of Grenache. Adam stared at the plate in front of him without taking a bite. She asked him, "Would you like one or two of my wine tastings? I hate to waste them."

"Sure."

She slid her two untouched glasses over. Ignoring the ongoing presentation, she asked Adam in a low voice, "So you're a native to Colorado?"

"Yup." He smelled the bouquet in Jane's first proffered glass, then took a swallow.

"You know everyone in Palisade?"

"Well, like I said, I come from Clifton, so I don't really know all the Palisade people." He drained the wine from the glass.

"Where's Clifton?"

"Between Grand Junction and Palisade, on the wrong side of the tracks, shome would shay." He was starting to slur his words. "My dad worked in a machine shop. He only understood what he could producsh with his hands, he didn't get it, that bein' a photographer was also workin' with the hands, the eyes, the lens, a masheen, even. I am also creatin' a commodity, so to schpeak." Adam picked up the second of Jane's wine glasses and took a healthy swallow. "He was right in one thing, I don't make alotamoney in photography, at leasch not yet."

She guessed him to be in his late thirties, early forties. A shame he was still concerned with what his dad thought of his profession, but maybe it was the drink talking or maybe caring about parental approval didn't stop at a certain age.

"Now, take Kirby." Adam slid farther down in his chair. "All that money Kirby's makin', and now he wantshs to be mayor, too. No one has run against a Barre for years."

"His art studio is in Palisade, right?" Jane knew that from his website.

"Yup."

"How can he run for mayor of Barresville if he's in Palisade?" Jane didn't think to ask Kirby himself and was glad for a chance to find out. All the towns blended together, they were so close to each other. She didn't know the boundaries.

"His studio is here but he lives in Barreschville. He bought a ranch on the edge of the township yearsch ago. Perfect for Kirby." He finally took a bite of the tenderloin.

"Why do you say that?"

Talking with his mouth full, he said, "Oh, very secluded and private estate. Hisss own ranch manschion."

She wanted to bring up the deaths again but felt at a loss for words. The last speaker took his seat, the presentation was over, and the diners proceeded to work on their entrée.

Dale angled toward Jane. "This meat is so tender."

He closed his eyes and licked his lips.

"Hon, do you remember Adam from the party? He's also the photographer Zeta hired for our wedding, and he was just telling me that he shares a studio with Kirby." Jane inched her chair back to include Dale in the conversation.

"Hello, Adam. Nice to see you again." Dale was always polite. "You were 'Fritz the Snitch.' I had a hard time telling you apart from Kirby's character because you were dressed alike. You both had on a black pin stripped suit and fedoras."

"Yes. We rented our coschtumes from the same placesh. Scho tell me about yourshelf. Jane let me do all the talking."

Jane glanced at Dale for his answer. He leaned forward in front of her to explain what he did for a living, in the way men do, and that he owned his own electrician's business. Eyes squinted into slits, Adam looked like he was having a hard time keeping up.

Before long it was time for dessert, chocolate cake paired with Cabernet Sauvignon. Jane asked for a to-go box for her piece of cake and refused the glass of wine. When coffee was served, Jane tried to encourage Adam to drink his cup, but his eyes were bloodshot and unfocussed, and he couldn't seem to concentrate.

When they were pushing out chairs and gathering jackets, Jane asked Dale, "So what do you think of this restaurant as Plan B?"

"It's a possibility. Let me talk to someone." He traversed the length of the dining room and approached the head chef. While Dale was occupied, Jane made sure Adam had arrangements for a ride home. She felt bad for offering him the wine she couldn't drink herself.

She didn't want any more mishaps to occur. They needed to get past these unfortunate events. The eclipse was tomorrow. Was it possible all these weird anomalies had been caused by the upcoming mysterious and mystical disruption of the sun by the dark side of the moon?

Chapter 12

"Holden's been at the police station for over an hour. I'm really worried." Olivia sagged against the kitchen counter beside the coffee pot the next morning.

Jane thought she'd only slept in a little, but the time must have been later than she realized. "Don't stress so much, Olivia. You know he had to give his statement."

She poured herself a cup of the energizing, dark brew, and the two women walked their mugs of coffee outside. Holden had left his guests a magnificent banquet on the patio, as usual. More quiche, banana bread, cut fruit, bacon slices, and orange juice. Also, a big bowl of ripe, juicy peaches.

Jane reached for a peach, but Olivia slapped her hand away with a shake of her head. "Remember yesterday, when you ate too many and had to hit the can on the four-wheel drive trail? Only, there wasn't a can."

"Oh, yeah." Jane slid a piece of banana bread onto her plate instead. "So where is everyone else?"

"Doug was concerned enough that he and Dale drove over to the police station. Dale said to tell you, 'good morning, sleepy-head,' by the way. You just missed the new guests, a couple visiting from Kansas. They left a few minutes ago."

"Dale and Doug are where?" Jane paused with her mug halfway to her mouth.

"Police Station. This is serious, Jane. Doug called from downtown. He talked to the investigating officer and..." Olivia's lips went wobbly.

"What it is? What'd he say?" Jane's heart did a little pitter patter.

"The police suspect Holden because he found the rock."

"Wait a minute, we all found it together."

"But Holden was the one who suggested looking for it. They said he manipulated us into finding the murder weapon. That he knew where it was because he's the murderer." Olivia's voice had risen to a high note. "And get this, the officer told Holden his fingerprints were on the rock."

Jane's eyebrows shot up to the skyline. "So you *can* get prints off a rock. Are the prints back from the lab already? How about the blood?"

"Doug didn't think it was possible to get the results so soon. He thinks the investigator made the whole thing up to get Holden to confess." Olivia squeezed her eyes shut.

"Did he touch that rock? After we told him not to?"

"He admitted he did. He turned the rock over, he said, when he was waiting in the field for the police. What are we going to do?" She trailed off, looking at Jane with anguished eyes.

Jane held up a hand. "Give me a second." She couldn't get her head around it. Why would Holden touch the murder weapon? Did he purposefully place his fingerprints on the rock because he knew his prints were there already? Was he worried the weapon would be found, so he navigated Jane and Olivia to the spot where they would find it and then claimed to have turned the rock over after sending them away? Thinking back to Rey's death, Jane couldn't help but believe Holden had the best opportunity to hide the necklace, knowing all the perfect hiding places. The inn was his, after all. Perhaps he'd snatched it up with sleight of hand when he was looking at Rey's body. Motive? His love for Zeta. Murder was usually committed for love or money. Was he the murderer? It was all too possible.

"What's this?" Isobel stepped onto the patio. She'd likely slept even later than Jane, but unlike Jane, she looked ready for a photoshoot with her fresh skin and slender figure, and in spite of having her hair in a scrunchy. She frowned with her brow wrinkled and her chin puckered. "Uncle Holden is at the cop shop?"

"Don't call it that, but, yes, he is." Olivia went on to make quick work of bringing her daughter up to speed.

"The cops can't believe Uncle Holden killed anyone." Her voice sounded faint. Her mother held her hand while her eyes blinked a mile a minute.

Jane's own eye twitched with a nervous tick, and she hoped her thoughts that Holden was the killer didn't show. "Are you going to have anything to eat, Isobel?" She prodded a plate of bacon in front of Olivia's rail-thin daughter.

"No. I'm not hungry."

"Let's clean up, Liv. It will give us something to do." Jane screeched her chair back from the table, picked up her plate, and headed toward the kitchen. The two women sealed the leftovers in freezer bags, stored the bags in the crowded fridge, and loaded the dishwasher, while Isobel sat outside with her cell phone. They didn't know if Holden would want to keep any of the food, but he could decide what to do with it later. Jane wiped down the patio table, and Olivia scoured the sink and scrubbed a sponge over the kitchen counters.

Jane started another pot of coffee. "I'm going to take a quick shower. I'll be right back." She climbed the stairs to her room two at a time. Once out of the shower, she stepped into a mint green sundress and her cowboy boots. She let her hair air dry for a few minutes, then blew it into her smooth, shoulder length bob.

Just as she returned downstairs, Dale and Doug trooped up the front porch steps. Both Jane and Olivia raced over.

Jane asked, "Well, what's the update?"

"Holden hasn't been arrested. At least not yet." Dale rubbed Jane's arm up and down in his reassuring way, although his words were anything but.

Doug added, "No need for any alarm, ladies. I'm sure he'll be released soon." But he was chewing on the ends of his mustache. Perhaps he was just trying to give his wife encouragement. Doug put his arm around Olivia's shoulder as they ascended the steps to their room.

"Do you want to go for a walk?" Dale asked.

"Yes, I'd like that." Jane went to get a light sweater and was back in a flash.

They set out toward Glen Oak Drive, jabbing their heels into the soft dirt on the side of the worn macadam, their footprints joining others who had trod the same way before them. The mid-morning sun reflected off the Bookcliffs a mile or two in the distance, but the radiant heat had a far reach, the brightness of the sun a blazing glare. Jane was comfortable in her thin, cotton sweater, but Dale was sweating slightly in a short-sleeved shirt. They turned off the busier Glen Oak Drive to walk along a less traveled narrow lane next to a fenced pasture. Horses whinnied in the field and birds sang from overhead. Lavender scented the breeze, although there was nothing around but rocks and dirt. Jane was missing her two dogs who usually accompanied her on neighborhood walks. She took hold of Dale's hand, determined to enjoy stretching her legs in the fresh air. After making the circuit back, they sprawled on the deck, Jane with a book and Dale with his laptop computer, the air between them thick with worry.

The hot sun soared high overhead, and Jane thought they'd have a stroke with all this anxious waiting, until Holden finally sailed through the door.

Dale and Jane hopped off their chairs, and the Ladners galloped down from the upper floor. Holden charged past them into the kitchen. "There's nothing new. Nothing to worry about." He waved off their concerns with a palm-up gesture. "Plus, there's no time to discuss it right now. No time. Help me get the food ready for the party. Good thing I had almost everything made in advance." He yanked two trays out of the refrigerator.

"Holden, we'll help, but tell us what the police said." Olivia opened a drawer, appeared to forget what she was looking for, and slammed it shut with a bang.

"I will. I will." He plunked the dishes onto the counter.

"What do you need done?" Jane asked as she tied an apron over her clothes.

"Follow me." Holden led the four helpers to the cutting boards, and he set peaches and tomatoes in front of them. "Can you cut these up, please?" He disappeared into the pantry and came back with a bag of toast rounds.

Jane asked, "So, Holden, about the police…"

"I know you're dying to ask, so I'll tell you. The investigator brought up my relationship with Zeta." Holden scowled.

Olivia took in a sharp breath and Doug stared at his brother.

"Well, you were expecting that. You said so yourself." Jane selected a sharp knife from the rack and began shaving bite-sized slivers from the ripe, juicy peaches. Olivia and Doug stood side-by-side together, slicing the heirloom tomatoes. Doug seemed to be holding his breath.

"I know. I know." Holden threw his hands up in the air, catching the pendant light over the sink, sending it careening around in a wide circle.

Jane took a deep breath. Cutting the fruit, the repetition of the movement, the knife slicing and dicing, the chopping sounds on the cutting board, all were soothing, in spite of Holden's rushing to and fro. Her stress lifted away. Why keep carrying it around? She chose to let it go. The eclipse party was about to begin and she was determined to enjoy it.

"Any more about the fingerprints?" Doug examined a Black Krim tomato as if he hadn't seen such a perfect specimen before. "The police were trying to trick you, I hope you know that."

"I told them I touched the rock. If they really did find my prints, they'll know I've been honest with them." Holden plopped two bowls of shredded cheese on the counter. "This one is for the peaches, this one for the tomatoes." He shook a finger first at one, then at the other bowl.

Dale helped Jane arrange the peach bites on toast rounds with shreds of fresh ricotta on top, while Olivia dotted the tomato wedges with the soft farmer's cheese. Jane tasted a peach round. The hard texture of the rounds contrasted with the creamy smoothness of the peaches and ricotta.

Dale sampled one of the Black Krims. "Where'd you get the cheese?"

"It's homemade. I make it myself." Holden pointed at a bowl of shredded bits of green leaves. "Sprinkle that chopped basil on the tomatoes. Then drizzle the balsamic vinaigrette on top and you're done."

"How do you make cheese? Do you milk the cow and churn the butter, too?" Olivia must have unloaded her stress, as well, because she was messing with her brother-in-law in her playful way.

"No, it's made from whole milk, buttermilk, some lemon juice. Simmer it, strain it through a cheese cloth." Holden had taken her seriously.

"Ooooh-kay." Olivia gave Jane a look that said, who-knew?

Doug said, "I'm glad you all are having fun, but we need to get back to the subject. So the police just let you go, and that was it?"

"They told me they'd probably have more questions for me later." Holden checked the time, then rushed the appetizer trays out to the patio. The other four stole outside after him, arranging skewers and serving forks on platters. Holden asked the men, "Can one of you bring out the basket of eclipse glasses?"

"I'll get it." Dale went inside and returned a moment later. He positioned the wicker basket next to an ice trough containing chilled bottles of wine. Next, the guys butted together the two patio tables with the trays of finger foods.

Once everything was arranged to his satisfaction, Holden said, "Whew. I can finally take a breather. By the way, thanks, whoever cleared up after breakfast this morning. That helped."

"Oh, sure," Jane and Olivia said at the same time.

When the sound of tires on gravel rang out, they all advanced to the end of the deck overlooking the parking lot.

"We finished getting ready just in time." Holden waved the guests over, then he greeted them all, saying, "Enjoy the eclipse," and "Welcome to my eclipse party," without one word of his ordeal at the police station that morning.

No one else seemed to want to talk about the homicide investigations, either, since nobody brought it up. The partiers appeared excited about the eclipse, chattering and jostling for position at the food table, lining up deeper than at a church potluck. Once their plates were stacked high, guests circulated, wine glasses in hand, munching on crackers and cheese and talking about the amazing celestial event they were about to experience firsthand.

Adam Aemes slammed a car door. Hands in his jeans pockets, arms straight and stiff, he climbed the stairs and made a beeline for Jane. "Have I got a hangover, and it's all your fault." He chuckled as if he had no hard feelings.

"Uh-oh," Jane groaned. "I couldn't drink all that wine. I thought you wanted it."

"I didn't realize how many glasses you were passing my way. I do have a vague recollection that my glass never seemed empty." He took one hand out of his pockets to knead a corner of his eye with his knuckles. "I can't remember the last time I had that much to drink. I hope I didn't talk your head off."

Heat rose to her face. She *had* gleaned a bit of information from him after plying him with alcohol.

"Did you hear the joke about the peach?" Kirby Potts grabbed their attention as he stood in the middle of the deck. The crowd smiled in anticipation. "It was pit-iful." Several women gasped, and one of the men coughed. Eek. Not an appropriate joke, considering the pit-in-the-throat death in the lounge just inside. A major faux pas for an aspiring mayoral candidate, but they all had on admiring looks, seemingly giving him a pass.

Skylar spoke up. "What do you call a fruit that's in love?" Isobel stood by his side, a rosy glow on her face. He gave the punchline, "Peachy-keen," and she smiled at him in an adoring way. He was tall and slim in his jeans and a T-shirt that read, "Go bohemian, dance in the sun."

Olivia cleared her throat and said, "Jane ate so many peaches, she was like a bottomless pit." No one laughed. Not having learned from Kirby's mistake and probably wishing to take back the word, "pit," she covered her lips with her hand and hunched her shoulders. Her cheeks flamed with a rare blush.

The corners of Jane's mouth twitched, then she laughed out loud. Her laughter was contagious, and the other guests started to laugh, too. When Jane couldn't stop, someone else let loose with a thigh-slapper guffaw, but not as loud as Jane. Only she knew that she'd been, literally, "bottomless." The laughter of the crowd sputtered out as individuals picked up their conversations.

Jane loaded a plate of food, but avoided the peach appetizers this once.

The photographer absconded with a full plate of his own to the other end of the porch where Dale and Doug were slouched over the railing. At least Adam's hangover didn't include a loss of appetite.

Skylar and Isobel stood off to themselves in quiet conversation. Should she take the opportunity to ask Skylar a few more questions?

Yes.

Jane tapped his arm. "Skylar, where did you go when you left your table at the cowboy steakhouse Saturday night?"

"I wanted to talk to Isobel. Isn't that right, Bell?" He winked at the younger version of Olivia, and she grinned back at him.

"Did you see anyone leave from the back of the restaurant?"

"No, but I wasn't paying any mind."

"You drive a Volkswagen van, don't you?"

Skylar's grin switched off, and he had a watchfulness about him, as if thinking hard. "I do."

"We saw a VW minibus up on the four-wheel drive trails above Barre Valley Ranch yesterday. An older model. Kind of beat up."

"I was never up there." His eyes darted left. "I swear, Jane. I don't have a four-wheel drive. You can't drive on those roads without a four wheel."

"I agree with you."

"That wasn't me. My old van wouldn't make it." He cracked a smile. "It barely makes it around town. Someone else was on the plateau. That, or you imagined it." He smiled more broadly. "An eclipse mirage."

Jane nodded. "Oh, man, nothing would surprise me anymore."

"I'm sure I'm not the only one who owns a VW van, but I don't know anyone else personally." He deftly changed the subject. "Isn't it awful what happened to Georgiana? I'm surprised Holden didn't cancel this party."

Jane glanced over her shoulder, but Doug was yards away and deep in conversation. Adam Aemes and Zeta Barre had their elbows propped on the banister at the end of the deck. Jane stepped nearer to the young man and kept her voice low. "Why do you say that?"

He smirked, like he was privy to a secret. "Holden being a suspect and all."

"He is not!" Olivia's voice rose and she drew her head back. Then she did a little shimmy around the table between them to get closer. "Are people saying he's a suspect?"

Isobel fanned her fingers out over her heart. "Sky, what's the word about my uncle?"

"Everyone knows about him and Zeta."

Jane's throat tightened. "What's this?"

"Rumors started going around right after the murder party. Right after Rey was killed."

"Well, that's tactless." Olivia flicked an angry hand in the air.

"As tactless as some of these jokes today." Isobel

aimed her blue eyes at her mother. She grasped Skylar's arm, and her sun tattoo peeked out from the edge of her sleeve. The two turned their backs on the pair of them.

Olivia gave Jane a confused look and shrugged her shoulders.

Jane pulled her friend away and said in an undertone, "Don't worry about Isobel. What I'm wondering is, who's spreading the rumors about Holden? Is it the same person who put up the flyers trashing the B&B?"

"Why would anyone do that?" Olivia's voice sounded faint.

They both jumped when Holden popped up next to them with another plate of appetizers, grilled peach slices on crusty baguettes. He stabbed a few more bottles of wine into the ice trough. Then, he pinched two fingers between his teeth and let out a piercing whistle, causing Jane to slap one hand over her ear. "People, listen up. Put on your eclipse glasses and follow me."

When the partygoers donned the protective glasses, Jane extracted a special pair from her purse and handed them to Olivia. "Here's yours." Olivia tucked the cardboard arms over her ears and peered through the lenses. The other guests laughed, nudging each other and pointing at her face.

"What's the matter?" She jerked her head all around and they laughed harder. She yanked the glasses off. Goofy eyeballs on see-through film were pasted to the outside of the lenses, unseen from the inside. Olivia slid them on and off her face several times in disbelief, then said, "You got me good with this prank. I think I'll keep wearing these." She held her head high, glasses on her nose, and proceeded to the end of the deck.

Emboldened by Olivia's joke, one of the townies said, "Well, I think I'll put on my hat, then." He unrolled a tin-foil hat and positioned it on his head. He got as many laughs as Olivia did.

"It's time!" Holden stared at the sun through his glasses, and all the other onlookers did the same. Jane held her breath, waiting for the heebie-jeebies that were supposed to accompany the celestial marvel.

The audience hushed.

The temperature dropped a teensy bit.

Tiny crescent-shaped shadows spotted the ground.

They all peered through their glasses, their conversations on hold, craning their necks, eyeing the sun in the way no one could without protection. If Jane hadn't been wearing the eclipse glasses, she wouldn't't've been able to tell that the lunar orb was advancing across the radiant ball of the sun, at least not until right before, at the last moment, when the moon inched forward ever so slowly, slowly, turning the blinding rays into a black ball.

Someone sang a song about flying a jet to an exotic place to see a total eclipse and all the guests burst out laughing.

Someone else said, "Yeah, just like Kirby. You did that once, didn't you?"

Kirby shrugged.

A sliver of burning white burst out from behind the moon. The eclipse was over, waning on the other side of the star that warmed the earth.

The dance between the sun and the moon hadn't been earthshattering. Jane had forgotten to notice whether the birds and animals had disappeared to sleep.

Even at ninety-something percentage of total eclipse, the light had only gone a shade darker and a touch cooler for a few moments. The world hadn't been cast into total inky blackness or come to an end. No alien spaceships appeared in the sky. No one collapsed to the ground. No illusory ghost child materialized in the peach orchard. No phantom VW bus zoomed out of nowhere. No one else died...Jane hoped, anyway.

Had all the sun worshippers on the Grand Mesa felt the same anticlimax as Jane?

Nothing alarming had happened...no aberrations. That is, until the police crashed the party.

Chapter 13

"We're looking for Isobel Ladner." The intimidating, stony-faced officer wore a navy-blue uniform and black, thick-soled shoes.

"I'm right here." Her voice hit a little girl's high pitch and her above-it-all affectation dropped away like a comet crashing to the earth.

Several more policemen stomped up the steps at both ends of the L-shaped deck. A mean-looking policeman with close cropped hair and rolls of fat at the back of his neck took her elbow. "Isobel Ladner, please come with us. We'd like to take you to the police station for questioning."

She wailed, "Sky! Let's make a run for it!"

Skylar's eyebrows surged up, and his eyes went so wide the whites showed. "Don't go wild child on me." He cast a terrified look at Isobel's father.

Doug shook his head. "Go with the officers, Isobel, and we'll follow you to the station."

Her face paled. "This is the weirdest eclipse manifestation yet."

The men and women watched in silence as the policemen marched Isobel to a patrol car. An officer yanked open the rear door and palmed the top of her head to keep her from banging into the roof of the car, just like on television.

The partygoers set down their wine glasses and

plates and started to shuffle off to their vehicles.

The police were party poison. A buzz kill. Casting a greater pall than the eclipse.

Olivia stood frozen, silent, as if she weren't breathing.

"Liv, sit down." Jane led her to a deck chair. "You look like you're about to keel over."

"What just happened?" Olivia was in a daze as she lowered herself to a seat.

"I honestly don't know. But they're only taking her in for questioning. Be calm. Yoga breath, yoga breath." Never once had Jane imagined that the innocent, angelic-looking Isobel Ladner would be taken in for a police interrogation in a double homicide, although she'd probably seen her share of the rough side of life living in New York City. All the same, fear gripped Jane's belly, and Isobel's mother must be feeling a similar panic.

"You know this is all your fault!" Olivia snapped, waving an accusatory finger at Jane.

She raised her voice to match Olivia's. "What did I do?" If she didn't have the heebie-jeebies before, she certainly had them now.

"You didn't find the killer."

Jane reared back in surprise, about to tumble over the edge of panic herself. "What about Doug? He's the ex-cop! He didn't find the killer either." She gave Doug a stern look, drawing her eyebrows in, lowering her chin, but his eyes were fixed on the police cruiser taking off down the street.

"My husband does everything by the book. But you sneak around and figure things out that no one else can." Olivia's face crumpled.

Jane had let her friend down. She would start to beat herself up if she wasn't careful, since disappointing others was on her top-ten-least-favorite-things list. She patted Olivia's hand. "I'm sorry, Liv. I'll get to the bottom of this yet. I promise." She wrapped an arm around Olivia's shoulders.

Doug seemed to come back to life once the patrol car sped out of sight. His footsteps pounded across the deck, and he barked out, "Holden, Dale, come with me."

Olivia's eyes showed hurt. "What about me?"

"You mean, what about us?" Jane corrected her. They gave each other a curt nod like they'd shared a single train of thought, like two minds in parallel universes. Had the vortexes between them come into alignment?

Olivia sprang into action. "Excuse me. Excuse me." She elbowed her way through the last stream of partiers heading out.

Jane made to follow, but Kirby stopped her with a hand on her arm. "I'm sorry Isobel was taken away by the police, but all of you should return to Denver, or wherever you're from, and stay out of the investigation."

"Why? What do you mean?" She pulled up short.

"Maybe if you hadn't asked so many questions, this wouldn't've happened."

Jane had no time to stick around. She shook off his grip and plunged through the patio door into the kitchen. Doug was yelling into his cell, Olivia was wringing her hands, and Holden wasn't doing much better. They hovered around, uncertain what to do next, waiting for Doug to get off the phone.

He hung up. His face was nearly purple with outrage. "Where's Skylar?"

"I saw him leave." Jane's heart was beating double-time. "Does Skylar have something to do with why the police want to question Isobel? Or does Kirby?"

"Skylar. The investigator told me Isobel lied for Skylar, said she was with him the whole time he was away from his table at the steakhouse, but she wasn't. A witness saw Isobel all alone in the hallway near the back door. Skylar found another alibi for himself, though, and left Isobel high and dry, with no alibi."

"Why would Isobel want to harm anybody? She didn't even know these people!" Olivia's voice sounded shrill.

Doug slapped the back of one hand against the palm of the other in a listen-up gesture. "Your daughter, the one with the high ideals, slammed the Barres on Facebook, warning people not to vote for a Barre. She called the Barres *hacktivists* and *harpocrites*, whatever those are. I guess they figure she has motive for Rey, so somehow she has motive for Georgiana, too."

Olivia's eyes were dilated in fear. She'd been a social worker before taking early retirement. She believed in helping the underdog. It wasn't hard to see where Isobel got her fondness for social causes. A tear spilled out and dripped down Olivia's cheek. Doug belatedly held his arms out, and she walked into his embrace. He patted her on the back, and she buried her head against his shoulder.

A worried frown pinched Dale's face. "What are you going to do, Doug?"

"Head over to the police station. If they don't

release Isobel right away, I'm calling a lawyer." Doug's gaze darted around the room over his wife's head, as if trying to find his keys. "Oh, I don't have a car. Sorry, Dale, can you drive me?"

"We're all going." Olivia pushed away from her husband and headed for the stairs. "Let me get my purse." While Olivia was making sure she had everything she needed, Jane returned to the porch where the last few party stragglers were scrounging what was left of the peach appetizers. When they clomped down the stairs to leave, she gathered up the leftover pickings and stuffed an untouched platter in the fridge and the rest down the garbage disposal.

The five adults piled into Dale's pickup, Jane squeezing in the middle of the back seat.

Rocks pelted the inside of the wheel wells as Dale gunned the engine and reversed down the driveway. He asked Holden, "Which way again?"

"Head toward town." Holden continued to give directions until they pulled up outside the tan and brick municipal building on Third Street. Just two happy days ago, Jane had watched the Peach Festival Parade march past this same building without thinking she'd ever step inside.

The police must not have been busy in this small community, since no one else was in the lobby. Doug checked in with the security guard at the desk, then the friends paced in opposite directions, turning around upon reaching the rows of hard, plastic chairs, and turning around again at the wall of dingy, narrow windows, dodging each other on the trip back.

The guard interrupted their race across the linoleum. "Is one of you Holden Ladner?"

Holden raised a hand. "Me."

"The investigator would like to ask you a few more questions, if you'd come with me."

With shoulders drooping, Holden followed the officer down the hall and through a heavy metal door. Jane exchanged glances with the remaining Ladners. Olivia looked like she was going to stroke out and Doug was breathing hard.

The wait seemed to take forever. Jane knew every crack in the tile, every scrap of litter on the floor, the brown edges of the fichus plant in the plastic pot at the door, the number of hard plastic chairs in each row. Olivia dropped into one of the chairs, then after Jane stopped next to Dale to stare out the dirty glass in the front window, Olivia disappeared. Jane figured she'd gone to look for a restroom.

The heavy door slammed at the end of the hall. Jane turned around in slow motion.

Isobel walked into the center of the lobby, her back ramrod straight, like the runway model she was. It was evident she'd been crying.

"Are you all right?" Doug held her elbow and led her to a plastic chair.

She nodded. "They kept asking the same questions over and over."

"What did you tell them?"

"The truth, Dad. I went to the john at the steakhouse. When I came out, I took a look out the back door, but that's all I did. I don't smoke anymore."

Jane's heart beat fast. She wished she hadn't told the police Isobel had left their table, but perhaps someone else had told them, too. Jane probably wasn't the only one to mention it. She asked, "No one else came in the restroom while you were in there?"

"Nobody. I was in there quite a while, but nobody came in."

"Weren't you feeling good?"

"I looked like crap in the mirror. Okay, call me vain, but normally I look great. So I scrubbed all my makeup off and reapplied it." Isobel ducked her head and put both hands to her cheeks. "It didn't help any. I looked just as bad as before. I was really in need of a make-up artist that day."

"Oh, Bell, that was the fault of the mirror." Jane stifled a laugh, in spite of the grim situation. "That mirror was worse than the dressing room mirror at the consignment shop." She took a quick look around for confirmation from Olivia, but her friend hadn't returned yet.

"Can we go?" Isobel leveled her chin at the door.

Her dad explained to her, "Uncle Holden is back there with the investigator now. We're waiting for him."

She stared up at the ceiling. "Wow. The cops really have it in for us."

"Why did you lie when you told the police you'd been talking to Skylar in the hallway the whole time?" Doug used his cop voice.

"Don't treat me like a suspect."

"Just answer the question," and he added at the end as an afterthought, "honey."

"Skylar told me that since neither of us had anything to do with it, we should just give each other alibis and avoid the whole police brutality thing." Isobel blushed, high spots of color on her face. "Sorry, Dad."

Jane threw a glance over her shoulder, but Olivia was still missing.

"The police think I had the necklace, since they found it in my bicycle basket. But I swear I never knew the necklace was in there."

"What basket?"

"The one on the bike I borrowed from Uncle Holden."

He slapped his thigh. "That's how the necklace was hidden. The killer opened the basement window, stowed the necklace outside in the bicycle basket."

Isobel's eyes widened, and she gave her dad a help-me look.

He pursed his lips. "How did they treat you?"

"Actually, they were pretty nice to me. They took my fingerprints, thanked me for helping them, and told me I could go." Isobel gave her dad a half smile, and he returned a comforting look.

Jane chimed in, "Her fingerprints won't be on the necklace."

Doug nodded, but said, "That's not definitive. Perpetrators handle objects with gloves or cloths."

Where did Olivia get herself off to? Jane rose from her chair and stared down the long hallway, looking for the restrooms.

An officer in a navy-blue uniform with a bright patch depicting the American flag, the Bookcliffs, and a cluster of fruit, strode past Jane and up to Doug. "Your wife confessed. We are holding her."

Doug's mouth gaped open in astonishment. He appeared as flabbergasted as Jane. "I've never heard of anything more ridiculous in my life."

Isobel burst into tears. Jane made light circles with

her palm on the young lady's back. Dale scrunched his shoulders up near his ears and lifted his palms skyward as if to say, *this-is-too-crazy-for-words*. She gave him a look that said, *I know*, and kept rubbing Isobel's back.

Jane knew what had to be done. "Now's the time to call an attorney, Doug."

"Right." He reached out to steady himself, then sank onto one of the hard chairs. "I don't know any around here, do you?"

"Yes, I do." As a paralegal she had many legal contacts, and the law firm where she worked in Denver had a satellite office in Grand Junction. "You're lucky. Let me make a call." She withdrew to a corner of the room and got busy on her cell phone. One of the lawyers agreed to meet if Doug was willing to take the short drive to his office in Grand Junction, since he didn't have the time to come to the police station in Palisade even though it was only a few miles away. She marched back over to the group. "You need to call him and confirm, Doug. Take the call outside for a private conversation."

Doug went out the front door and was only gone a little while before he returned. "I have an appointment in thirty minutes. Dale, can you drive?"

"Sure thing. We can drop off Jane and Isobel at the B&B on the way."

"What about Mom? And Uncle Holden?" Isobel choked back a sob. "When are the cops going to be done doing the *Law and Order* thing?"

Jane's lips quivered, but she held them still. She didn't want to join Isobel in her crying jag. She needed to be strong. "I'll stay here. I bet they'll let Holden go any minute now. And, maybe they'll let me see Olivia."

"That might not be a bad idea, Jane." Doug tugged hard on the end of his mustache. "You can let them know we're going to talk to an attorney."

"Right. I can do that." She took a step back, and her heel bumped into the metal leg of one of the plastic chairs. She sat down hard. Dale leaned in to give her a quick hug before following Doug and Isobel out the door.

Jane's spirits were low, but dropped even lower after they left. This must be some kind of a mistake. The police would soon realize the confession was unbelievable and none of the Ladners were killers. She had wondered about Holden herself. But if the police were questioning him as a person of interest, as mistaken as they were about everything else, they were likely wrong about him, too. He dropped way down on her suspect list. She half expected Olivia and Holden to be released and come walking through the metal door, arm-in-arm, any second. She sat in the closest chair facing the hall in anticipation.

Voices floated out from behind the closed door. Jane also heard clanging sounds, but they might have been street noises from outside. Beyond the window, cars flew along the street and pedestrians drifted along the pavement. She felt so alone, although she was in the middle of this cozy town. People were everywhere, going about their business, and hopefully she'd be joining them with her friends shortly. But right now she'd been left by herself with nothing to do but wait and worry. She asked the officer at the desk if she could talk to Olivia, and the officer promised to check.

If the time weighed heavily before, the clock dragged even more as she kept checking her phone for the time and her text messages. She gripped the phone tighter when she noticed her cell showed a slim red bar at four percent power. She'd forgotten to plug in her phone and didn't have a charger in her purse. Her car charger was in Dale's truck. She sent a text to Dale, but after five minutes he still hadn't responded. She called his number. He didn't pick up and neither did Doug when she called him, or Isobel when she called her. The power went down to three percent. She messaged Dale again. Maybe he couldn't take her call because they were in the meeting with the lawyer.

She couldn't keep her eyes off her phone. The power dwindled to zero and then the cell phone shut off. She inserted it into her purse and crossed her arms to wait. She started to sweat from the stifling air in the lonely lobby.

At last, Jane was allowed to speak with Olivia. She retraced her friend's steps on shaky legs down the hallway behind a police matron, who locked her into a small, but amazingly clean, comfortable-looking room, with cheery yellow walls, a scrubbed oak table, and two wooden chairs. A coffee pot was on a corner shelf with the usual powdered creamer and stirrer straws. Olivia was seated at the table, still in her regular, street clothes, a chunky yellow mug in her hand. Under Olivia's eyes, dark circles made black crescent moons like the partial eclipse, but at least the room wasn't as grim as Jane imagined it would be.

"What are you thinking, Olivia?" Jane rushed up and jabbed her index finger into her chest so hard that her friend rubbed the spot and gave Jane an aggrieved look.

"I killed him. I killed them both."

Jane rolled her eyes. "Okay. How'd you do it?"

"I pushed that Barre fellow, like Holden said." Olivia sank back into her seat, fiddling with her coffee mug, not looking Jane in the eye. "And I hit the woman over the head with that rock we found."

"Why?" Jane flopped into a chair on the other side of the table, wrapping her arms over her chest and tucking her hands under her damp armpits.

"They were having an affair. That was wrong." She gave Jane a triumphant see-there look.

"You knew nothing about that until Holden told us."

"I did too know." The triumphant look expanded. "So I pushed him and he fell. He was holding onto the necklace and I wasn't sure whose it was. Maybe it was yours. So I went back for it. I wanted to make sure I didn't leave any clues behind."

Jane stretched over the table, snatched the coffee mug out of her friend's hand, and got up in her face. "How did you hide the necklace?"

"I stuffed it in my bra."

"In between your boobs?"

"Yes. But don't say it like that."

"It got lodged in your ta-tas." Jane clenched her jaws so hard her muscles popped. This was the most absurd antic her friend had pulled yet. She hoped Olivia had given the police this version of her story, so they'd know she wasn't telling the truth.

"I'm serious!" Olivia had the grace to look ashamed at how lame her confession sounded.

Jane took a calming breath. "What's your motive?"

"I wanted to see the other guy win the race for mayor, ah, what's his name."

"You don't even know his opponent's name."

"You are getting me all flustered," Olivia shouted.

"You don't care about local politics. You don't live here. You can't vote here. You don't have a dog in the fight. You are only trying to protect your daughter." Jane's voice had gotten louder. What could she say to make Olivia come to her senses? She glanced around the pleasant room with Olivia sitting across the table from her as if they were in someone's kitchen. She sighed and hugged her arms tighter to her chest. "I'm surprised they let me in to see you."

"I told them you were my lawyer."

"What? And they believed you?"

"I gave them the name of your law firm. They seemed to recognize it."

"That's because we have a satellite office here in Junction." Jane grasped her hair in her hands and gave her head a violent side-to-side shake. "Olivia, I can get in a lot of trouble for impersonating an attorney. They probably think I'm giving you legal advice."

"Yeah, right. Turn this around so it's all about you, all about your problems."

Jane flung out her hands. "You are the cause of all the problems. Isobel was released. She left with the guys to head into Grand Junction and talk to a real attorney. You're only making matters worse. Isobel hasn't been arrested and she won't be. She's innocent, and the police have to know that."

"Well, they don't. They're focusing on Holden and my daughter," Olivia said with a whine in her voice. "And I killed those two people."

"You would think being arrested once before was enough." Jane narrowed her eyes, recalling Olivia's bad luck in a prior murder investigation, and said in her most stern voice, "You know they have the death penalty in Colorado."

"They do?" Her friend gulped in air for a moment. Then, she swallowed and gave Jane a shrewd look. "I don't remember hearing about anyone being put to death."

"Well, nobody has been in the last twenty years or so, but that doesn't mean they won't do it." Jane glared at her lunatic friend who was playing with fire.

"See, you are giving me legal advice."

Jane ground her teeth. "Just think about wearing the orange jumpsuits. Going potty in a metal throne in your cell." Olivia clutched the pearls around her neck, prompting Jane to add, "Your only accessories will be handcuffs and ankle bracelets. Talk about living in a gated community."

"Please understand." Olivia blanched, but her expression remained stoic. "Holden and Isobel are my two favorite people in the world. Other than you, Jane."

"What about Doug?"

"Oh yeah, him too." She squiggled in her chair.

"You're being foolish!" Jane jumped up, hands on hips, bent forward at the waist. "You're an idiot."

Olivia leaned over the table. Her voice was low and determined. She gave Jane a pointed look. "I've given you more time now. If you're so smart, figure it out."

"Quit it, quit it, quit it!" Jane slapped her friend across the face.

Olivia's hands flew to her red cheeks and her mouth dropped open. They both stared hard at each other, lips blowing out, faces heated, just as the police matron rushed in.

"That's the first time I've ever seen attorney-client abuse." The officer tskked. "You"—she indicated Jane—"Come with me." She propelled her out of the room. The door shut with a loud click of a lock behind them. "You're going to have to wait in the lobby."

The matron deposited herself in the empty seat behind the security desk, darting looks at Jane to make sure she didn't go postal.

She asked, "Is Holden Ladner going to be released soon?"

"I can't answer that." The look in the policewoman's stony eyes gave nothing away.

Jane couldn't stay at the police station another minute longer or she would go crazy. She banged out the front door and dropped onto the blue metal bench between the bike rack and a trash can that held old newspapers and the smell of a dirty diaper. She checked her phone once more, but it was now a total black screen. She nearly growled out loud.

Chapter 14

Jane lifted her cell phone up to the sky and shook it.

What did people do before cell phones? Nothing…just like it felt she was doing now.

She stomped down the sidewalk, passing into the heart of downtown Palisade, and entered a java joint. "I need a large, two-pump, non-fat, mocha latte. Add an extra shot, please." She handed the barista a five dollar bill and stuffed a dollar into the tip jar.

What to do?

Patience, she scolded herself, you need patience. Waiting, waiting, waiting, and doing nothing was the hardest test of all. She sipped her drink, looking out of the window. The caffeine made her heart beat faster, the thumps seemed irregular, off beat. Thump, thump.

Think. Think. She told herself, think.

Should she head back to the station to wait for Holden or walk over to the B&B to charge her phone? If she had a phone that worked, Holden could call her to let her know when he was released and Dale could call to let her know about the attorney.

The B&B was probably not that far from downtown, between two and three miles. She walked that many miles on her lunch hour almost every day.

Piece of cake.

Taking her to-go cup in hand and hitching her

purse higher on her shoulder, she emerged from the coffee shop and charged up the street. Six blocks later, when she cut across Palisade Memorial Park, her stiff cowboy boots made their presence felt. A blister on the back of her right heel grew bigger with each step, and then one rose on her left little toe. The sun burned her shoulders, bare under the straps of her sundress. Sweating at the police station was nothing compared to her perspiration from the heat radiating off the macadam without the benefit of shade. She continued along the side of Highway 6, limping now, the dusty gravel crunching, the cars speeding by, the drivers and passengers comfortable in their air-conditioned seats.

She studied every truck that passed so she could wave Dale down if he happened to be on his way back to the police station. What if he took a different route? What if he arrived at the station and didn't know where she was? Should she have stayed put? What if the police had released Holden, he found himself stranded, and felt abandoned by his friends? Olivia, too. Maybe the police had released both of them. They certainly should. Would her friends be angry that she'd left her post?

She fretted with each painful step, but there was nothing to be done now. She was at least halfway to the B&B...surely within the next few blocks she would come to the busy road that led to the inn.

"Hey, lady! I like your boots." A driver waved one hand out the window and beeped his horn making her jump. She had a feeling the man's words weren't a compliment. Yes, she was regretting her choice of footwear.

She came to the corner, turned down Glen Oak

Drive, and hobbled the additional mile or so to the inn.

As soon as she entered the front door she kicked off her boots and went looking for the Ladners' daughter, but Isobel was nowhere to be found. Not in her room, not on the patio. Jane located her charger in her bathroom and plugged her phone into the wall socket. Since the phone was so dead, the screen remained black. She washed her feet in the bathtub, cleaning the blisters, then put on some Band-Aids and comfortable flip-flops. She pressed a cold washcloth over her sweating face and neck, then went outside to wait on the patio.

Melting ice floated in the semi-freezing water that filled the mini trough where the wine had been kept chilled for the party. She leaned back in a chair, toed off her flip-flops, and submerged her feet in the water. Ahhh that felt good, cooling off her whole body. Her hair rose in the breeze, blowing around, caressing her neck. Her nose perked up with the sweet scent of ripe fruit wafting over from the peach orchard. She would've liked a little company about now, even the company of the ghost child.

Words from the party that morning rang in her ears. Isobel had given her mother the cold shoulder, but now was quite concerned about her. Olivia had been on Jane's team, but now had gone rogue. Holden had acted as host, but was now being held hostage by the police. Isobel and Holden had both been interrogated as if they were persons of interest. Olivia had confessed to a crime she didn't commit. What a difference the eclipse had made in the end. After the obstruction of the sun, their world had shifted on its axis.

And Jane couldn't get a hold of anyone to find out

what was happening, not until her phone charged. There was no land line at the inn.

She pulled her toes out of the icy water and lowered the soles of her feet to the deck, then put her head in her hands and studied the ground beneath the floorboards. No answers were written in the dirt, but Jane could write down her scattered thoughts on paper. Back in the kitchen, she nabbed a bottle of water from the refrigerator and a few leftover rounds of toast topped with slivers of peaches. Her pad of paper was in her room, so she went to get it along with her tablet computer.

Spreading out at the patio table, she chewed on a peach round and reviewed her suspect list.

Zeta Barre…owner of the vineyard where Jane and Dale were to be married in four weeks…could've killed her husband so she could run for office in his place. Her political ambitions overshadowed any love she still felt for him, especially if she knew about his affair with Georgiana. She may have killed Rey in a fit of jealous anger, although Holden didn't believe she was capable. Perhaps she saw Rey and Georgiana together. Rey had the gold chain with the peach pendant in his hand when Zeta shoved him, then he fell and hit his head. She returned to the scene in a fit of rage and jammed the pit down his throat. When Jane discovered the body, Zeta dashed back for the pendant, perhaps to hide the evidence of his affair, opened the basement window, and stowed the necklace in the bicycle basket. Later, Zeta killed Georgiana because she'd seen something…or Zeta simply killed her out of jealousy, too.

A compelling theory.

Kirby Potts…successful sculptor running for mayor against Rey Barre. He could've killed his opponent so he'd assume the office of mayor by default. He realized whose necklace it was, thought Georgiana may have seen him shove Rey, and so he went back to recover the necklace and had to kill her, too, to keep her from talking. Maybe Georgiana threatened to expose him.

Adam Aemes…the photographer. Did he hide out in the lounge, disguised not as Fritz the Snitch, but as a Kirby Potts look-alike? Adam idol-worshiped Kirby. Did he kill Kirby's political opponent and then *off* the eye-witness to his crime? The gangster murder party may just have put him over the edge of his obsession and given him the idea…

Holden Ladner…Doug's brother, Olivia's closest thing to a sibling, Isobel's favorite uncle and one of Olivia's favorite persons…had to be considered. He was once engaged to Zeta and thought the world of her to this day. He could've killed her cheating husband and his lover. His fingerprints were on what very well could be Georgiana's murder weapon. He seemed more concerned about losing bookings than he did about the death of his friend. The simplest explanation of all. But it couldn't be Holden. He was Doug's brother, Olivia's, too, and Jane's friend now, as well. The police investigation seemed to be focusing on Holden, and the police were so wrong about everything else, the investigator was probably mistaken about Holden, too. She was now certain of it and ashamed of herself for even suspecting him.

She should consider Skylar Straite. He cared deeply about many issues. Maybe Reynard wasn't showing enough concern for one of his causes. Did the environmental crusader feel betrayed by his boss? Did the young man defect to Rey's opponent? Did Rey threaten Skylar's job or even use his great influence in the valley to compromise Skylar in another way? Even if so, the young man didn't have a motive for the second death. He had no reason to kill Georgiana. The hippy-dude was a peace-loving and pacifist type. There wasn't a more unlikely killer in the bunch, yet he'd asked Isobel to lie to give him an alibi. That was suspicious.

None of these theories accounted for the peach pits or the pendant necklace. That piece of the puzzle didn't make sense. Were there other suspects not on her list for reasons Jane didn't know about? Such as the person who posted the flyers around town disparaging the inn. The negative sentiment smacked of Kirby Potts. She could picture him using such tactics, but why? Was the person someone else who had a grudge against Holden? Could there have been two killers?

Had she considered every angle?

Was there more on the internet to be discovered?

She pulled her tablet computer closer and opened the Facebook application. It was too bad Georgiana hadn't posted any revealing snapshots of herself with Rey or any other man. Adam's Facebook page had quite a few photos of Georgiana pictured with horses, perhaps at the wild horse sanctuary or maybe at the Barre stables, it was difficult to tell. Maybe Rey wasn't the only man interested in her. The horses were something Adam and Georgiana seemed to have in common—she must've liked horses if she worked in the stables and he must have, too, since he took so many pictures of them. Could the photographs have something to do with the double homicide?

She clicked around different Facebook pages, then drew up short after spotting pictures of Isobel on Skylar's page. Humph. She was starting to feel as prejudiced against him as Olivia did.

Adam had told her that Skylar was the wedding caterer. A curious piece of information. She exited Facebook to search for caterers in Palisade and scrolled through the results. One called, "Organic Catering," shouted out to her, so she clicked on the website. Skylar was identified as the contact, and he claimed to use organic produce grown from his own garden. Nothing surprising or sinister.

Not sure what else to query, she leaned her chin in her hand and stared between the slats in the deck flooring below to where the bicycles were stacked together. After returning her computer to her room, she shuffled the pages of her suspect list and folded them into her purse, then descended the steps. Bypassing the gardening shed, she stooped low to look at the bikes and behind them, the narrow casement window to the lounge. Large paw prints—a dog's, she guessed—and imprints from a couple of different shoes pockmarked the dry dirt around the window, and probably Isobel's footprints were among them.

Several bicycles had wire baskets strapped to the handlebars, but Jane recognized the one with side-by-side wicker baskets flanking the rear fender rack. Isobel had ridden that bike to the festival. Jane lifted the wicker lids by the leather straps and peeked inside. Of course, the baskets were empty, now.

She emerged out from under the deck and covered

the ground past the gardening shed to the back door, then went into the basement area with the lounge and fireplace. A sturdy accent table was positioned under the window, and when she climbed on top, she could slide the window open and reach the bicycles. Someone taller than her and with longer arms—just about everyone else—would've been able to reach any number of the bicycle baskets.

Olivia's story of hiding the necklace in her blouse didn't hold up, and the police couldn't possibly take her seriously.

All the same, Olivia was in the slammer, Holden was also being targeted by the police, and the other two men were busy writing a large check to an attorney. Isobel had vanished like she always did, and Jane was the only one left to investigate the crime, if the police were looking no further than an almost comical confession. The dinner club's extended weekend trip, which was scheduled to end tomorrow, was coming unglued at the seams. She needed to insist on Olivia's release from jail, and now.

She'd already questioned Kirby and Skylar about their alibis, but not Zeta, a suspect at the top of her list, and the one whose guilt would totally nuke the wedding plans.

Tired of playing the waiting game, she bolted from the basement and out the door around to the stack of bicycles. A few of the bikes were heavy cruisers. They looked trendy, but would be difficult to pedal, so she chose a lightweight Schwinn mountain bike with upright handlebars and a wide gear range. After untangling the bike from the pile, she tossed her purse in the basket, slung one leg over the frame, tucked the skirt of her sundress under her bottom, and took to the road.

The sweeping turns of the Fruit Loop were easy to navigate by bicycle, although there were some tough inclines. She met a car on a ninety-degree bend, but the driver was gracious, giving her the right of way. The lavender scent in the air and birds singing from the peach trees calmed her racing thoughts. Having written down the suspect list on her pad of paper and heading out to question a suspect, actively *doing something*, was soothing and energizing at the same time. She breathed the fresh air deep into her lungs, propelling her faster. Catching up with other cyclists on the road, she followed the pack all the way to Barre Vineyards.

She leaned her bike against the beam holding up the pergola and made a bee line for the door.

The rest of the cyclists ponied up to the tasting bar, but Jane hesitated near the gift shop. Just then, Zeta and Betsey came out from a backroom, the woman's heels making clip-clopping noises and her dog's nails clickity-clicking on the hard cement floor.

Zeta greeted her with a warm smile. "Hello, Jane. Are you here to talk about your wedding plans? Did you want to make any changes?"

"I hope not." Jane didn't want to tamper with the arrangements, or more likely torpedo the arrangements, if she didn't have to. Although, there was a strong possibility she would—between the vineyard owner, the caterer, and the photographer, all on her suspect list. But she wasn't ready to abort Plan A just yet. She needed more facts.

She studied Zeta's face. Although the woman did not have the appearance of a grieving widow, Jane wondered if it would be too tactless to bring up the death of her husband. Zeta had seemed to put his death out of her mind. Not knowing where to start, she stroked one of Adam's photographs hanging on the wall, a shot of the wild horses with their legs gathered under their bodies, their manes streaming behind, as if in a gallop. A powerful sun glowed in the background. The wild horses she'd seen in real life had their heads down to the ground munching on tuffs of dead grass, not so picturesque. "I'd like to buy this photograph."

"Yes, Adam captured the horses at a rare moment." Zeta laughed. "He sells a lot of that one." She removed the picture of the galloping mustangs from the wall and handed it to Jane.

"You arranged for Adam Aemes to take the wedding pictures." Jane tapped the heavy frame with her finger. "This photographer. I ran into him at the antique store in Grand Junction, and he told me. He asked me what pictures we wanted for the wedding."

"That's right."

"He also said that Skylar Straite is our caterer."

"I like to throw business to people I know and trust." There were creases above Zeta's smile, but not around her eyes. "Are you inviting anyone from Barresville to the wedding?"

"No. I don't know anyone from there, other than you, I guess." The business relationships in the Grand Valley may be incestuous, but Jane wasn't in the gene pool. Her wedding guests weren't from the Western Slope and wouldn't afford Zeta any opportunity to win more votes. As a politician, Zeta was likely well versed in masking her true feelings, since disappointment didn't show on her face.

"That young man at the tasting bar will ring up your purchase. If you don't need anything else…" Zeta turned as if to leave.

"Wait, please." Jane clutched the framed photograph to her chest. She took a big breath, then her words tumbled out. "I have a couple of questions for you."

"Yes?" Zeta's politician's smile slipped.

Jane's words came out in a rush. "I'm trying to help Holden. His business is suffering and he's been grilled by the police too many times. But he didn't harm anyone, you know that." Zeta nodded. After another deep breath, Jane added, "May I ask, who do you think killed your husband?"

The widow sighed, looking down at her hands. Her shoulders slumped and the muscles in her face went slack. "It's bad enough that all the locals are stopping by to chat me up. Now you? Why do you care what I think?"

Zeta *was* grief stricken—underneath the veneer. Peeking out was a sad and suffering widow, managing a business alone, running a political campaign, having to endure the aftermath of her husband's violent death.

Jane, also a widow, felt a sudden kinship. "I'm sorry if my questions are upsetting, but Holden's niece was taken in for questioning, too. I'm worried about both of them. They would never harm your husband, but the police seem to think they had something to do with it." Jane didn't mention Olivia's confession, too ludicrous to acknowledge. Had Olivia been released? What about Holden? Were her friends all waiting at the inn, safe and sound, wondering where she was?

"I know Holden wouldn't hurt Rey. They were

friends." The widow's gaze traveled around the room as if she was considering her words, then she said in a low voice, "I think Georgiana did it. I found out from the police Rey had Georgiana's necklace, the one with the peach pendant. It was in his hands. I believe he was trying to leave me a message that she was the murderer. Her nickname was Peaches."

Jane prodded, "How did he get her necklace?"

"He told me he was going to ask for it back and I guess she gave it to him." Zeta flattened her gray-auburn hair against her skull with both hands, smoothing it toward the knot at the top of her head.

"Ask for it back?"

"Yes, he had given it to her."

"Then you knew about their affair."

With her chin tucked in, Zeta once more flicked her gaze around the tasting room. The customers at the bar were marking their selections on the order sheets, laughing loudly and enjoying the wine tasting. She swallowed a couple of times, then her voice came out shaky. "What was that? What did you say?"

"Your husband and Georgiana were having an affair. You knew about it." Jane's words were soft, almost a whisper.

"Y-y-yes. I knew."

Chapter 15

She and Zeta exchanged look for look.

Jane asked, "How long had the affair been going on?"

"Long enough." The widow folded her arms around herself. Betsey whined at her feet. "I'd discovered he'd given her the necklace months ago. I insisted he break off the relationship and get it back from her."

"The pendant was expensive."

"That's true. It cost a lot of money. I imagine when he asked her to return it, she flew into a rage and pushed him. Then, she left him to die, bleeding on the floor." Zeta's feet were aimed at the door.

Jane gave her an encouraging nod. Keep her talking. Hope she doesn't walk away. "That makes sense."

Zeta blinked back some tears and slid a hand over her eyes. "That's exactly what I think happened. The police asked me about the necklace when they told me it was in Rey's hands, but it wasn't returned with his personal effects, so I don't know what happened to it."

Jane kept the information to herself that the police had found the pendant. "Didn't you wonder where Rey was all night?"

"I took a sleeping pill. I was dead to the world." Zeta blushed. "No pun intended. What about the rest of you? How come no one else heard anything? You'd think someone would have heard or seen something."

Jane nodded. "We were all asleep on the second floor and Rey was found in the basement." Since none of the guests had heard anything, she couldn't criticize Zeta for being oblivious. "It's hard to believe someone assaulted Rey right under our noses without getting caught. And then got away with it a second time. Did you know that the auction barn is within walking distance from the cowboy steakhouse?"

Zeta inclined her head. "Everybody around here knows that."

"Did you meet Georgiana at the barn? One of the waitresses said you left your table." Jane's heart rate hiked up and she found herself crossing her fingers. Did Georgiana kill Rey and then Zeta killed Georgiana? But if so, did Zeta steal the necklace from her husband's fingers and hide it in the bicycle basket? She probably did know where it had been hidden because she had been the one to hide it. Was her purpose to conceal her own motive for the crime?

Jane took deep calming breaths. The cyclists were talking in loud voices at the bar. She wasn't alone in a dangerous place with this potential killer. Nothing could happen in the presence of all these witnesses, even though no one was paying them any attention. Her heartbeat returned to normal.

Zeta's lips trembled, and she gave Jane a grave nod. "Yes, you guessed it. I asked Georgiana to meet me at the barn on Saturday night when I bumped into her at the Peach Festival on Friday. Then I made plans with Rey's campaign manager to go out to dinner with me at the steakhouse." Oh my. Was this a confession?

Jane's heart raced once more. "But Georgiana was alive when I left her. On the way back I met Isobel in the hallway outside the restroom. I told the police all about it, and I took a lie detector test. They believe me. You should, too."

Shoot. This wasn't a television drama where the killer confessed at the slightest provocation. "So you are Isobel's alibi!" Jane raised her eyebrows.

"I'm afraid not. Isobel could've run over to the auction barn after I left her in the hallway. The police asked me about that, and I told them."

Jane bristled. "That's why they took Isobel in for questioning. That's about as crazy as believing Olivia did it!"

Zeta's jaw dropped. "I never said Olivia killed Georgiana."

Jane backpedaled. "Yes, well, um, neither of them have a motive, that's what I meant."

Zeta's eyes turned shrewd. "Isobel has a little crush on Skylar. He might have influenced her. He backed Kirby in the election, you know."

"Skylar backed Kirby, even though he worked for you?" Jane already knew this, but lifted her eyebrows to feign surprise.

"My employees can vote for whoever they want."

Both women fell silent as the cyclists told the server behind the bar they'd come back for their purchases later, then the group headed outside. Next thing she knew, the clerk had vanished through a door behind the bar.

Zeta moved over to one of the high top tables in the corner of the now vacant room. "I need to sit down."

They were alone. Even the wine server had left.

Should she have escaped along with the other cyclists? Maybe she should follow them and make a run for it? Yes? No?

Jane hesitated for a few seconds.

Her yellow belt in Krav Maga defensive training came to mind.

The decision was made for her when another group of wine tasters entered the winery and the server scuttled back into the room like a prairie dog popping out of its burrow whenever anyone approaches. The group was noisy at the bar, leaving the two women alone in their quiet conversation.

Jane hitched herself onto the stool across from Zeta. "What did you talk to Georgiana about at the auction house?"

"I confronted her about the affair, asked her if she had anything to do with Rey's death. She admitted meeting Rey in the basement after the party. To hear her tell it, she was the one to break off the affair. She said she threw the necklace at him." Zeta shook her head slowly as if she didn't believe it. But the young lady was no longer alive to confirm or deny this story. "I still say she killed him. She put that peach pit in his mouth just to be hateful. She was spiteful and vindictive, you know."

Jane couldn't comment on that. She didn't know the woman. "But then, who killed Georgiana? Who would leave a peach pit in her mouth?"

Zeta put her head in her hands. "The peach pit was obviously a copycat crime."

"But what does it mean?"

"It points to Georgiana."

Jane could understand that, what with her

nickname. "She worked in your stables at the ranch. Why didn't you fire her when you heard about the affair?"

"I had just found out about it." Zeta took a tremulous breath, and Betsey seemed to shudder along with her, the dog's body jerking as she thumped her tail on the floor. "But when we were at the auction barn, I told her she'd worked her last day at the Barre Ranch and to clear her things out of the stables."

"So you did fire her?"

"I did, but I didn't kill her." Zeta was vehement in her denial.

And Jane had no proof otherwise. There was something she was missing. "Well..." She chewed on her thumbnail. Oh yeah, she thought of a good question. "Was Rey in favor of oil development? We saw some oil company trucks on your land."

"When was that?"

"Yesterday."

Zeta's eyebrows drew in. "What do the oil surveys have to do with anything? There's nothing in the city ordinances against having studies made. They've been testing, that's all."

"What are oil surveys?"

"Rey commissioned some geophysical surveys to gather information. They're used for locating oil and natural gas deposits. He scheduled an environmental assessment along with the oil studies. He was trying to gather all the facts. He cared about the land, about the people. Everyone here loved Rey, they worshiped the Barre family, the founding family."

"No one is perfect. He had to have had enemies. And oil development causes a lot of controversy."

"You're wrong. Nobody wanted him dead. Except maybe Georgiana." Zeta obviously wanted to believe his lover was the murderer. Maybe she was, but that solution didn't tie up all the loose ends, like who killed Georgiana.

Jane looked around the room, trying to think of more questions. "What about the vineyard? Did anyone have a grudge against the business? What about competitors?"

"I told you, Rey didn't have any enemies. The business owners in the Grand Valley are a tight knit group."

Jane said, "I'm not so sure about that. Someone put up signs making fun of Holden's bed-and-breakfast, calling it 'deadfast.'"

Zeta had on a pained look. "I'm sorry to hear that, but I'm sure whoever did that was not from around here. As I said, the businesses support each other. The vintners in Grand Valley help each other out. Most of the customers travel the circuit on the Fruit Loop, going from one tasting room to the next. If the neighboring wineries are successful in bringing in people who also stop at my place, and vice-versa, all the wineries benefit. Rey was always popular with the other owners."

"It looks like you were the one who operated the winery, not Rey." Jane clasped her hands together and angled her forearms on the edge of the table. *Come on Zeta, give up a clue. Everything couldn't have been that peachy.* Jane groaned inwardly at her own pun.

Zeta shook her head. "It's still the Barre name. His name and his involvement. That's why this vineyard is successful. It's not because of me. Georgiana was the only one who wanted to ruin Rey's success. She killed him." She stubbornly wanted to believe the rival for her husband's affections was guilty. And maybe she was, or maybe she wasn't.

"Do you think Kirby could have killed Rey? Or was it Skylar?"

"I don't know."

"What about you, Zeta? Did you kill your husband and his lover, so that you could take over as mayor?" Jane held her breath. Had she gone too far?

The widow's eyes turned black with anger. "Jane, we had a strong marriage. Georgiana knew it, and that's the reason she killed him. She pushed the peach pit in his mouth out of spite."

Georgiana had told Jane the opposite, that the Barres' marriage was in trouble. She sighed. "Then who killed her? Shoved a pit down her throat, if not you?"

"That's the question. I don't know." Zeta's hands went to her own throat. "But I'm afraid that I'm next."

"Why would you be next?"

"I don't know, but I'm frightened." Zeta's eyes were round and wide.

The widow seemed believable, truly rattled, but Jane reminded herself of the saying that politicians and sociopaths, both, were excellent liars.

*****

A cool wind kicked up when Jane unlocked her bicycle and wheeled it over the gravel drive past the rows of grapevines. Dark purple clouds covered the sky and concealed the Bookcliffs. Once she left the gravel drive behind, she climbed onto the bicycle and pushed off. Riding at the foot of the obscured cliffs, the rhythm of the wheels and the flying sensation, feeling like a kid again, carefree, was a balm to her soul, soothing, keeping her peaceful and rooted. If only the sky wasn't threatening to rain. Her legs pumped at a speedy clip and the skirt of her sundress fluttered as she bounced along the track. She took her fingers off one handlebar to tuck the fabric tighter under her bottom.

A sudden deluge began to pour down, raindrops stinging the backs of her hands and the tops of her knees with sharp, cold pinpricks. The wind buffeted the rain against the bike like a whiplash. Cold water soaked her hair and the tops of her shoulders, and she shivered. Her flip-flops were soddened, slipping on the pedals. Would the rain damage her Adam Aemes framed photograph tucked into the bicycle basket? Should she seek shelter under one of the peach trees in the orchard bordering the Fruit Loop?

She squeezed the handbrakes to halt the bike. She was almost at a stop when a banged-up VW van emerged out of a hidden driveway, narrowly missing her front wheel. If she hadn't slowed at just the right moment, she would've been run over. She jerked the bike to a complete stop and had half a mind to use a finger sign she'd never used before as the van, covered with rivulets of rain and red dirt, burnt rubber down the road. How many broken down, dirty old vans were there in this small town? Was it the same VW van they'd seen on the trails above the wild horse refuge?

Yanking the bike after her, Jane scrambled under a thick peach tree to wait out the storm.

What time was it getting to be? How were the others doing? Was Dale miffed at her for leaving and not letting him know where she was going? Were Holden and Olivia mad that she'd left them stranded at the police station? Would Doug be angry she'd questioned Zeta? She wished for her phone and vowed never to let the battery die again, but it was easy to forget when she was out of town and in a different routine.

Surely by now everyone had made their way back to the inn. Likely, the attorney was able to convince Olivia to recant her silly confession. Probably the police had released both Holden and Olivia. Were all of her friends warm and dry waiting for her at the B&B? The dinner club friends could very well be watching the downpour without her as they relaxed with a glass of wine under the awning covering the deck. Jane pictured Isobel there, too, cracking jokes about this crazy weather starting with the eclipse.

Which were they, mad or happy? If only she knew.

Before long the sprinkles thinned, then stopped. The clouds disappeared, and the sun shone out of a blue sky in the way the rain quits and the sun appears suddenly in Colorado. Jane wheeled the bike onto the road to head for home, her soggy flip-flops about to fall off her feet.

When she pedaled the bike across the driveway at the B&B, Dale's truck was absent, Holden's car wasn't parked in his spot under the peach tree, and the deck was deserted. The picture in her mind with everybody waiting for her went "poof."

Where were her friends?

She stowed the bike with the others, grabbed the framed photo from the basket, then dashed inside, her flip-flops squishing with each step. In the common room, couch cushions lay on the floor and a lamp was overturned. Had she left a window open, allowing a gust of rain-driven wind to do this damage? Her cell phone was ringing from the second floor. She dropped the framed photograph and kicked off the water-logged flip-flops. Taking the stairs two at a time, breathless, she hoped she could reach her phone before the call went to voice mail. She crashed through the bathroom door and slid across the floor, plucking the phone off the counter.

"Hello."

"Jane, where have you been?" The caller's voice was frantic.

"Who is this?"

"Isobel."

Jane gave her head a shake and laughed with relief. "Where are you?"

"I'm at the emergency room at St. Mary's in Grand Junction. How come you haven't answered your texts and calls?"

"You're where?" Jane looked in the mirror above the sink. Her hair was glued to her head like a wet dog's and water dripped down her back.

"I'm at the hospital. Dad and Dale were in a car accident. They were brought in by ambulance. Uncle Holden is here with me."

"What happened? Is Dale all right?" Jane couldn't take it in. Her heartbeat hammered in her ears.

"He's in radiology. Getting a CAT scan of the head, I think."

Oh my God! That sounded bad…

"What about your dad?" Jane was shaking, so she jerked a towel off the rack and threw it around her sopping wet shoulders.

"He's been admitted with a concussion."

"Is your mom there?"

"No, I was hoping she was with you. She's not answering her phone, either. Crap. That means she's still in custody." Isobel drew in an audible breath.

"I'll let the police know about the accident and ask them to get a message to your mom. It's going to be okay, Isobel. Stay with Holden and I'll get there as fast as I can." Jane pressed the button to disconnect and toweled the rain from her hair.

She tore the phone charger out of the wall socket and stomped out of the bathroom, searching for the police non-emergency number. She punched the call button, but was only able to leave a message, so she asked for the homicide investigator—she couldn't remember his name—to call her back. Sitting on the side of her bed, shivering, she scrolled through multiple text messages from Isobel. There were none from Olivia. Her friend's phone was probably in a sealed property bag.

However, a text from the attorney read: *Your friends didn't show up after I rearranged my schedule to accommodate them. Don't expect any more favors.*

She'd call the lawyer back later and explain. She couldn't think about that now.

It was then she noticed the pillows on the floor, the lumpy, flower-patterned comforter askew, and an edge of the oval rug flipped over. Had someone been in her room looking for something?

She cracked open the doors to the other bedrooms. Each room was a mess. Hardly daring to take a breath, with her cell phone at the ready to hit the call back button for the police, she went through the entire inn. Every room had been gone over, but none of her friends would have created this chaos and whoever had tossed the place was long gone.

She returned to her room to finish toweling herself off and finally stopped shaking. She threw the pillows onto the bed and jammed everything that had been removed back into her suitcase, quickly examining her things for anything missing. Nothing appeared to be unaccounted for.

If she called the police to report what may or may not have been a burglary, she wouldn't make it to the hospital for hours and hours. She'd call them at her first opportunity, but not right now.

She slid her feet into a pair of sandals, then threw a couple of bottled waters into a tote bag. After scampering up and down the stairs a few more times for a sweater, then her phone charger, she headed out the front door.

But her car wasn't parked outside. Dale had the only vehicle on this short trip to the Grand Valley wine country. Where was his truck? Was it totaled?

A wrecked vehicle was the least of her worries.

She had to see about Dale and Doug and comfort Isobel and find out what the police had wanted with Holden and force Olivia to come to her senses. And report the ransacking of the B&B...and find the killer!

What to do first?

Track down a ride.

An anxious taxi trip later, she walked into the emergency entrance and up to the registration desk. The nurse on triage asked what her relationship to Dale was, then explained the only information she could provide was that he was in radiology and hadn't yet been assigned a room. Doug had a room assignment. She was able to wrangle his room number from the nurse.

She hopped into a waiting elevator and moments later stepped out on Doug's floor. She searched the hallway for his room number. The door was partially open, so Jane knocked softly.

Isobel's voice came through the crack. "Is that you, Jane? Come on in."

Jane threaded herself through the doorway. She took in the IV drip in Doug's arm and the bandage on his head. He was in a hospital gown under a thin blanket, and Isobel sat on the edge of his bed holding his hand.

Holden slumped in a chair at the foot of the bed, his feet stretched out in front of him. He stood. "Here, take my seat, Jane."

"That's okay." She motioned for him to stay where he was. Her heart in her throat, she asked, "Doug, how are you feeling?"

"I've got a pretty good bump on my head." He rubbed the top of his head with his free hand.

"What happened?" She set her bag of water bottles on the floor.

"A vehicle made a left turn right in front of us. He came right at us, out of nowhere. Crashed into the front of the truck pretty hard, almost head-on, then the moron left the scene. I'm not sure how he was able to drive away. Dale's truck was heavily damaged and the other vehicle had to've been, too."

Holden's arms were crossed over his chest. He said, "He must've had a pretty good sized vehicle to hit Dale's truck and still drive off."

Questions screamed in her head. "Did you get a look at the driver? The kind of car?"

Doug answered, "No, Jane. It was like, bam! My head hit the windshield. I might have blacked out for a second. He was gone. His car must not have had airbags, an older car, I guess, for him to take off like that. The police probably have evidence from the scene, like a broken headlight or paint transfer or even a witness. Let's hope they do. It's pretty hard to get away with an accident like that, but it does happen."

Another mysterious, unexplained event. Another phantom vehicle. Another unidentifiable driver. This was one too many crazy eclipse catastrophes. Maybe there was something to Isobel's theories of vortexes and chakras after all.

The young lady herself interrupted Jane's thoughts. "Did you get a hold of Mom? Does she know?"

Jane said, "Not yet. I left a message."

"I don't want her to worry. It's best she doesn't know." Doug's voice was tired and his eyes droopy.

Jane put her hands on her hips. "If Olivia knew, she might tell the police the truth and get herself over here."

"She'd better." Isobel plucked at the thin blanket on her dad's bed.

"Do you have any news about Dale's condition? The nurse at the station wouldn't tell me anything." Jane glanced at each of them.

"No. I'm sorry, Jane. We don't know anything either." Holden tucked his legs under the chair and leaned forward, elbows on knees.

A doctor charged into the room, and they immediately gave him their attention. "I need to speak with the patient and the family. Would you please wait outside, ma'am?"

"Certainly." Jane backed away from the hospital bed. She hated to be called "ma'am." "I'll wait in the hall." She left the room and let the door fall shut behind her, but after a few long minutes, she took off down a maze of connecting hallways. Maybe she could uncover news about Dale.

Thankfully the hospital didn't smell like rubbing alcohol and disinfectant. The walls weren't painted institutional green and the floors covered in ugly tile. Just the opposite, the walls were a cheerful yellow and the carpet a pleasant gray. Jane even got a whiff of the calming lavender scent that seemed to permeate the Grand Valley. After wandering in circles, she arrived at a nurses' station in a calm and tranquil area of chairs next to tall windows overlooking the Monument. Skylights in the ceiling threw light onto the floor, and above the squares of glass the sky was capped by a brilliant blue. Behind the nurse's station was a buzz of activity.

"Is Dale Capricorn out of radiology?" Jane leaned on the counter.

Peering at her computer screen, the nurse moved the mouse across the pad and made a few clicks. "No. It's going to be a bit longer. Why don't you go get a cup of coffee and come back later? Once he has a room assignment, you'll be able to see him. The doctor will stop by and explain the results of the tests then."

She gave Jane a reassuring smile, but Jane wasn't buying it. Why were the tests taking so long? Why couldn't she get more information right now?

Was it because they weren't married and she had no rights as his wife?

Chapter 16

An orderly finally wheeled a sleeping Dale into his private room, and Jane spent the dark hours curled in a chair at his bedside.

She never did get a chance to speak to a doctor. None had stopped by after they'd parked Dale in the bed, although nurses came and went once or twice in the night. The nurses assured her in their helpful way that Dale only had a concussion and needed to rest.

She tried to sleep, too, but just managed to thrash around in the chair while letting her imagination run away. What if Dale had a worse traumatic brain injury than what they were telling her? Like the brain bleed that killed Rey Barre? Her exaggerated worries kept her awake along with her guilty thoughts.

If only she'd found an attorney who was willing to come to Palisade. If only she hadn't sent the guys off in Dale's truck to Grand Junction. If only she'd solved the murder.

Isobel had stayed in her dad's room, but Holden had driven his car back to the inn, since he was expecting more guests to arrive in the morning. He'd explained his neighbor, the police dispatcher, had given him a ride yesterday afternoon from the station to the inn where he'd picked up his car and headed to the hospital. Jane had forgotten to ask why the police questioned him for so long. She'd get another chance, since he'd promised to come back for Jane and Isobel in the morning. This morning, that is. What day was it, anyway?

She shook the cobwebs out of her head and wondered where to get coffee. Consuming several cups of the canteen brew before trying to sleep hadn't helped her rest either. Maybe the cafeteria served up a more palatable version.

The sun was shining a bright beam through the gap in the curtains, so she unfolded herself from the chair, stretched, and drew the drapes back, hoping the light would help Dale to wake up.

Isobel poked her head in the door. "Jane?"

She waved her in. "How's your dad?"

The young woman cast a couple of quick glances at Dale. "Step out in the hall with me."

They both slid into the corridor.

Isobel explained in a low voice, "They decided to keep Dad a full twenty-four hours because of his concussion. The doctor told us he would be released this afternoon." The young lady's eyes were bloodshot, but her features were relaxed and she still looked adorable, her hair in a scrunchy. You'd never know she'd slept in a hard chair like Jane had.

"That's good news. The nurse said Dale has a concussion, too, same as your dad, so hopefully they'll be released at the same time. Heard anything about your mom?"

"Nope." Isobel's forehead tightened.

"She'll be out today, I'd bet a million dollars. One night in jail and she'll be screaming, *get me outta here!*"

Isobel's mouth twitched. "You are so right. She's

actually getting what she deserves for her stupid confession."

"True." Jane laughed for the first time in a while, then sobered. "What are the police thinking, keeping her at the jail?"

"I haven't a clue. Skylar's been interrogated again. He told me you've been going around asking a lot of questions, as if you suspected him, or something. Is that true? Why would you do that?" Her soft voice now had an edge.

Jane gave an intake of breath. "Isobel, you want your mother out of jail, right?"

"Dad said the police can only hold her for so long before they need to press charges. She'll be let go, he's sure of it. Maybe this morning."

"So they aren't going to book her?"

Isobel shrugged. "Uncle Holden's back and we're going over to the police station to find out." She jerked a thumb in the direction of her dad's room. "We're heading out in a few minutes if you want a ride to the B&B."

"I do. I'll be right there." Jane breezed into Dale's room to gather her tote bag and sweater. She kissed his forehead. He looked peaceful, as if he wasn't in any pain. The hospital was taking care of him through the IV drip and a clothespin-like clip on his finger, monitoring whatever it was that they monitored. Hoping and praying he was in good hands, and knowing there was nothing she could do but wait, she stopped at the nurses' station to notify them she was leaving for a while and would be back shortly, and then she steered straight for Doug's room.

Holden stood outside in the hall. "Jane, were you

looking for something at the B&B yesterday?"

"Like what?"

"I don't know. When I got back last night, it kind of looked like the place was tossed. I had to do a lot of straightening up before my new guests arrived this morning. You left your boots and your flip-flops by the front door, so I put them in your room."

Jane smacked herself on the forehead. "Oh, no! I forgot all about that. When I got back to the inn yesterday, it was messed up already. Was anything taken?"

"Nothing that I could tell." He pursed his lips. "I was going to call the police, but I thought maybe you'd moved things around looking for something, so I wanted to talk to you first."

"No. I wouldn't make a mess of your place." Reproach was in her voice. "I didn't call the police, either, because I was in a hurry to get over here to the hospital."

He nodded, but held her gaze, his eyes narrowed to slits. He continued to give her the stink eye, tight-lipped and cautious, and she returned the look. Would Holden have ransacked his own place to throw suspicion off himself? He looked as if he was thinking the same thought about her.

Jane asked, "What did the police question you about yesterday? You were at the station for quite a while."

"Just the same old questions." He found something interesting to stare at on the floor. She looked away, rolled her shoulders, and massaged her stiff neck. A moment of mutual suspicion passed before Isobel rejoined them in the hall. They took off in his car and minutes later Holden halted his Subaru in front of the B&B.

Isobel said, "After we spring Mom I'll give you a call to let you know when we're on our way back for you."

"Sounds like a plan. And, Holden, tell the police someone searched the B&B. You should let them know." Jane flung herself out of the car, and the other two sped out of the parking lot. She rushed inside, bypassing the new guests in the common area, and climbed the stairs two at a time.

A lot had happened since Jane had made herself pretty in her mint green sundress the day before. Now the dress was stinky from sweat and limp from being rained on and slept in. After showering and feeling like a human being again, Jane put on the only clean clothes she had left, a T-shirt and a pair of boot-cut jeans. Her flip-flops were in shreds, but she wanted to wear something sturdy anyway, so she bypassed her thin ballet flats and flimsy sandals for her cowboy boots, hoping the Band-Aids would protect the sore spots on her feet from the stiff leather. Once she looked around to make sure she had everything she needed—the charged phone was in her pocket—she descended the stairs to the kitchen to make a fresh pot of coffee.

Waiting for the coffee to brew and the phone to ring was nerve wracking. No phone call, but the coffee was soon ready, so she poured herself a steaming mug.

And waited.

Isobel didn't call. The hospital didn't either. No word from Dale.

She waited some more.

Please, God, arrange for Olivia to be released this

morning. Let Doug be discharged. Let Dale get out of the hospital, too. *Please, please, please.*

She stared out the window. Surely Isobel and Holden would show up soon with Olivia, then they would all head to the hospital to pick up Dale and Doug. Her mind spun until she told herself, *just stop worrying so much! If you're going to worry, concentrate on finding the killer.* She gulped down a few more fortifying swallows of coffee, grabbed her purse and went out to the deserted patio. She set her cell phone in the middle of the table, never to be out of her sight again. She was able to read through her suspect list one more time, studying each name, before tires scrunching on the gravel made her look up.

Skylar's VW van parked in front of the steps. He loped up to the door and bent his elbow, about to knock.

She leaned over the corner of the deck railing and hollered, "Skylar, are you here to see Isobel?"

He turned in her direction. "Yes. Can you get her?"

"She went with her uncle to the police station."

He looked toward the Heavens and clenched his fists at his sides. "Not again. Are the cops still questioning her?" He strode over, digging his heels hard into the dirt with each step, then he climbed the stairs to the deck.

"No. I guess you haven't heard the latest." Jane directed him to a patio chair and forced him into it. "Isobel's mom confessed to killing Rey and Georgiana. Incredible, isn't it?"

"Isobel told me. Why would her mom do that?"

She stabbed her fingers through her hair. "Because the police implied Isobel and Holden were involved.

And for some stupid, stupid, misguided reason, she thought she'd save them and sacrifice herself." A vision of her friend alone in the lockup swam before her eyes. A part of her scrunched up inside. She grasped Skylar's elbow. "I have some questions for you, young man, and you're going to answer them."

He drew back. "What?" His eyes had a wary look.

"Why in the world did you ask Isobel to lie for you and say you were together at the steakhouse? Do you know how much trouble you got her into?"

"I thought the police would leave us alone if we gave each other a rock solid alibi. It was to help her, too, not just me." He slid his arm out of her reach and held himself at a distance.

Jane glared at him. There was no way she was letting him off the hook that easily. "Somehow I find that hard to believe, Skylar. I heard you have yourself another alibi."

He crossed his arms and hunched his shoulders. "Well, when I wasn't with Isobel, I was with Kirby or Adam the whole time." He shook his head with force. "Isobel has nothing to worry about, I'm certain. What can the police have on her?"

"She posted some nasty comments about the Barres on Facebook. Now, where did she get the idea to do that, I wonder?" She glared at him some more.

His hands fell to his sides, but he didn't come up with another lame excuse.

Jane brushed her fingers against her eyes, still tired and foggy. "I need more coffee. Do you want some?"

"Sure."

They went in through the patio doors. Jane poured a fresh mug and handed it to Skylar, then topped off her own. She put her head in both hands and took in a deep, steadying breath.

"What's the matter, Jane?" He gave her arm a light tap. "Are you all right?"

"Isobel's dad and my fiancé were in a car accident yesterday afternoon. They're in the hospital. Doug's going to be released today, thank God, but I don't know about Dale yet." She slumped against the counter.

"I'd better give Bell a call." Skylar slid his cell phone out of the back pocket of his worn jeans. He strode out onto the porch, lowered himself onto the top step, and put his cell phone to his ear.

Jane climbed the stairs on shaky legs to her room. After splashing some cold water on her face, she went downstairs and carried her mug back to the front door, but Skylar had vanished.

Darn.

There went a potential ride. Dale's truck was in the police impound lot, she'd found out. Holden's car was at the police station. Skylar's VW van was speeding down the road away from the inn. Did she know anyone else who had a vehicle so she could cop a ride? No, except for Kirby and Zeta...her top two suspects...

Olivia had given the police that bogus confession so Jane could have more time to find the killer. She might as well make use of it.

Jane googled Kirby Potts' business address. His studio was located off Glen Oak Drive, an easy bike ride. She texted Isobel what she was about to do, grabbed her light rain jacket, just in case, and headed for the bicycles.

*****

Her bike coasted under a post with a sign swinging

in the wind, "Kirby Potts Art Studio," and she made the turn down a rough dirt lane between tight rows of thick evergreen trees.

The pines only allowed slivers of light to seep through the branches, but afforded protection from the gusts of wind that blew in from De Beque Canyon. She glimpsed bits of color and odd shapes between the trees. Halting the bike and planting both boots on the ground, she peered past the boughs. Giant sculptures rose from the ground in a groomed, park-like area on the other side of the trees. With renewed energy, she pedaled over the bumpy track until she came to a building that was all sharp angles. Solar energy panels lay at a flat angle on the steep roof; a stone sculpture of a blue heron in the traditional one-legged pose stood in a bed of flowers beside the door.

She parked the bicycle against a tree and rang the bell.

Kirby answered, wiping his hands on a white towel. "Hello, Jane."

"Can I come in?"

He regarded her for a moment, then opened the door wider and stood back. "I'm not holding any classes today, so I have a minute."

Jane entered into a massive room with floor to ceiling windows, drawing her eyes back to the outdoors where Kirby had positioned modern statues among standings of pines. The sculptures looked like they belonged with the others in front of the historical buildings in downtown Grand Junction. She turned from the windows to survey the inside of the studio. Smaller sculptures on pedestals filled the center of the room, and shoved against the windows were work tables with scattered hooked or flat tools that looked similar to dental instruments, likely implements for working with stone. Framed photographs hung on room divider panels, Adam's allotted space.

Jane stepped up to a picture of two horses, one brown, one speckled gray, their noses touching. "I just bought one of Adam's photographs at the Barre Winery."

"He sells his photos around town." Kirby adjusted a small metal sculpture of a wild horse centered on a marble base. The bronze horse wasn't the typical bucking bronco tossing a rodeo rider in the air, not the typical galloping mustang with mane and hooves in flight. The horse had no saddle or rider and stood as if alert, as if listening, maybe listening for danger, and its eyes appeared to be looking directly at Jane, asking if she would try to capture him or let him remain free.

Jane spoke into the silent moment. "A lot of artists around here use horses as their subjects."

He nudged one hand under his chin and grasped his elbow in his other hand, seeming to consider her. All he needed was a beret and a paint brush. Then he would tell her to move her chin ever so slightly up and out, make a square between his hands, and say, *perfecto!* What he did say was, "This is the Western Slope where everyone loves the outdoors."

She acknowledged that fact with a nod. Might as well be bold. Maybe he was a famous sculptor, but he was still a regular person. He put his pants on one leg at a time, just like everybody else, and all that. "Kirby, why did you warn me to quit asking questions yesterday at the eclipse party?"

His hands balled into fists. "Don't tell me you

came here to ask me more questions. Why do you keep going on and on? You didn't even know Rey or Georgiana."

"But you did."

"Of course. This is a small community." His face was hard like his stone sculptures.

She held his gaze. "Someone's confessed."

His eyebrows climbed up and his expression became animated, interested, and almost friendly. "You can tell me about it over coffee. Come with me." He threw open the door to a backroom, a kitchen area with shining appliances, wine glasses suspended bottom sides up under a wine rack, and a coffee bar. And the aroma of coffee beans. Seemed safe enough. She followed him in.

He went up to the industrial-sized espresso machine and started pulling levers. "Tell me, then, have the police made an arrest?"

"I haven't heard anything about an arrest. My friend, Olivia, confessed, though. She did it to protect her daughter because she thinks the police are focusing on Isobel. Which is ridiculous. She didn't do it. I expect the police will let her go today."

Disappointment showed in his eyes. He emptied two espresso shots into a mug.

"You didn't see or hear anyone the night Rey was killed? Right?" She examined his face.

"No." His expression was stiff.

"Skylar told me you alibied him at the steakhouse, but you said Skylar was out of your sight for a while."

"Yes, he was." He poured steamed milk over the espresso, then topped the cups with foam.

"For how long?"

Kirby handed her a mug. "So you think you can find the killer, put the police to shame, and rescue your friend?"

She smiled. "Something like that, I guess."

A bell rang from the front of the studio. "I need to see who's here. Sometimes I make random sales." He backed through the door which swung shut after him.

Jane examined the kitchen, opening drawers—if caught, she'd say she was looking for a spoon—and poking her nose in cabinets and the side-by-side refrigerator. All right, she was just being nosy now. Nothing out of the ordinary. But just around the corner, behind a row of cabinets, was an arched doorway opening to another workroom.

She didn't hesitate.

Bulky mounds were covered, ghostlike, in white sheets, casting different sized shadows from the light through the high windows. A chalk-like scent was thick in the air. She lifted several of the cloths to reveal marble busts, with heads and necks in progress. Likely, this was a classroom.

Jane approached one that stood taller than the others and gave the sheet a tug.

The face of Georgiana was chiseled in stone, a beautiful face with a tender expression, her hair cascading down her back, her shoulders beginning to take shape.

"There you are." Kirby came around the corner from the kitchen.

Jane turned and looked at him. "Did your customer leave already?"

"Just a package delivery."

They both stared at Georgiana's form. Jane asked,

"This is yours, isn't it?"

"Yes." He stroked his fingers over the hard stone, caressing the smooth lines, over the top of the head, down the locks of hair, over the shoulders, to the sharp, unfinished marble at the base.

She narrowed her eyes. "You cared about her, didn't you?"

"You can see it in the stone, can't you? Not everyone can see it."

"But she was having an affair with Rey."

He looked past Jane out the window. "It was over. Georgiana and I started seeing each other at the beginning of summer. She'd ended the relationship with Rey. He wasn't happy about that. He'd even given her an expensive necklace to try to win her back."

"She seemed upset when he died. She teared up and everything."

His voice rose, indignant. "Of course she was upset. We all were, and she was a very caring person." Kirby jerked the sheet over the head of the statue. "Come on, your espresso is getting cold."

Jane was fine with following him back through to the comfortable kitchen because it seemed safer than the classroom with the ghost shrouds.

The sales floor would be safer yet. She crossed the kitchen in a few quick strides, carrying her mug of espresso into the studio.

Kirby came through the door after her.

Was she alone with the killer? Did he poison her coffee or would he stick to his usual mode of killing by shoving her and bashing her on the head? She felt a creepy prickling at the back of her neck. *Krav Maga, don't let me down now.*

She stationed herself with her back to the window in view of anyone coming up the drive. She pretended to take a sip of the espresso, trying not to form a defensive stance, but unable to keep herself from rising onto the balls of her feet. "Kirby, put aside politics. Who do you think killed Rey? Could Georgiana have had anything to do with his death?"

"What? No." Kirby shook his head with some force. He was painting a different picture of the Peach Festival Queen than Zeta had described.

"Then who?"

"Zeta, of course. She killed them both. The ironic thing is, she didn't need to. The affair was over."

"Tell me what was special about Georgiana. Why did Rey care about her? Why did you?" When his eyes narrowed, she backpedaled. "I'm not trying to be rude, I'm just trying to understand."

He seemed to drift away. "We were soulmates, Georgiana and I. I'm what they call a big fish in a small pond. I'm rather a big deal around here, at least in the art community. But all I want is to be left alone. People are so aggravating, always hanging around, not giving me a moment to myself. Georgiana felt the same way. She was a bit of a dignitary herself, having been one of the queens of the Peach Festival. She understood me."

He took on the look of a man who had suffered much, but Jane was having a hard time feeling empathy for his first world problems and his first rate ego. Being too popular and in demand…well, boo-hoo-hoo.

"What's up with running for mayor? Nobody will leave you alone once you're in office."

His attention returned to Jane in a long, level stare. "I might be an important celebrity, and the good citizens may like to drop my name and invite me to parties, but I don't stand a chance against a Barre. I'll never be elected."

Chapter 17

"What?" Jane gripped her espresso mug to her chest. "You don't think you can win?"

Kirby snatched up one of his sculpting tools, something that looked like a serrated trowel or a flat knife. He slapped the tool against the palm of his hand a couple of times. "Not a chance."

She stepped a few paces back, bumping into the hard glass window. "Why all the billboards? Why the negative campaigning?"

"I'm trying to get people to think instead of blindingly voting for the Barre name. Maybe someday they'll elect a person who will make a difference for the valley. If you're looking for a scapegoat, I did not kill Rey. If I did, why would I kill Georgiana and why wouldn't I kill Zeta?" He wiped the tool with a white rag.

"Well, Zeta is worried someone will come after her." Jane tried not to have the same fear. Had she put herself in danger, alone with a killer who was trying to convince her he didn't do it? While holding a deadly, pointed object in his hands?

"Not likely. The person you should be questioning is Zeta. Not me." His voice came out sharp. He picked up another tool with a wicked-looking hook and began polishing. Impatience and irritation had taken the place of his prior interest, which had not been exactly

229

friendly, but at least he had behaved well enough before. Not so much now. His civility was long gone. And the tool in his hands looked lethal. "You have no business asking me about anything."

Jane's back pressed against the glass window, her breath caught in the back of her throat.

The door banged open with a loud scrape and Jane yelped.

They both whipped around as Adam Aemes bounded inside, a backpack riding on his shoulder. "Hello, Kirby. Jane, what are you doing here?"

"She came to accuse me of murder," Kirby said in a dry tone.

Adam's gaze volleyed between the two. "You're kidding, right?"

Jane slipped her mug onto the table. "I'm just asking a few questions, I'm not accusing anybody of anything."

"See, Kirby, she didn't mean it." The photographer dipped his head, curving his shoulders inward.

Kirby dropped the blunt tool onto a bench and stood with his chest out, his head high. He wheeled around and angled for the kitchen. "I've got work to do." He swept out of the room with an I'm-the-head-of-the-food-chain attitude.

Adam lifted one curved shoulder and let it fall. "He's a busy man."

She sighed heavily and prodded herself away from the window. "I had no idea he and Georgiana were an item." She might as well test the waters.

He glanced away, taking in a deep breath.

"Kirby already admitted it. He's not keeping their relationship a secret."

Adam relaxed and lowered his heavy pack gently onto the table. "You know he's not a killer, Jane. He would never have hurt Georgiana."

"You must've cared about her, too." Was it possible three different men could have feelings for the same woman?

"She was a friend, that's all."

"You took so many pictures of her." Jane drifted along the panels of photographs of the wild horses and the beautiful woman with the setting sun over the desert. She glanced at the kitchen door, but Kirby remained out of sight.

"She loved the horses." He shadowed Jane's steps as she inched along the displays. "And since we knew each other for years, she never charged a modeling fee. I was lucky she was so photogenic. I really miss her, and not just because of my pictures."

"Were you jealous of Kirby's interest in her?" Jane threw the question over her shoulder. Now her suspicions were turning in his direction. She tensed, listening for his reaction.

"Not at all. I was happy to be the one who introduced them."

She stopped in front of a familiar photograph of wild horses on the plateau high above the valley. She may have seen this image before, but now the pictures were starting to look alike. "What's in the corner of this photo?" She edged closer for a better look, then tapped a fingernail against a corner of the frame.

"Let me see." Adam scrutinized the images. "I wonder. Let's look at the original on my laptop." He ushered Jane over to the work table. She stood to one side as he extracted his computer from his pack and turned it on. He scrolled past dozens of folders, then clicked one open and found the file he was looking for. He hit a button on the keyboard to enlarge the picture. Together they gazed at a tiny chassis behind Georgiana's head, an oil exploration company truck.

"Huh. I never noticed that." Adam blew up the photo even more, to the extent it became blurry.

"You didn't know about the geophysical surveys?" Jane tried to keep the skepticism out of her voice and couldn't help but ask, "Were you up on the trails spying on Barre, taking photos of the oil trucks?"

"I took lots of photos in lots of places, but honestly, I never spied on the Barres. I never saw the trucks." He rocked back on his heels, arms crossed. He appeared distracted, like his mind was racing.

"Do you think Kirby knew? I mean, this picture is hanging right here for anyone to see."

"No, no. Kirby didn't know." He gave her a quick look and threw his arms out. His voice grew loud. "I've walked past this photo how many times and never noticed that tiny truck in the background. And I'm certain Kirby didn't either." Adam's voice went from loud to low. "He probably never even looked at this photograph."

Jane could accept that about Kirby, but not Adam. "It's hard to believe you didn't see the truck, you being a professional photographer. Don't you look closely at the pictures you take? Examine all the details?"

"I was concentrating on the subject." He turned his palms up in a so-what gesture.

"Did you put other copies of this print out for sale?"

"I don't remember if I did." He shook his head.

Jane pointed at the screen. "I think I've seen this photo before. I'll bet you have more like it."

"I'll look through my pictures and let you know. I'm interested myself." His eyes took on that faraway look again.

Kirby barged back into the studio and gave Jane a neck-jerking glance. "Why haven't you left?"

Adam waved Kirby over while Jane cowered, making herself small. "Come here and look at this."

Kirby made a pointed study of his watch, then moved to stand in front of the computer screen, center-stage, arms crossed, obviously still annoyed. His head jutted forward, and his impatient look suddenly morphed into outrage, his eyes bulging. "Those Barres! They're going to ruin my ranch." His voice echoed in the large room with the high ceilings.

Adam reached out as if to pat Kirby's shoulder, then withdrew his hand. "You'll win the election now for sure."

Kirby gave him an approving smile.

Adam beamed and said, "Zeta's the one you should talk to, Jane."

Kirby said, "Right. Someone needs to confront her."

"Thanks for your time." Jane backed up and headed for the door. The two men didn't seem to pay much attention as she took off. Probably Kirby was thinking about more campaign slogans and slap-you-in-the-face billboards.

She tugged her bike to a stand and climbed on. A corrugated steel outbuilding caught her eye. A bent bumper protruded slightly out of the doorway. Curious, she hopped back off, casting a fleeting glance behind her back, but neither of the men was looking out the studio windows to make sure she'd left, so she wheeled the bike over. The barn-like door was cracked open and she peeked inside.

Partially hidden under a tarp was a rusted out VW bus with its front hood crunched upward and back, the bumper hanging by a thread and the body caked with red dirt.

The van prevented the door to the shed from closing completely. There was only a smidgeon of space between the vehicle and the walls, not enough to squeeze in for a better look. She crept along the outside perimeter until she circled back to the front, but didn't find any windows.

Was this broken-down vehicle the one that smashed into Dale's truck? Was this the van on the four-wheel drive road? The one that almost ran her over yesterday in the rain?

She hopped back onto her bike and sped away, the bike shaking and knocking like a rattlesnake's tail, like she was running from a rodeo bull. Blood thundered in her ears as she pedaled hard, darting quick looks behind her, breath rasping. Sweat trickled along her hairline, down the back of her neck, and the front of her shirt. Her slippery hands gripped the handlebars, and her thigh muscles screamed with the effort as she bounced down the track. The tall pines on either side of the road cast sinister shadows, and the lonely gravel drive felt like a trap. She didn't slow up until she hit the main road, and even then she only slowed a little to try to catch a breath, to think.

A mile or two later, she let the bike coast along busy Glen Oak Drive until the wheels rolled to a stop on the shoulder. Her muscles had cinched up, her legs frozen, and she almost fell over onto her side, but at the last minute managed to untangle one boot from the pedal and land it on the pavement. She stood above the bike as the traffic whooshed by, shooting dirty blasts of hot air against her jean-clad legs. She let go of the handles and the bike frame clattered to the ground.

It was a stretch of the imagination to think she'd found the vehicle responsible for Dale's accident, but if someone was in a hit and run, they would store their car out of sight in such a place.

Who would do that?

She thought back to Skylar's VW van parked at the B&B only an hour ago. It did not have all this road grime and damage. So Skylar wasn't the only one with a VW van.

The obvious person was Kirby Potts.

Kirby had driven a VW van in the Peach Festival parade. Zeta had ridden in a pickup, but Kirby led the procession in a classic VW with a bullhorn on the roof. Doug would tell Jane in his cop way not to jump to conclusions. Not to assume the van was Kirby's. He could've borrowed a vehicle for the parade. This could be a different vehicle he was storing for someone else.

Who? The killer?

The suspects were limited to those staying overnight at the B&B, of course. Kirby, Zeta, Skylar...

And Holden. Just because he wasn't at the steakhouse didn't mean he couldn't've been the one to kill Georgiana. Anyone could've come from town to meet the woman in the auction barn after Zeta had finished talking with her. Holden didn't drive a VW van, though. He drove a Subaru, plus he was at the police station at the time of the accident, she realized with relief.

If only they had seen who was driving the van on the plateau…and it was too bad Doug couldn't identify the driver of the hit-and-run.

Rage reared its head. Dale and Doug could've been killed in the accident. That would have been two more deaths. The hit-and-run driver would not get away with this! No one could hurt Dale!

Dale. How could she have forgotten about Dale alone in his hospital room? He was probably awake by now and wondering where she was. Was he about to be released, staring at his watch, tapping his foot? Or Heaven forbid, did he take a turn for the worse? Did his concussion become exacerbated somehow? Traumatic brain injuries could be deadly. The doctor could've moved him to ICU. Was he on a feeding tube and oxygen? Life support?

Jane recalled the news of an actress who fell and hit her head, who initially thought she was fine and joked about the fall, who then died a day or so later…and that could happen to Dale, too.

And what about Doug? Did the killer go back to finish the job? Was the murderer standing above her friend right at this moment with a pillow over his face? And then there was Olivia. Was she in a sheriff's transport van, being moved to a maximum security prison, her feet and hands shackled, or was she loose, at the mercy of someone who could now be called a serial killer?

She gave herself a mental slap. Too much imagination. A dose of reality was needed here. All she had to do was pick up her cell phone and call around.

She had the capability this time.

Two more pickups flew past, kicking up gravel. She scooped up the bike and rolled it over to a fence post away from the edge of the road. Then, she dialed the hospital. First things first. She'd find out about Dale.

The call was connected right away to his room.

"Hello?"

His voice was a balm to her soul. She relaxed against the fence post. "Dale?"

"I'm glad you called, hon. I'm going to be released soon. Just waiting for the doctor to sign off."

"You're out of the coma?" Her back slid down the fence post until her bottom rested on the heels of her cowboy boots.

"What? I was never in a coma. Where'd you hear that?"

She shook herself and refocused. "Oh, what I meant to say…is your concussion better?"

"Just a small headache. The nurse told me you spent the night in my room. She also told me I slept like a baby even though she woke me up a few times to check on me. I barely remember that. I do feel rested. I'm going to be released soon. Can you catch a ride to the hospital?"

She jerked herself to a stand. "I'll get there as fast as I can."

"The doctor hasn't signed my discharge papers yet, and no one seems in a rush around here, so I guess there's no hurry. But after I get out, we'll need to take a look at my truck and make arrangements to get back to Denver…"

"I'll figure it out, Dale." Jane would've been

beside herself if her cute, lime-green car had been banged up in an accident, but she said anyway, "Don't worry about your truck."

"All right. Love you."

"Love you, too." Jane disconnected.

She hadn't told him about the VW van in the storage shed at Kirby's art studio. She'd decided not to mention it, not to concern him. He had enough to worry about.

A text from Isobel waited for her in messages. *Mom still in slammer. If not out soon, then heading 2 hospital 2 get Dad. I'll text when we get close & we'll pick U up on the way. It might be awhile <impatient face>emoji*

Why was it taking the police so long to figure out they should release Olivia? A slow boil simmered through her blood, but she needed to look at the bright side.

At least one thing was going right...the guys were okay. Dale and Doug were going to be discharged today. The group was supposed to check out of the inn this morning. They could probably stay another night, there'd been so many cancellations. They'd need to sort out Dale's truck so they could return to Denver. Work, home, puppies...responsibilities awaited.

But the murderer was still at large and Olivia was still in jail.

If Jane uncovered the murderer, the police would have to let Olivia go immediately. She couldn't count on the police to get it right. She planned to report the VW van, but needed to get a few more of her questions answered first. Now was the time to do it. Dale even said there was no rush to get to the hospital.

She turned the bike around and headed for the Fruit Loop, her mind spinning along with the bicycle spokes.

Jane needed to pin down just what was going on with the oil trucks. What did oil have to do with either of the deaths, if anything?

Kirby's surprise seemed genuine, so believable, when he saw the truck in the picture. And Adam would've shown it to him sooner if he'd known. Jane was now convinced neither knew about the oil until today. If they had, Kirby would have used such knowledge in his negative campaigning before now. She wasn't impressed with Kirby. For all his rhetoric about helping Barresville, he only cared about his own ranch.

However...someone else could have recognized the trucks in the picture. Someone else could have observed the activity in the valley.

Even though Adam denied seeing the oil trucks, Georgiana could've spotted them in the distance during the photo shoot. The picture proved her presence when the oil company was performing surveys, or worse, planning to drill, although Zeta didn't admit to that. If she hadn't seen the truck during the photo session, Georgiana had plenty of opportunity to observe what was going on since she worked on Barre Ranch. And of course, Zeta knew all about it.

Here was a new idea. What if Zeta was in a power struggle with her husband over oil development? Maybe they argued over who owned the mineral rights? The motive of the affair was always a possibility, too. Perhaps Zeta owned a VW van. And—this was a brilliant brain flash—Zeta could have arranged for the VW van to be hidden on Kirby's property to frame him!

Adam was right. Zeta was the one she needed to talk to.

Murder *was* usually over love or money or power, and all were Zeta's motives, no one else's.

Oh, dear—if Zeta had eliminated her husband and his lover, Plan A would be eliminated as well, and Jane had no Plan B in place.

Back to the Barre Winery.

Chapter 18

She milled around the gift shop side of the Barre Winery tasting room and examined Adam's triptych of photographs on the wall, but none of the three had hidden images of oil exploration trucks.

A crowd of twenty- and thirty-somethings had their elbows propped up at the tasting room bar, laughing and sipping samples, while a young man Jane didn't know poured the wine. There was a time when her cuteness captured others' attention, but that had faded in her fifty-somethings and now she felt like a middle-aged woman shopping for knick-knacks. She picked up a ceramic salt and pepper shaker set of Lucille Ball stomping grapes. Too adorable! But no one else was around to ring up purchases, and the wine server was paying her no mind, so she put it back down.

Being invisible had its perks—she was able to slip unnoticed through the door into the back room to spy out the wine cellar for clues.

The door shut behind her with a cringe-worthy bang. Oops.

She held her breath as she stood stock still for a moment. The room was vast, dimly lit, and cool, with concrete floors sloping to drains and giant, stainless steel tanks reaching high to the ceiling. No windows were in the cave-like space, and the tall tanks appeared in the shadows like stalagmites or fairy chimneys. Had the noise awakened someone in the cellar? She half expected to hear drums in the deep.

"Hi, Jane. What are you doing here? Can I help you with something?" Skylar trundled up behind her.

Jane's heart rate accelerated and she jumped a mile. As she patted a hand over her chest, her voice came out wobbly. It was just Skylar, not a goblin. "I'm looking for Zeta."

Betsey trotted out from behind the row of wine barrels and licked Jane's boot. She leaned over to rub the friendly beast for a little dog therapy. Her heart slowed back to normal.

"She's not here right now." Skylar gave her a reassuring smile. A clipboard was under his arm, and he was once again wearing one of his hippy shirts, this time with a buffalo pictured on the front and the words, "Stand Up, Be Herd." A beaded choker hung around his neck, the beads spelling out the words, "peace, love, and hope."

"I guess I should've called first." She tried not to hide her disappointment. She wasn't going to be able to snoop around after all, and so little time was left. She nodded toward his clipboard as she scratched Betsey's head. "You have some more of your petitions? Need some signatures?"

"No." He glanced at the pages and chuckled. "This is for checking the barrels."

"What's that mean?" Jane untangled her fingers from the dog's long hair and straightened to a stand. Betsey whined in protest.

"I'm recording the temperatures. Zeta should be back soon if you want to wait."

Jane glanced at the time on her phone. "Okay. If

she's not back in a few minutes, though, I'll need to take off. Dale and Doug are getting out of the hospital today." She smiled in anticipation of seeing Dale back on his feet.

"That's right. Bell told me her dad hasn't been released yet, that there's a lot of waiting around."

Dale had said the same thing. She might as well hang out here rather than at the hospital. Maybe Zeta would show up soon, and in the meantime Jane could ask Skylar some more questions. "Can I watch what you're doing while I'm waiting? I do need to learn more about wine."

"Sure. Come this way." He moved halfway down the line of tanks with Betsey and Jane trailing behind.

"So I thought barrels were made out of wood." She tapped a fingernail on the metal barrel with a ping-ping sound. She'd try to put him at ease, then work her way back into the murder investigation. Yep, that was the plan.

"Zeta uses the stainless-steel drums with the open tops. Vintners will argue about working only with wood, but most use both. We have some of the smaller oak barrels in another room." He stared at the temperature gauge on the barrel in front of him and scribbled down the numbers. "So what were you going to ask Zeta?"

Ah, the opening she was looking for. "Actually, you might know the answers to my questions, Skylar." Jane followed in his steps while he continued to the next tank. "You're concerned about environmental issues and all. You're probably way ahead of me." She checked the time again before sliding her phone into a pocket.

"What do you mean?"

"Remember, I asked if you had your VW van up on the cliffs overlooking Barre Valley? When we had Dale's truck up there we saw some oil exploration trucks on Barre land."

He rolled his fingers into balls of fury and swung his head back and forth. "It's terrible! I don't want to look over the valley and see oil rigs all over the place! We have too much drilling already and now they want Barre Valley, too. We need to keep Barre Valley clean, we need to protect the wildlife and the water." His voice was sharp, like he was over-the-top angry.

"I know. I know. Skylar, I'm not arguing with you. I get it. I understand." She tried to make her voice soothing. "I'm glad someone cares. You, and Isobel, too."

He nodded and peered at the temperature gauge on the tank in front of him. He jotted something on his clipboard with such force his pen tore through the pages.

Betsey shook herself, starting at her tail end, giving off a flapping sound and ending with her tags jingling around her neck.

"Zeta told me they were doing seismic surveys, but she said Rey also had an environmental study done, too." Jane examined his face. His temple muscles worked like he was grinding his teeth together. "I figured you already knew about it even if you haven't been on the plateau because one of Adam's pictures shows the oil trucks on Barre land. Do you know which picture I mean? Have you seen it?"

His gaze darted left, then back to his clipboard. "No."

How was it possible the club members had sighted the oil company trucks, but Skylar, an environmental watchdog, had not? Whoever drove the VW had to have seen them. Skylar drove a VW van. But, Jane reminded herself, there were two vans...

"Skylar, I think I found the vehicle involved in the hit-and-run accident. I just came from Kirby's art studio. I saw a VW van with a lot of front end damage parked in a shed. I think whoever killed Rey and Georgiana drove that van into Dale's truck then hid it." Jane strolled after Skylar to the next barrel. "I need to call the police and let them know. They will figure out the owner by the VIN."

Skylar drew in a sharp breath. His eyes were wide, his lips in a deep frown. Sweat beaded on his forehead and tension seemed to grip his body. A frisson of energy whisked between them on a wave of fear and danger.

And everything clicked into place.

Skylar was an eco-warrior, someone who would fight to stop oil development in Barre Valley.

She pictured Skylar—not Zeta, not Kirby or Adam or Holden—down in the lounge.

Skylar faced Rey, who had his bottom hitched up on the table, right next to the candle and framed photograph. Jane concentrated on the picture, recalling the details, the wild horses high above the valley, the tiny oil trucks off in the distance hidden in plain view.

And Rey Barre, owner of Barre Valley Ranch and mayor of Barresville, with the western frontier mentality of fierce independence...arguing with Skylar Straite, who was telling him what he could and could not do on his ranch or in his town, both controlled by the family for generations.

Was Skylar fiercely passionate enough in his beliefs to hurt Rey that badly and leave him to die? Killing to prevent extraction of the oil was not out of the realm of possibilities.

Of all her suspects, Skylar was the last one she had imagined could be the killer, the most unlikely, the most improbable. Even Holden had been higher on her list. But the murderer in the mystery parties was always the one least suspected, the one with the fewest amount of clues stacked against him.

She narrowed her eyes.

He could probably read her mind. She never did have a poker face.

"Skylar."

"What?" His shoulders were tensed, his fingers holding his pen in a death grip.

"Did you hear what I said? I found the hit-and-run vehicle."

"I heard you." His eyes were aimed on the barrel, but he was watching her, too.

She knitted her eyebrows together. "You left the B&B this morning before I had a chance to say goodbye."

"You went upstairs so I thought I should leave." He moved to the next steel barrel and squinted at the gauges, but was no longer writing anything down on his clipboard.

"Why did you really stop by today? Was it to make sure no one suspected you'd searched the B&B?" He turned to stare at her. She continued, "At first I thought the killer came back for the necklace, not knowing the police had already removed it. But that wasn't the case, was it?"

Skylar lowered his clipboard an inch. "I have no idea what you're talking about."

"You stole the photograph from the lounge and tore the place up so it wouldn't be obvious the picture was missing. Holden couldn't tell anything was taken, but he might've noticed if the candle hadn't been thrown on the floor and the rest of the place in a shambles, too." Her heart started to race as her thoughts jumped forward.

"Why would I do that?"

"Because I talked to Zeta about the oil surveys. She told you, didn't she? She told you I was asking questions. The picture was a clue. Present at the scene. The subject of Rey's last conversation with the killer. You thought you'd better get rid of it. But I didn't see the photo at the B&B, I saw it at Kirby's studio. So you needn't have bothered taking it."

"I don't know what you mean." His voice was insistent, his eyebrows drawn tight. The clipboard shook in his trembling fingers.

"The drilling is the key. It wasn't about love or political power or any of that." Her heartbeat hammered in her chest so hard she was sure they could both hear it. "You killed Rey to prevent drilling in the valley. You crashed into Dale and Doug, too. Pretty clever of you to use a different van. Not the one you drive around town. The police will find out you own two of them. I was getting close to the truth, so you staged the accident to intimidate us, so I would be distracted and quit asking questions. You didn't find out from Isobel that Olivia had confessed until afterward."

His glower deepened. "Isobel told me you were

investigating the murders and would probably figure it out."

"She did?" Her tongue felt thick in her dry throat. If she wasn't petrified, she might have felt a little pride.

He set the clipboard down on the edge of a metal table, fisted his hands, and glared at her. The chilly room was suddenly even colder. A dangerous light glinted in his eyes and his face contorted in anger.

Jane stepped toward the door. "You can't get away with murder, you know."

He reached behind his back, under his T-shirt, and yanked a gun out from the waistband of his jeans. He aimed it at her.

A red hot bolt of absolute fear took off from her head and shot down to her toes. She heaved big gulps of air in and out. "So I'm right. It *was* you." Her voice cracked, breathless. Betsey whined, sensing her distress.

"You're going to walk ahead of me." He flicked the gun to his left. "Go that way and stop at the end of the barrel racks."

"I know the reason why you killed Rey, but what did you have against Georgiana?" Her voice came out high by an octave.

"Get moving."

She hated to turn her back to him, but did as he said, proceeding with leaden feet farther and farther away from the door of escape to the tasting room, the mountain dog following close as if heeling. "Skylar, you don't want to do this."

"Shut up and keep walking."

Her footsteps were heavy and the aisle between the wine barrels was all too short. She approached the keg at the end of the row and swung around to face him. "Now what?"

"Climb that ladder."

She inched over to the ladder running up the side of the last barrel. Betsey sat on her haunches to watch. "What if I don't want to? Are you going to shoot me?" Her pounding heart would probably give her a heart attack first. Her heart pelted around in her chest like a gunshot ricocheting around in an empty wine barrel.

"Yes, I will."

"You didn't use a gun on Rey or Georgiana. Why change up your method with me?"

"I didn't have a gun at Holden's party. All I had was that stupid, plastic Tommy gun. Besides, this gun's not mine. It's Zeta's. I got it out of her office. If anyone finds your body, which they won't, but if they do, the bullet will have come from her gun." He had on a satisfied, tight-lipped smile, but the gun wasn't even pointed at her. The heavy weight of the pistol caused the muzzle to drop toward the floor.

Skylar probably didn't know how to shoot a gun. Probably never had a lesson in his life. Maybe the safety wasn't even off. Jane stared hard at the pistol, but she didn't know anything about guns, either.

If he wasn't capable of shooting her, maybe she could keep him talking until Zeta returned. She tried to use telepathy to tell Betsey to go get Zeta, but the mountain dog plopped on the floor and buried her face in her paws.

"Climb the ladder."

She moved another millimeter. "So you went down to the lounge after Georgiana came up. Did she see you or something?"

"Move it!"

"Answer me and I will." Her heart threatened to thump right through her chest.

His face scrunched up some more, like a child debating with himself, then slyly bargaining for his own way. "All right. I'll tell you. Then. You. Will. Climb. That. Ladder." He emphasized each word, as if in doing so he could make her jump to it. "You were right about the photograph. I saw it on the table when we were having a last drink, and I noticed the oil trucks in the background. After the others left, I watched Rey and Georgiana head back down to the lounge. So when Georgiana came up the stairs, I went down to ask Rey how he could allow drilling in the valley." He waved the gun around. He obviously didn't know how to handle a weapon. "Now, climb the ladder."

Jane put one hand on the metal rung and clutched her pocket for her cell phone with the other, giving herself away.

"Give me your phone." His voice sounded flat, unnatural. "Now." She passed it to him. Darn. It was fully charged, too.

She tried to stall for more time, hoping against hope that Zeta would show up. "You probably didn't mean for Rey to hit his head."

"I walloped him in the chest hard, I was so angry. He went down heavy and cracked his skull on the cement hearth. He was bleeding from the back of his head."

"That sounds like an accident. Why didn't you call for an ambulance?"

"I wanted him to die. I even went back in the middle of the night to make sure he was dead." Skylar's own face was waxen with a gray, dead cast. "I got rid of the one guy who was bent on ruining the land. I've talked Zeta out of allowing any drilling, so I don't have to worry about her. Just in case, I decided to back Kirby for mayor. Really, Jane, it was for the best. You have to understand that."

"Murder is never justified, Skylar." Jane tried to take a few calming yoga breaths, but was possibly hyperventilating instead.

"This time it was." He seemed to believe it.

"If it was all about the oil, what was the deal with the peach necklace? Why did you go back and hide it after I found Rey's body?" Jane held onto the metal rung. "You were taking a risk."

"I didn't. That was Georgiana."

Jane's mouth dropped open. "Did she see what happened?"

"No. But after you found the body, she panicked and thought the police would assume she'd killed him. She figured the necklace would be proof she was the last person to see him alive, so she ran downstairs and hid it."

"How do you know about this?"

"She texted me from the auction barn when I was at the steakhouse and asked me to meet her. Her text said she'd seen me at the B&B in the middle of the night coming up the steps from the lounge. So I left the steakhouse and headed over to the barn. That's when she admitted she'd moved the necklace."

"She never told the police she saw you?"

"No. And a good thing she didn't. She thought I might've had an explanation for being in the basement. She wanted to meet and talk to me about it. So I needed to get rid of her. I grabbed a rock on my way to the barn. I hit her until I knew she was dead. I took her phone with me so the police would not find her texts. The silly woman was using a disposable phone, untraceable. Now, I've told you everything. Get yourself up that ladder." His voice came out loud. He stepped closer, practically shaking the gun in her face.

Betsey got up and inched away, then slumped back down.

Jane put her boot on the bottom rung and pulled herself up the first step. "What am I supposed to do when I get to the top?"

"Climb inside the barrel."

She would no longer have to worry about her heart ripping a hole through her rib cage if she drowned in a wine barrel. "Why, Skylar? Olivia's confessed. The police aren't even looking any further. You can just disappear, no one will suspect you or come after you. Georgiana can't talk now. And I won't say a word. Who would believe me, anyway?" Jane hoped he didn't know that Olivia was likely on her way out the door of the jail at this moment. At least, Jane hoped she was.

"Yeah, right." He edged closer. Maybe he did know.

Betsey lifted her nose out from under her paw. Where was Zeta? She usually had Betsey with her. Jane prayed Zeta would come looking for her dog any minute now.

She wrapped an elbow around the chest-level rung. "Your customers in the wine tasting room will hear the shot, so you can't shoot me."

"They're probably long gone."

"Why don't you shoot me then?"

"There'd be blood all over and I don't need the police looking at yet another murder."

"Good thought." She reminded herself she had the upper hand, so to speak, but she wished Olivia, who surprisingly was a sharp shooter and had a concealed carry permit, would walk in the door along with Zeta.

He didn't take his eyes off of her. "Look, this barrel is empty. All you have to do is climb in."

She would not, absolutely not, climb into the gigantic wine barrel. It probably wasn't empty. Would she drown in wine? Would her body ever be found? And if they did find her, what would she look like all stained red and everything? Eugh!

"Even if your customers have left, more people will come, and I'll bang on the metal, or climb out, or yell or something."

His eyes made a quick dart to the thermostat on the tank.

She kicked herself for pointing out the weakness in his plan. "Oh, so you're going to turn up the temperature and I'll die from the heat. Why not just lock me in that cooler over there?" She gestured to a walk-in refrigerator. "I've heard that freezing to death is painless, you just fall asleep." That didn't sound so bad. After the heart attack she was about to have she'd need a long rest.

"People are in and out of that cooler, but this drum is not going to be used until the next batch. No one but me checks these barrels. The police won't look for you in there. Like you said, the police won't investigate since Isobel's mom confessed and your body won't be found. No one will know what happened to you, and the best part is, no one will suspect me. You're right about that. You're the only person nosing around."

She hung onto the rung with such a tight grip her shoulder ached. "What about cadaver dogs? A cadaver dog will sniff out my body. It's a bad plan!" Jane's eyes went to Betsey.

He snorted. "The Palisade police don't have a cadaver dog."

"The FBI will get involved in a missing person search and they use cadaver dogs all the time." She didn't really know if this was true.

Skylar yelled, "Get in the tank and shut up!"

"All right, but I'm going to kick the sides and make a lot of a noise," she shouted back at him.

Skylar jerked the pistol up. "Heck with it. I don't care about the blood. I can get the hose out and spray it down the drain." He trained the gun in her direction, his finger hovered over the trigger. He was in point blank range, so close she could count the number of beads in his choker necklace. Even if he didn't know how to shoot, he couldn't miss.

She might as well give in. Her arms were tired from hanging off the side of the ladder and one of her blisters had burst. She hauled herself up one more rung.

He squinted his eyes and puckered his lips. He looked like her older son looked at age three when he didn't get his way. She shoved her boot onto the next step. Would she ever see her sons again? Dale was waiting at the hospital for her. What would he think when she didn't show up? Her other boot clanged on the next rung. She'd never get to marry Dale. Suddenly she didn't care about getting married in this beauty spot. She wanted to be far away.

The young man, gun in hand, strayed even closer.

He'd screwed his eyes completely shut in his temper tantrum, just as her son used to do. She swore her heart really did stop beating as a moment of clear opportunity miraculously presented itself.

She swung around and drove the heel of her fancy new cowboy boot straight back.

The hard heel caught him above the eye and he dropped like a stone to the floor. The gun flew out of his fingers and skidded across the cement, ending up well underneath a barrel rack. She jumped down, hitting the concrete floor with a bang.

She'd used a Krav Maga technique called the "spinning back kick." Her instructor would've been proud.

"Help! Help!" Jane screamed.

Betsey darted over with a loud growl and hopped onto Skylar's chest. The large dog had him pinned to the floor, but Skylar wasn't resisting. Jane had knocked him out flat.

"Good girl, Ms. B! Don't let him up." Jane sprinted the length of the wine barrels and burst through the door to the tasting room. All of the customers had left, just like Skylar said. The wine server had disappeared and the room was empty.

She rummaged through the goods, tossing aside wine bottle openers, coasters, and T-shirts with the Barre Winery logo. A pile of knick-knacks littered the floor. She yelled, "Where's a rope when you need one?" but no one was there to help her. Had the tasting room server disappeared completely down his rabbit hole?

An extension cord was taped along the wall from an outlet to a swag lamp decorated with grapevines. She

255

yanked the cord out of the wall socket and charged back through the barrel room.

She let out a breath of relief to see that Betsey still had Skylar pinned to the floor, but he moaned and his eyes fluttered open, then he tried to elbow his way up.

Betsey took one of his hands in her mouth and Skylar cried out. Jane grabbed his other hand while Betsey gnawed away, a low rumble still in her throat. With both of his hands restrained, Jane was able to tie his wrists together with the cord. After she made a tight knot, she let go and trembled back against the bottom of the wine barrel where she'd almost met her death.

Betsey hopped down from Skylar's chest and licked Jane's hands in her comforting canine way. But with the weight of the dog no longer an impediment, Skylar kicked his feet and got up to a half stand.

Jane yelled, "Get him Betsey," but the mountain dog must not have been used to guard dog commands since she only lashed her tail. Her job was done, wasn't it? She'd helped when Jane asked.

Jane lowered her head and rushed at Skylar, knocking him once more to the ground with her shoulder. Then she assumed the Krav Maga fighting stance, feet apart, hands curved in front, palms ready to strike, almost like a boxer but without the clenched fists.

"I give up, Jane. You got me. Who knew I'd be beat up by an old lady."

That earned him a slap on the hand like her son used to get during one of his tantrums. "Mind your manners. Fifty is the new thirty."

Chapter 19

"I'm married."

Jane could tell Olivia was shocked speechless for a moment.

Her friend's face was a picture. "Is this a prank? Or some kind of a joke, or a mistake, like when you told everyone at the mystery party you were the murderer?"

"No. I'm married. It's for reals." Jane laughed.

Olivia's astonishment gradually combined with dawning realization. "I knew it! I saw you and Dale coming out of his room this morning. You were hanging on to each other like newlyweds. I wasn't going to say anything with you being a churchgoer and all."

"There's more to going to church than that, Liv." Jane leaned her head back on the seat bench and gazed out of the glass ceiling as a view of mountain peaks and blue sky sailed past. The two friends sat across from each other in a booth in the observation car of the Amtrak train to Denver as it rocked on the tracks with a clackety-clack rhythm.

The desert scape of the Western Slope had given way to the dark green pines climbing up the sides of the mountains, side-by-side with the viridian aspens, almost spring-like in color, even though it was nearly the end of summer. The flowers also looked like spring mixes. At the high elevations, the mountain lupine and columbine were just blooming purple among the yellow sunflowers and buttercups, with the occasional Indian paintbrush, a rare red beauty. The train was snaking through the pass, tunneling into the granite that made up the Rocky Mountains, on tracks some distance away from the highway over terrain unseen by humans…except for those traveling by train.

"So how…when…what…" Olivia sputtered. "How did you pull that off?"

"After the police arrived, they let me leave Barre Winery without having to give a statement. They were so nice when I explained I needed to pick up Dale from the hospital. Of course, I had to promise to stop at the station later. So I called an Uber driver who came and took me over to St. Mary's Hospital. Holden and Isobel had just picked up Doug. So Dale and I went over to the court house in Grand Junction. We went inside and got married." She wondered if she was the only bride ever to go from a hospital to a wedding ceremony to a police interrogation before stopping at a hotel for the honeymoon.

"Just like that?" Olivia snapped her fingers.

"Yup." Jane gave her a wide grin. "We already had the marriage license. We got that in advance. Plan A was getting married at the winery. I almost lost my life there, so we came up with a Plan B at the last minute."

"All these wedding preparations for nothing. You didn't even get to wear your dress." Olivia was going to be stuck on that; Jane knew she would never hear the end of it.

"We'll have a reception at home." Jane's thoughts were already turning to planning a party. "The dress will be perfect for that. It's a cocktail dress, tea-length, remember?"

"I sure do. I helped pick it out." Olivia took a different tactic. "Why didn't you tell me you were getting married by a justice of the peace? Doug and I would've been your witnesses." She popped her wide eyes like a teenager in a sulk.

"Well, if I would've asked you, the rest of the dinner club and my kids would've complained that we didn't invite them, too. So we used the Uber driver and one of the courthouse employees as witnesses. Turns out, a courtroom deputy recognized me from a trial I worked on a couple of years back, so she wasn't exactly a stranger, but anyway, you can help me plan the reception."

Olivia looked slightly appeased. Jane laid her cell phone flat down between them. "You want to see the pictures?"

"I do." Her friend stretched over the table to get a better view of the screen.

Jane opened a cloud site named, "Capricorn Wedding," and entered a password. "Here we go."

Olivia nudged her reading glasses farther up her nose and made a trombone sliding motion with the cell phone forward and backward. "Did you at least get married in front of a window with a view? I don't see a view."

Jane made a pee-eew face. "Who cares?" Plan B had ended up at a place with no view.

"You did, once. How about your name? What name did you put on the marriage certificate?"

"Marjorie Jane Marsh-Capricorn. I know it's a mouthful and hyphenated names went out with the eighties, but I'm thinking of using Jane Marsh for short.

Don't mention it to Dale. Yet." Jane put a straight-up finger against her lips.

"My lips are sealed." Olivia zipped her fingers across her mouth. "Ha. You got married in jeans and your green boots. Cute. Who shot these photos? They look professional." She arched an eyebrow.

"Well, umm." Jane chewed on a thumb nail and felt her cheeks burn. Oh dear, she was busted. "Actually, I called Adam on the way and he met us at the courthouse." Jane flushed hot, but she was saved when Olivia's phone rang with a text.

Olivia peered at her messages. "Isobel's plane landed in New York."

"She beat us home."

"That's the difference between trains and planes." Olivia tucked her phone back into her pocket. "Isobel and her choice in men. Imagine her hanging out with the killer!"

"That is a scary thought," Jane agreed. "But it's over now."

"She claims she was never interested in him, that she only cared about his causes. Humph!"

"Your daughter is a good person and her heart's in the correct place. She knows the right way to make a difference in the world, unlike Skylar." Jane patted her friend's hand. "I wonder who put up the Deadfest signs downtown. I didn't ask Skylar if it was him and I don't know why he would've done that, anyway."

"Holden never found out. He thanked me for taking them down. He said his business has picked up already. A lot of reservations have been coming in through his website." Olivia broke into a smile.

"That's good. Because I cancelled the reservations

I'd made for the wedding, since I'm already married." She twirled the ring on her finger. "Zeta refunded all our money."

"As well she should have," Olivia huffed.

Jane nodded in agreement. "She had to since the caterer turned out to be the killer." Of all the luck.

Once they had scrolled through the fifty or so images and Olivia picked out the ones Jane should have framed, they opened up a long cardboard box with, "West by Northeast, Murder on the Train Tracks," written across the lid. They'd purchased the game at the train station. Olivia extracted the four clue books and handed one to Jane.

Olivia said, "We aren't wearing costumes." Her 1920's flapper dress hung in a garment bag ready to return to the costume shop; Jane's tired, old black dress was rolled into a ball in the bottom of her suitcase ready to be sent to the cleaners.

"We don't need costumes." Jane set the clue books for the men in their places on the table. "What's taking the guys so long, anyway?"

"Maybe they can't find the corkscrew." Olivia had sent Doug back to their compartment for a bottle of wine and some paper cups. Dale had gone with him.

Jane glided her elbow onto the table and propped up her chin, while Olivia extracted the rest of the game pieces along with paper and pencils. They were in for a long haul on the train over the Divide to the Front Range, and a game would make the time go faster. While Jane was reading the instructions, the men returned to the observation car with a bottle of wine and a small bag of peaches.

Doug parked the bottle in the middle of the table.

"I had to go to the snack bar for the paper cups."

"I knew you'd want a peach, Jane." Dale bumped the sack in her direction and beamed at her with love-struck eyes.

"Thanks. You're so thoughtful." She gave him a full-on grin, all gooey-eyed.

"Okay, love birds." Olivia took up her pencil. "So you're the train conductor, Doug. And Dale, you're the Cary Grant character, the stowaway on the train."

Jane asked, "So, Doug, did you ever hear if the police found fingerprints on the rock?"

"What rock?" He thumbed through his list of clues as if he was behind, trying to catch up with the score.

"The weapon Skylar used to kill Georgiana."

"Oh, that rock. No, the rock was too porous. No fingerprints. The police only said they found some prints to trick Holden into giving them information. They found Georgiana's fingerprints at the B&B on the window sill and the slide to open the window, just like Skylar explained to you. Her prints were on the pendant, too, but since it was hers, no one thought anything of it."

"I guess Skylar's confession was enough, then. They don't need any more proof." Jane had heard the statement he made to the police while she was waiting for the Uber driver.

Dale slung his arm over her shoulder and gave her a squeeze. "That, and the front end damage on Skylar's second van. I'm amazed he was able to drive it over to Kirby's studio after ramming into us and totaling my truck. That was a good find, Jane. By the way, I was able to make a claim against Skylar's insurance."

"I'm glad you took care of that, Dale." Jane gave

him a kissy face.

"Thank you for getting the train tickets." Dale hugged her tighter. They exchanged a flirtatious look.

"Bleeck. I think I'm gonna barf, you two." Olivia made a finger-down-the-throat, gag-me gesture.

Jane drew in a deep, satisfied breath and snuggled closer to Dale.

Doug brought them back to the murder. "Kirby told the police he didn't even know Skylar hid that van in his shed. And since Skylar had two VW vans that looked alike, one was just a few years newer than the other—Volkswagen doesn't change models often—no one realized he was missing one."

Olivia asked, "Did Skylar admit he drove up on the cliffs?"

Jane shook her head. "He never admitted it to me. I asked him twice and he denied it both times. The phantom VW and the ghost child in the picture remain unexplained manifestations of the eclipse."

"Isobel will be happy to hear that." Olivia stuck her nose in her clue book. "So, Mr. Train Conductor, did you find the missing key to compartment 13?"

"What? Oh. Let's see." Doug tucked in his chin and looked over the game book.

Jane bit into a soft, juicy peach and made a loud slurpy sound. Olivia handed her a paper napkin. She wiped her chin and said with a smile, "I was right about something else, too. Doug, you were convinced Georgiana couldn't've witnessed the murder because she would've told the police and not held back. You slammed my theory down, but I was right. She was killed because she was a witness."

"She didn't actually see the murder," Doug

reminded her.

Dale stood up for his new wife. "Georgiana may not have seen Skylar kill Reynard, but she'd seen him leave the scene of the crime, which was just as good and signed her death warrant."

Doug rubbed his mustache, and Jane recognized that habit of his when he was annoyed. "The police told me they were closing in on Skylar. They only kept Olivia in custody to make him feel safe and draw him out."

Olivia jotted a note down on her pad of paper as if she'd actually uncovered a clue in the game. "Doug knows about the peach pits. Tell them, Douglas."

He perked up. "Skylar had the pit in his pocket at the murder party because he started an organic orchard and wanted to ask Holden some questions. He never got around to asking and thought that shoving the pit in Rey's throat would throw the police off his trail."

Dale rolled his eyes. "Humpf. Why would he ask Holden about growing peaches? Why would he bring along a peach pit? Holden runs an inn."

Olivia leveled a finger at Dale like she had a gun in her hand. "Hold it right there! Now, back off, city boy, reeeal slow-like. Holden has a couple of rows of peach trees. He doesn't use pesticides or chemicals and knows about organic stuff."

"Whoa, Nellie! I was just askin'." Dale held up his hands in mock surrender. "Is this part of the murder game we're playing? I'm lost, here."

Jane squeezed his arm. "Not part of the game, but I think you've been outdrawn. Anyway, I agree with Dale, why would Skylar want to ask Holden anything about a peach pit?"

Doug said, "Skylar was experimenting with peach wine and wanted to supply the wineries with organic produce. That's why he happened to have another pit on him when he killed Georgiana, too. He was carrying them around, talking to other organic growers whenever he got an opportunity."

"Oh, that makes sense since he has that organic garden." Jane nodded.

"Not anymore, unless there's a farm at the prison." Olivia rocked to her left as the train jolted along the tracks.

"Well, you should know." Jane flicked a page of her clue book. "The key to compartment 13 was found in your pocket, Olivia, I mean, Eve Killright. You were the one who stole the key from the conductor. Isn't that where the dead body was found?"

"I had the key?" Olivia stared at the pages of her booklet.

Jane reached for another peach. "And Mr. Thornkill here…" she poked Dale with her elbow. "I saw him sneaking out of compartment 13 right after the bloodcurdling scream rent the air." She sank her teeth into the juicy peach.

Their passenger train rolled to a stop on the side of the line to wait for a freight train to go by. The cargo boxes swished past their windows blocking their view for everything but the blue sky above. Jane felt a rumbling in her tummy that matched the reverberations of the train speeding alongside. "Uh, I need to hit the little girl's room." And fast.

She jumped out of her seat and took flight down the passageway through the vestibule to find the toilet at the end of the next carriage. She barely made it in time and swore off peaches for good, or at least for the rest of the train ride home. Palisade peaches were the best, but she'd need to show moderation in the future.

She made her way slowly back to the observation car. When she scooted into their booth, Olivia said, "You're the murderer, aren't you, Jane?"

"How'd you know? Did you cheat and look at my clue book while I was gone?" Jane pursed her lips, her cheeks puffing out. It seemed she always drew the role of the murderer.

"What if I did? Are you going to slap me again?" Olivia pushed back from the table as if preparing for the blow.

Chastised, Jane said, "No, but seriously? How else would you know? We just started playing the game."

"You left your clue book open to the last page, Jane." Dale laughed. "We all saw the answer. We couldn't help it."

"You did it again. You gave away the murderer." Doug folded his book closed and stuffed it back into the box looking a bit relieved.

"Any-hoo, you deserved to be slapped silly, Olivia." Jane cuffed her friend upside the head with a gentle upsweep of her hand.

"Hey. Watch it there." Olivia fluffed up her hair.

"How did you like spending a night in jail? I was getting all ready to explain to our friends why you couldn't make it back to Denver, because you were still in the slammer." Jane scrutinized Olivia's face for tell-tale signs of trauma. Olivia gave a lady-like shiver and touched a napkin to her lips. Jane had to wonder if the whole thing was a dream. Her elegant friend couldn't possibly have spent a night in the big house.

Doug raised his wine glass. "To busting Olivia out of prison. Escape from Alcatraz." The glasses touched rims as they met in the middle of the booth.

"Did they take Skylar to jail or is he still in the hospital?" Dale asked.

Doug had the answer. "Skylar ended up with a concussion and five stitches in his head. He's still in the hospital waiting for transport to jail. That was some kick to the noggin you gave him, Jane."

"I forgot I had on my cowboy boots. The heel caught him right above the eye."

"Don't worry about him. He was threatening you with a gun and you were only defending yourself. Thank goodness you had on those boots, Jane," Dale said with a strained laugh. "He deserved a hard knock on the head of his own after giving me and Doug concussions."

"I guess you're right." Jane peered down at her feet and tapped her toes together, like Dorothy in Oz, except her feet were clad not with ruby red slippers but with green tooled boots. "I'm glad I bought them, even if people made fun of me."

Doug tapped on his cell phone. "Talking about being made fun of, you should see how many people have viewed your bull-riding video. I added some hashtags, #GotHerBootsOn and #fierceboots. The number of views went up another thousand."

Dale threw back his head and laughed. Jane laughed along with him, holding his hand. They were making new memories, forever-in-life-together memories. The best things in life were the people you loved and the memories you made together.

Getting married trumped solving the murders as the

most memorable event of the weekend, but capturing the killer certainly came in second. Jane had tried to make the solution too complicated, but the crimes had turned out to be so simple.

The peach pendant necklace was only a necklace.

The total eclipse was only an eclipse.

The pit in the throat was only a last-minute thought.

The phantom vehicle and the ghost child, those were still unexplained.

Jane planned to celebrate by getting a tattoo, a design to commemorate the trip, something with the feel of a mystery. Maybe an eclipse…like Isobel's tattoo with a star, a moon, and the waves of the sun in the sky.

Peach Crisp Bread
Contributed by Rosie Hoehne Alcaraz

Preheat oven to 350 degrees. Use 9x5 loaf pan or 4 mini loaf pans. Spray bottom of pan(s) with cooking spray.

Bread ingredients:

1 cup fresh peaches, peeled and diced
2 eggs
1/2 cup vegetable oil
1/2 cup sour cream
1 teaspoon vanilla
1 1/2 cups flour
3/4 cup sugar
3/4 cup chopped pecans
1 teaspoon baking powder
1/2 teaspoon cinnamon
1/4 teaspoon nutmeg
1/4 teaspoon ground cloves
1/2 teaspoon salt

Crumble Topping ingredients:

1/3 cup brown sugar
1/4 cup flour
1/4 cup oats
1/2 teaspoon cinnamon
1/2 teaspoon nutmeg
3 tablespoons soft butter

Directions:

In a large bowl, combine peaches, eggs, oil, sour cream, and vanilla. Mix thoroughly. (I used a large spoon to mix and the bread came out with whole chunks of peaches. If you use an electric mixer, the peaches will blend in more.) In a separate bowl, combine flour, sugar, baking powder, cinnamon, nutmeg, cloves, and salt. Gradually sift flour mixture into peach mixture. Stir in pecans. Don't over mix or you will get large air bubbles in bread.

Pour batter into 9x5 loaf pan.

For topping, combine brown sugar, flour, oats, cinnamon, nutmeg, and butter until crumbly.

Top batter with crumble topping.

Bake in preheated 350-degree oven until golden brown and toothpick comes out clean (about 1 hour). If using mini loaves bake 35 to 40 minutes.

When bread is done let cool 10 to 15 minutes on cooling rack then turn out of pan.

Freezes well.

Farmer's Market Tomatoes
with a side of Homemade Cheese
Contributed by Mary and Dean Harris
Great for an eclipse party...

Tomatoes by Mary:

Buy a variety of a several kinds/colors of tomatoes. I like the orange/yellow ones a little better, and Dean prefers the green ones. Serve them sliced, with some homemade cheese, basil grown on the patio, and some good balsamic.

Cheese by Dean:

Ingredients:

    1-quart whole milk

    1-quart buttermilk

    1/8 to 1/4 cup lemon juice (or vinegar)

    1 teaspoon of rosemary or thyme or herbs de Provence

    Cheesecloth

I make it up as I go, but I usually use a quart of whole milk and a quart of buttermilk. It can be pasteurized but NOT ultra-pasteurized. That is why you cannot use cream instead of milk. It is impossible to find cream in the store that is not ultra-pasteurized. The other key is that you must add an acid to make the curds coagulate. This is where you can start customizing the flavor. A lot of people use vinegar. Flavored vinegar will give subtle notes. I usually use lemon juice. It gives a very subtle lemon taste. Finally, I often add some herbs wrapped in cheesecloth to add more flavor. None of these ideas will make a strongly flavored cheese. I have not used loose herbs, but I don't see why it would not work. I usually use rosemary, thyme, herbs de Provence, etc.

Directions:

Heat whole milk and buttermilk until simmering. Use a slotted spoon, ladle, etc. to skim the curds and put them in a strainer lined with cheesecloth.

I just fold the sheet double and put it in a strainer and pour the curds and whey through that so it drains into a bowl and leaves the cheese in the cheesecloth.

Let it drain to suit the consistency you want. The first time I made it, it seemed so wet that I squeezed liquid out of the cheesecloth. Mistake. Made a dry cheese that resembled cottage cheese.

I like it creamier, so I just let it drain for about 30 minutes and put in a container. More liquid will leach out, but just pour it off.

If you have chopped herbs, you could add them directly to the cheese loose so that the herbs are in the finished cheese. I usually pick the herbs whole and put them in the cheesecloth when straining the cheese, so I can remove them when the cheese is done. Voila.

A bit of trivia. People refer to this cheese as homemade ricotta. That is actually incorrect. Ricotta means "recooked" in Italian and in the original Latin. Ricotta came about when cheesemakers used the whey left over from making cheese and recooked it similar to above to draw out additional curds. The cheese above is really a soft farmer's cheese. I have never tried recooking the whey to make a second batch, but it is possible. It seems you would need even more whey the second time around to make any amount of cheese.

Grilled Chicken and Peaches for Two
Contributed by Karen Whalen

Ingredients:

2 chicken breasts (I buy a bag of individually frozen chicken breasts to have on hand and defrost the number I need)

2 oz. peach jam (1-ounce equals about 2 tablespoons, but I use a 1.5 oz. jar of Colorado Mountain Jam, organic Peach Jalapeno, from Palisade, Colorado. Other kinds of jam would work, such as orange marmalade or apricot)

1 teaspoon honey mustard

1 large garlic clove, diced

2 peaches

Directions:

Preheat grill to medium heat and brush on a little olive oil on the grates to keep the chicken from sticking.

Stir together jam, mustard, and garlic to make a sauce.

Cook chicken until done, flipping on both sides.

When done, brush one side of the chicken with peach sauce and let warm, then flip and brush other side.

In the meantime, cut peaches in half and remove pits. Once chicken has been coated with the sauce, place peach halves on grill to warm.

Remove chicken and peach halves onto plates to serve.

Note: the peaches taste almost like dessert when grilled.

Karen C. Whalen

Easy as Canned Peach Pie
Contributed by Karen Whalen

Ingredients:

Prepackaged pie crust (I use Pillsbury's, which has 2 crusts per package)

2 cans of peach pie filling (21 oz. each)

2 tablespoons brown sugar

1/4 teaspoon ginger

1/8 teaspoon nutmeg

3/4 teaspoon cinnamon

Directions:

Preheat oven to 425°.

Place one crust in bottom of pie dish (large size dish for 9-inch pie) and poke holes in bottom and sizes of crust with a fork.

In a large bowl, add pie filling and spices. Turn with a large spoon several times to distribute spices evenly.

Pour pie filling into pan. Top with second pie crust and poke a few holes in top. Pinch edges shut. (You can press a fork against the top edge all around the crust to pinch it shut.)

Bake for 45 minutes. I always put a cookie sheet on the oven rack below the pie to catch any drips.

This will taste better than regular canned pie filling. Everyone will compliment you on your "homemade" pie.

Streusel Cake
Contributed by Debra St. John

Debra St. John has been reading and writing romance since high school. She always dreamed about publishing a romance novel someday. Her dream came true when she started writing sultry contemporary romance with sexy heroes and spunky heroines for The Wild Rose Press. Although she's a country gal at heart, she lives in a suburb of Chicago with her husband, who is her real-life hero.

~

Ingredients:
1 stick margarine
1 cup sugar
1 egg
2 cups flour
1 tablespoon powdered sugar
1 teaspoon baking soda
1 teaspoon vanilla
Pinch salt
1 cup sour cream
Peaches - 2 or 3 - Peeled, pitted, and sliced.
(Can also use apples, plums, or just plain)

Directions:
Cream margarine, sugar, egg, & vanilla. Sift dry ingredients. Add alternately with sour cream. Dough will be thick. Grease jelly roll pan and spread evenly. Line peaches (or other fruit) in rows on dough.

Streusel topping ingredients:
1 stick margarine (I used butter)
1 cup flour
1/2 cup sugar
1 teaspoon cinnamon

Directions:
Combine all with pastry cutter until crumbly. Spread on top of peaches. Bake 350 for 25 minutes. When cool drizzle with a little frosting made of powdered sugar and milk.

Spicy Peaches and Cream Trifle
Contributed by Kathy Gaworski

Cake Layer

    1 boxed spice cake mix

    1 cup vanilla Greek yogurt (I used light)

    1 cup ginger ale (or the amount of water on the cake box directions)

Mix all three ingredients and pour into lightly sprayed 13 X 9 cake pan and bake according to instructions on the box. This can be made ahead of time since you want it to be cool for assembly. Cut into 2x1 inch bars.

~

Peach Layer

    4 large peaches

    1 pinch nutmeg

    1/4 teaspoon cinnamon

    1 pinch of cardamom (opt)

    2 tablespoons brown sugar

    2 tablespoons ginger ale

    2 tablespoons peach brandy or if don't want to use brandy can add fruit juice of your choice

Slice the peaches into thin wedges about 1/4 inch thick (don't have to be too precise).

[Karen's note: I did not peel the peaches first.]

In a saucepan over medium heat, combine the peaches with the sugar, juice, spices and brandy or juice. Bring to simmer and turn down to low heat, cover and simmer approximately 5 minutes or until the fruit is tender.

Remove from the heat and set aside to cool.

(You can also make this a day ahead of time since you want it to be cool for assembly.)

You will want to divide this into 3 portions.

~

Cream Layer

8 oz. of Mascarpone cheese (room temperature)

2 cups whipping cream (this is 1 pint)

1/3 cup confectioners' sugar

1 teaspoon vanilla

In clean mixing bowl with an electric mixer whip the whipping cream and powdered sugar until you have soft peaks, add the Mascarpone cheese and vanilla and continue to mix until smooth and the mixture holds a peak. You will want to divide this into 3 portions.

~

Crunch Layer

1/2 package of Speculoos Cookie

[Karen's note: I used Archway Crispy Windmill cookies]

Pulse cookies in a food processor or put them into a freezer bag and crush with rolling pin until you have course cookie crumbs.

~

Assemble Trifle:

In a trifle or other glass bowl, line the bottom and sides with the cake that is cut into rectangles, and divide the rest of the cake into 2 portions. Top the bottom layer of cake with 1/3rd of the Peach layer and 1/3rd of the Cream Layer and repeat until you have 3 layers of each ending with the Cream Layer on top. Chill at least 1 hour and before serving sprinkle the top with the Speculoos Cookie crumbs.

[Karen's note: for an even spicier dessert, bake the cake using the ingredients called for on the box instead of the ginger ale and yogurt.]

A word about the author...

Karen C. Whalen is the author of a culinary cozy series, the "dinner club murder mysteries." The first in the series, *Everything Bundt the Truth*, tied for First Place in the Suspense Novel category of the 2017 IDA Contest.

Whalen worked for many years as a paralegal at a law firm in Denver, Colorado and has been a columnist and regular contributor to *The National Paralegal Reporter* magazine.

She believes it's never too late to try something new. She loves to host dinner clubs, entertain friends, ride bicycles, hike in the mountains, and read cozy murder mysteries.

Thank you for purchasing
this publication of The Wild Rose Press, Inc.

For questions or more information
contact us at
info@thewildrosepress.com.

The Wild Rose Press, Inc.
www.thewildrosepress.com

To visit with authors of
The Wild Rose Press, Inc.
join our yahoo loop at
http://groups.yahoo.com/group/thewildrosepress/